Eighteen Wishes

THE DJINN OF LAS VEGAS
BOOK ONE

C.K. SORENS

Books By C.K. Sorens

THE DJINN OF LAS VEGAS SERIES

Eighteen Wishes

***

TRIMARKED SERIES

Trimarked
Afflicted

This novel contains content that may be triggering.
For a list of possible triggers, please visit
https://www.cksorens.com/djinn-series-trigger-warnings
This is a work of fiction. All of the characters, organizations, and events portrayed in this novel
are products of the author's imagination.

EIGHTEEN WISHES

Edited by Whitney O. McGruder via Wit & Travesty
Proof Edits by Katherine D. Graham

Cover design by Rebecca Kearney

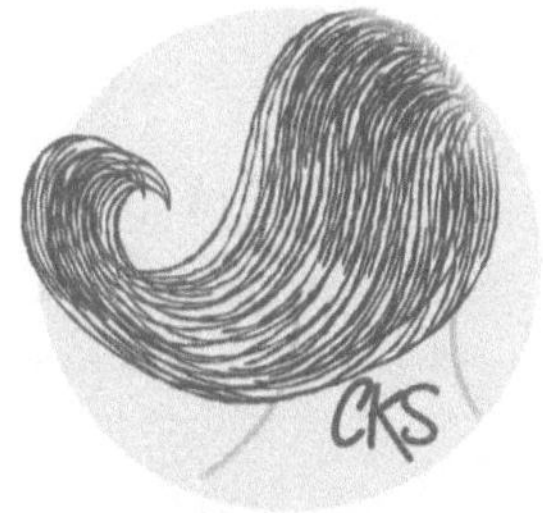

www.cksorens.com

ISBN 978-1-954054-07-3 (Paperback)
ISBN 978-1-95404-06-6 (Hardcover)
ISBN 978-954054-08-0 (ebook)

To Quill & Cup, who brought me balance.
And Lauren, who loved this story before I did.

CHAPTER 1

Jacoa

J acoa Wicker checked the digital display on his smartwatch. 8:47.

His birth time was 8:43. He had been in his eighteenth year for four minutes. There'd been no flash of light. No sudden presence at his side batting dark lashes over pale, yellow eyes.

He rested in disappointment, standing on the shadowed landing of the staircase, his back against the tiled wall to absorb the cool touch of polished stone. He studied the people drifting from the grand entry hall to the chef's kitchen in the large, open-planned space of the main floor, hoping to find an unfamiliar face.

The view was gorgeous, no matter the perspective. A high-end house in the high desert outside Las Vegas. Painted and jeweled guests had driven to his remote house in expensive cars. They showed off their gold-plated smartwatches, flashed diamond-studded phone cases, drank from crystal glasses, and ignored the mess they left behind as they laughed into the night.

Boring. Not a bit of uniqueness in the sea of generic beauty. Human.

Jacoa searched for a fairytale. Or was she a monster?

He hadn't always believed he had a genie. His mother had

sent him to bed with stories of her, but he'd thought they'd been fantasy. At sixteen, he inherited a stack of old journals that told similar tales, but in real time. To his ancestors, the curse tormented them.

Whether he was fulfilling the dream or ending the nightmare, Jacoa was determined to end the cycle. First, he wanted to meet the legend and take his own measure of her character—a plan that required her presence.

Jacoa straightened from the wall and descended the thick planks of the floating steps, illusions of wood clad steel cantilever from the wall. Slipping into the crowd as if he'd always been amongst them, he braced against a few shoulder slaps and leaned away from loud exclamations of birthday greetings. A Jacoa Wicker party was a rare occurrence that brought in crowds. Not only was he rumored to be the heir of a massive fortune, but his personality shift from four years ago was still a topic of discussion.

In his early teen years, Jacoa's presence made the party. With a neglectful aunt and uncle as his guardians, Jacoa had grown up on his own and taken advantage of the freedom. With a very large allowance, he had funded quite a few illegal trips to liquor stores and street-corner salesmen who offered non-regulated pharmaceuticals.

What the crowd didn't know was his fortune was the least interesting part of his inheritance. After his lawyer threatened to withhold it, Jacoa chose to clean himself up. He put aside the drugs and alcohol, but he hadn't given up all fun. He still popped up at a Vegas party every now and again, usually when he wanted to find someone else's bed to share, then crawl out of.

One couple Jacoa had indulged himself with before sandwiched him in a group hug, whispering promises of birthday suits and tangled sheets. Though he'd once experimented with them for a few satisfying hours, a repeated experience was not on his mind tonight. He made sure they had their cups refilled, and then directed the pair to enjoy their evening without him.

The bartender had claimed the long granite island-turned-bar.

Jacoa picked an empty barstool on the patio side of the island, despite the bodies that leaned next to him as they shouted drink orders. He turned out drinks with admirable speed, keeping the party guests flowing in a smooth exchange between the patio and the bar, the direction of their feet guided by the level of liquid in their cups.

The stool to Jacoa's right changed occupants, the new seat-mate pressing against the bar to spin in the chair. Ward Emrick had put product in his shaggy brown hair for once, slicking the thick mop away from his face and leaving the buzzed sides free. He'd also worn his nice pair of jeans and a fitted navy Henley in the same dark blue shade as his eyes.

"Why are you so fancy?" Jacoa asked.

"Special occasion. When was the last time you threw a party?"

"Two years ago."

"Right. When we met."

Ward soft-punched Jacoa's shoulder. Jacoa rubbed the spot and grimaced in mock pain, which only sent Ward into a fit of laughter.

The bartender set a beer on the counter. Without looking, Ward grabbed it from behind him. His ability to sense the surrounding environment always intrigued Jacoa. No matter the noise or distractions, his friend was never taken by surprise.

"I thought I'd get here and find the gate closed. I didn't think you'd go through with it," Ward said.

"It's customary to celebrate certain birthdays. Sixteenth. Eighteenth."

"Right," Ward teased with a smile. "I'm here when you're ready to tell me the real reason."

Jacoa didn't plan to explain that the gathering had nothing to do with his birthday, and everything to do with the expected arrival of his family's curse. He'd read djinn preferred the night, and though they hated human crowds, they loved a good party. So to welcome his genie, he'd thrown himself an evening birthday bash. Ward would laugh the story away, or demand to be included. Jacoa didn't want to deal with either.

His genie's entire purpose was to grant him eighteen wishes within his eighteenth year. If she could do that, she would be free of her imprisonment. None of his ancestors had allowed that to happen.

Djinn often twisted wishes to punish their captors, but in this case, it was more. To free this genie meant to release all imprisoned djinn, and as Jacoa's bloodline had created the method of their enslavement to begin with, having hundreds of freed, angry reality-creators after him was not ideal.

Jacoa was intent on not repeating history. He'd end the curse one way or another, even if that meant the Wicker line was to end with him, and the journals destroyed.

If his genie was amiable, Jacoa hoped she could help him. If not, he would go through with his plans anyway.

Jacoa hooded his eyes and searched for a pair of non-human irises amongst the crowd comprised of just-graduated high school students and a few college undergrads. Of course, genies could control a human's perception of reality through their powerful illusionary magic. Even though he couldn't see her didn't mean she wasn't present. Jacoa rubbed his stubbled jaw, an idea forming.

His plan didn't require wishing, but one might draw her out.

"I wish I had a drink right now."

Ward's brow rose, and he pulled his bottle to his chest. A second later, a whiskey sour with a single, oversized ice cube appeared at Jacoa's elbow, but not by magic.

"No need to wish," the bartender grinned. "You're paying me, after all." He left to fulfill another order.

Jacoa wrapped his fingers around the glass with a frown. Ward laughed at his expression.

"Yeah, you're enjoying your party." Ward's phone buzzed and he glanced at the screen. With a sigh, he took one last pull from his beer, then slid it to the barman, who caught it and tossed it into the trash.

"I have to go check on my brother. Are we still set for tomorrow?"

"Yeah." Jacoa clasped Ward's hand. "Is everything okay with Will?"

As long as Jacoa had known Ward, his brother had been in a special hospital. Though Ward had never been able to fully explain what was wrong with his brother, Jacoa had the impression it was a lifelong ailment.

"I'm sure it's fine. Thanks for asking. I'll be here in the morning and we can take your car into Vegas."

Ward walked off, dialing a number on his way out. Jacoa gripped the rim of his glass with his fingertips and turned it clockwise, ignoring the people easing up to the bar, then withdrawing in alcohol driven waves.

Even outside Las Vegas, the drinking age was twenty-one. With a cash payment, finding a bartender who aged people by looks rather than drivers' licenses wasn't hard. Of course, every underage person in this room had a fake ID. The secluded location of his house ensured there wouldn't be an angry neighbor calling the cops to put pressure on the validity of their identification.

So well planned and nothing to show for it, except for one wasted wish on the attentive mixologist.

Then again, Jacoa studied his glass.

How had the bartender known to pour a whiskey sour? He didn't drink alcohol anymore, but when he went out, he'd often order this to stop people from asking the ridiculously tiresome question of 'where's your drink?' Was this a matter of serendipity, or was the genie happy to hide her presence for now and keep the granting simple?

He studied the bartender. About Jacoa's height at around five foot seven, the young man had a narrow frame and bronze skin only slightly darker than Jacoa's own. Long black hair was twisted into a half bun that let the length fall along the back of his neck, the ends pure white. Slender, agile fingers danced with incredible dexterity. He wasn't one of the more showy mixologists who flipped and tossed for entertainment, sacrificing flair for pure efficiency. The number of drinks he moved was impressive. A time or two, he swapped out a drink, dumping the untouched original into the sink. He'd whip up another with a quick apology about the first being mixed wrong, and ignored the acidic glares.

Roofied cast-offs, Jacoa guessed. He'd happily pay for the booze to be clean.

"What's your name?" Jacoa asked. The bartender looked up and winked a golden-green eye.

"You want my number, too?" He moved along without offering either.

Jacoa couldn't deny the man had amazing eyes, a color he'd never seen. His ass curved just right in his belted jeans, revealed by a tucked-in long-sleeved polo shirt that hugged his flat abs. If Jacoa wanted the bartender's name and number, he would have gone for it. Tonight, he was looking for a girl. He thought.

The crowd had thinned. A splash from outside told him his guests had found the pool on the lower patio. Jacoa lifted his glass and caught the transparent twists of melting ice as they shifted into the golden whiskey.

"You don't like your drink?" the bartender asked.

"I'm wondering if it's safe," Jacoa admitted.

"You think I roofied you?"

Jacoa laughed and shook his head.

"Your hands are fast, but I've kept up with them. I don't mind a few sacrifices in the name of clean drinking."

The bartender grinned, displaying his full, sharp-edged smile.

"Glad to hear it. So, what's up with your whiskey?"

"I'm hoping to keep a clear head tonight."

The bartender grabbed an empty tumbler and dropped in a clean ice cube from the machine on the counter. He wiped out the shaker, then splashed in pineapple juice before adding orange bitters and crushed ice. After a few shakes, he poured the mix into a glass and topped it off with the fizz of a ginger ale and an orange slice for garnish.

"Mocktail for the boss." The man traded glasses and claimed the whiskey for himself. His eyes caught Jacoa's as he pulled away.

"How did you get your eyeliner so thin?"

"I was born with it." Jacoa answered with the dry, breathy exasperation of a question over-asked. People often mistook him for wearing eye makeup because of the thick, dark line of his lashes that surrounded light green eyes.

"It's a shame," the bartender continued, though Jacoa had tuned him out. "I bet a tutorial on how to copy your look would go viral."

Jacoa nodded and twisted his stool. His house was filled with people he didn't care about. Boredom sank into his bones. The conversation was too familiar. The gathering was too typical.

"I wish I'd never thrown this damn party."

Jacoa's ears rang in the sudden silence. The press of bodies exchanged with a cool evening breeze. No coats flooded his dining room. No drinks lined the kitchen island. The accordion doors were closed.

The front door burst open. Jacoa eased from the stool, his hand still holding his mocktail. Ward toed his shoes off on the rug in the entry hall, his laughter filling the space.

"I knew you'd cancel at the last minute! You should see the text chain. You aren't popular right now."

No problem. He never was.

What mattered was that Jacoa remembered.

He'd thrown the party. He'd hated it so much, he'd wished it away. And his djinn had granted it, leaving only his drink.

But where the hell was she?

CHAPTER 2

Isra

A cloud of heavy vanilla-laced tobacco filled Isra Almasi's lungs when she walked into the bar. The building nestled deep into a coastal city, hours away from where Jacoa spent his evening at his desert home. She stopped just inside the door and loosened the top knot she'd worn for the party. Inky black hair grew to her shoulders, then shifted to white wavy tresses that poured over her back in contrasting tones. Her male frame softened at the edges, the width deflating and breasts curving out, filling the heather gray polo shirt in a different way.

Using her eyes wasn't helpful at this moment. The bar appeared empty, not even a single member of the waitstaff present. The illusion of vacancy hid the powerful djinn. Scented vanilla smoke acted as a calling card for the strongest power in the room. Isra wasn't familiar enough with names or features to know which djinn used the vanilla essence, only that it wasn't the one she came to meet.

That she had to be here at all was an affront to her instincts. She hadn't been born djinn, and did not enjoy being cursed to be one, locked not only into the form of one of these creatures, but bound by the genie curse as well. They thought she should be glad to have a taste of their power.

The djinn could not change the physical world, but they could cast illusions on top of it. Their creations were so accurate, even a human could get caught up in the magic and do the impossible, like walk on clouds or survive deadly falls. The illusion only lasted as long as a djinn held it. Convincing humans of one thing and revealing the truth in a devastating manner was one of the djinn's favorite games.

When djinn got together, their illusions pressed against each other. The older the djinn, the stronger their creations. Like crowded bubbles in a bathtub, they each fought for space, some expanding and others contracting as their magic collided.

Magic flowed into Isra through her chakras, connecting her to the universe with *Sutara* above her head and *Vasundhara* below her feet. She synchronized the nine central disks.

A counterclockwise spin pulled in the surrounding energy, helping her discover how many djinn hid within the human-made building. It wasn't packed, but the walk to her table would be interesting.

Her chakras reversed into a clockwise spin and fortified her aura, creating a small barrier between herself and the other djinn. She would maintain her form and have to tolerate the rest.

A few steps in and the flavored smoke changed into a damp heat. The illusion of an empty bar disappeared, and Isra diverted her gaze from the group of naked djinn relaxing in a sauna. Only one appeared humanoid; the others took on various creature forms, but Isra didn't look long enough to pick them out. Laughter at her discomfort followed her into the next bubbled reality.

The damp heat gave way to cold wet. Isra thickened the weave of her clothes to guard against the slushy marsh she trudged through. The creatures here sat in a semicircle around a stone table. They had pale skin and brownish-green hair, holding cups with spindly fingers as they glared at her intrusion into their space.

"Who are you?" The djinn sitting in the middle of the five leaned forward, squinting her orange tinted eyes at Isra.

"It's the Wicker genie," another answered, a curl on her lip.

"Get out!" one of them hissed. "Go back to your master and do your job."

"Do you think she can even count to eighteen?"

Cackles filled the space. The center djinn glared, and with a sharp jerk of her chin, thrust Isra from the marsh. She bent against an increase in gravity, pressing through the new, pressurized reality. Her heavier clothes imprinted onto her skin. With tiny movements, she struggled to unfasten her belt, wincing as she loosened it and its hold on her hip bones.

"Take it off!" Maram wrapped her arms around Isra, her reality pushing the rest away. The sudden relief of weight allowed Isra to straighten her spine just as Maram slung her smaller frame on Isra's back. Isra laughed against the energetic hug and flung the leather of the belt over Maram's shoulders, pulling both ends to lock them together and ensure Isra held on to the protection of Maram's greater powers.

The djinn were only as powerful as their order of creation. Not born, a djinn formed when the energies of the universe fell in perfect alignment on the Earth, a rare and notable occurrence. Isra was the youngest, by far, created by a curse rather than nature. It's why she hadn't slipped between the bubbled realities of the djinn. Maram's age gave her the natural ability to push them all away. Though Isra wasn't sure where Maram landed on the hierarchy, she was likely one of the older ones, the way she threw around her power.

"They really hate you," Maram announced cheerily.

"Yes, so thank you for inviting me here, deep in the den of my enemies."

"You were only born an enemy. If you embraced the djinn life and granted all your wishes, we wouldn't despise you as much."

"Finding a place amongst the djinn will never be my goal."

"That's good, since I lied about learning to tolerate you. At least you've decided to go after your freedom after five hundred years."

Isra pressed her lips together. Trapped by the genie curse, her contract with the universe stated she could only engage with the firstborn son of the current generation of Wickers. Of course, not all firstborns were sons, limiting her chances. Sometimes, the first-born son died before he turned eighteen, and once again Isra would be imprisoned in the netherworld.

She'd been bound in the nether for the past three generations of Wickers. Deprivation reigned in that darkness. No sight, no touch, nothing. Caught in a formless essence until the stars aligned and allowed her release.

Her centuries trapped in the netherworld left her desperate for freedom. However, she was not as dedicated to the djinn's plan as Maram thought. Though Jann had made Isra the key to freeing all djinn from their genie curses, she had no intention of playing their game. Unfortunately, she had done poorly on her own. Only a fool followed a failing strategy repeatedly. She needed help and Maram was willing. Never mind that their plans did not actually align.

Isra dispelled thoughts of the nether and erased any sign she meant to betray the djinn. She focused on the sensations that came with freedom: Maram's weight against her back, actively pulling her long hair as it caught between their bodies.

Maram squeezed her thighs, then let her legs drop and her reality soften to allow Isra space. Her belt became a silk scarf that she looped around her neck. Cloth thinned and rippled into a wine-dark satin sheath, displaying the wide brassy bands that encircled Isra's forearms just above her wrists. The silky slide of fabric brought goosebumps to her skin. She shifted until her lips almost brushed the djinn's, reveling in the simple enjoyment of tactile contact.

"He asked for two wishes," Isra said.

"So he didn't know you were there."

"Hmm," Isra hummed in agreement, her eyes narrowing as

she allowed Maram to lead her to the double couch with a curtained alcove. A hookah sat on the round coffee table but remained untouched. The permeating vanilla scent meant someone here was stronger than Maram, bringing a mix of emotions to Isra. Maram would be frustrated that she wasn't the strongest, and there was joy in that. However, it was nerve-wracking that Isra's benefactor was outmatched.

Maram fell into a sitting position on the curved couch. She wore a black jumpsuit that fully covered the left side of her body but broke into thick strips that wrapped around her to cover the most intimate places. Once Isra sat, a soft sigh parted her lips as she reveled in the velveteen caress of the upholstery, swaying in her seat to keep the friction moving.

Each change in the environment was a well-studied phenomenon. Even the trek through the different illusions within the bar had proved a lovely adventure. This was life.

She swore that this time, she would not return to the netherworld.

Isra leaned her head onto the curved back of the seat, softly rubbing away an irritating itch. There were reasons she kept returning. She refused to remember them. For now, she only wanted to immerse herself in the experience.

Maram, however, wanted to talk.

"We shall see if he continues the pattern. Two thoughtless wishes in less than an hour are promising. Perhaps the fact that there was no living male Wicker to guide him will be our saving grace."

"And if he catches on?" Isra asked.

"A problem for a different day."

Maram fell silent and Isra let it wrap around her as she flattened her hands onto the cushion, her palms warming the velveteen. She ignored the weight of the djinn's study. Maram had never been bound to a vessel, or beholden to a contract forged between her captor and the universe to define the terms of her servitude.

Like other djinn, Maram bent reality and created her own illusionary world within this one. A genie could change reality with the will of their master. Nothing was stronger than a wish. But the trade for such awesome power was to become a slave.

To wear the copper and iron cuffs that marred Isra's wrists was the stuff of nightmares. Isra couldn't alter them. They turned invisible only if the rest of her was, as well. They remained a constant sign of her captivity and bound her to a vessel held by a human.

Each genie had different expectations. Three wishes, then back to the nether. A human's lifetime, then trapped. Freedom that came one year at a time, but only with the existence of an eighteen-year-old Wicker son.

Isra's contract was unique. It allowed for a chance at freedom. All she had to do was grant eighteen wishes within one year. She'd failed twelve other times. In five hundred years, this was her thirteenth release from the nether. Her thirteenth opportunity.

She'd arrived at dawn, though Jacoa's birth time hadn't been until the evening. Early entry was a perk she used well. Isra had been exiled from this world for almost one hundred years and she needed to catch up on the missed history. She'd been awed at human innovation, and learned how to pass herself off as a modern mortal.

Maram had found her at the edge of the Indian Ocean. When the djinn pressed plump lips into the curve of Isra's ear, it had been her first skin to skin contact of this escape. It was no surprise Maram realized Isra had been released from the nether. The Wicker line had been watched long before Isra had become a genie for their long-dead ancestor's role in betraying the djinn.

It was a plan with multiple stages. Isra should hide herself instead of revealing herself and see if her master's casual vernacular would lead to enough wishes. For the next phase, Isra would appear in his life and urge him directly.

But then there was part three.

Try to kill him.

Isra's contract forbade her from murdering her master. Maram insisted she didn't intend the current Wicker to actually die, just to fear he might. Humans did silly things when faced with death - like wish to stay alive.

The djinn had been surprised with her easy agreement to trick the new Wicker. Isra gave Maram the expected rationale. Being bound as a genie meant she only existed for someone else. An accumulated four hundred and eighty-eight years in the realm of darkness was enough.

Isra was tired, and needed assistance, but didn't have faith in Maram or her motivations. Wishes were the only magic stronger than a djinn's. If the game went too far, Isra would have to convince her master to wish to stop it. That required trust and some kind of relationship.

An unpleasant twist burned Isra's core at *Svadisthana*. She hated getting that close.

"Maybe you should watch him at night," Maram suggested, twisting a lock of honey brown hair around her finger. "Maybe he sleep-talks in wishes."

"I'm not sure I want to waste any of my time watching a human snore."

"It's not a waste if it ends Jann's game." Maram slumped in her seat even as Isra straightened at the mention of the First Djinn's name - the very creature who had cursed her to this life.

"What is Jann up to these days?" Isra asked. Maram's dark brown eyes narrowed. She snapped the straps of cloth against her thigh.

"I thought you were focusing on pleasure."

"It would be remiss of me to ignore the one we're defying."

"Jann's game keeps djinn as slaves," Maram sneered. "As First, one would think they'd be more eager to free their people. I'd thought they meant for your contract to do just that, but—"

Maram popped her lips without continuing.

"He's a djinn," Isra said. "You all enjoy your games too much."

Maram's frown darkened her face and Isra wondered for a moment if it had been wise to remind her companion of their differences. Isra had not been born djinn or genie, which is likely why she hadn't been offered 'help' before.

"Jann is at their palace in the clouds." Maram glanced around as if to catch any possible eavesdroppers. "They haven't had to track down and imprison any rogue creatures since the last time you were out, and have settled in. They prefer to bring beings to them, so you should be safe as long as you don't spin new worlds for your human. You'll likely want to get those last wishes done in quick succession, though. I doubt their disinterest will continue beyond the fifteenth or sixteenth granting."

"They didn't interfere the one time I'd gotten to seventeen."

"What? With the savvy businessman you fancied yourself in love with? We all knew he'd swindle you in the end. It wasn't even worth betting on."

Isra closed her eyes to hide her flinch. She hadn't been in love with Gunter as Maram suggested, but she had believed he would complete the contract. Granting all eighteen wishes was not how Isra meant to escape, so she'd left before he asked for his last wish.

She intended to find an honorable way out of this trap, one that didn't free the genies or leave her trapped in the nether. With Maram's magic working so close to hers, she had a chance.

There were no good choices in this world. Regardless, the most important decision was made. Use the djinn to draw the attention of their only enemies—the draconian djinn-hunters.

Otherwise known as her family.

CHAPTER 3

Jacoa

Ward stayed until he got a text saying he needed to check on his brother. The déjà vu moment sent goosebumps prickling over Jacoa's skin. He had truly gone back in time, then. The rest of the world moved as though the only thing that changed was whether he'd thrown a birthday party or not.

Magic was amazing. If only he had some of his own so he could track down his genie. He'd tried a wish to bring her out of hiding after Ward left, but nothing had happened. Whether it was because she was gone, or had some choices, he wasn't sure.

Either way, with that option unavailable, Jacoa locked up the house and made his way downstairs to surround himself with the mystery of his family. Maybe the old pages he'd gone over a million times would share some more secrets now that he was officially eighteen.

The office was on the lowest level of his three-story home. The back wall comprised a wide sliding glass door with an in-ground pool set into the simple patio that spread from the house to the base of the rocky hill bordering his yard. To the right, a wall of hand-carved bookcases hadn't been replaceable, but his interior decorator had worked magic, blending his modern style with the traditional features. His glass-top desk paralleled the shelves, and on the opposite wall, a pair of mid-century modern chairs sat on either end of a custom coffee table that echoed the bookshelves.

Jacoa swayed in his ergonomic chair as he glanced over the stack of old ledgers, mounds of open journals, and scattered forms littering the room. Only a small fraction fit on the desk. The rest sat in piles atop the wood-finish tile floor.

Documents meant for the first son. The facts behind the fairy-tales his mother had used to send him to sleep.

His ancestors hindered the genie from completing her contract, though there was a pattern in those granted.

Bank statements, investment reports, real estate portfolios, and off-shore account numbers linked to wishes for wealth.

Wishes for health attached to x-rays, lab tests, and records of miraculous recoveries.

News articles about uncommon luck amidst fires, earth-quakes, and tornadoes were evidence of wishes for protection.

He collected notes on what couldn't be wished for. Unnaturally long life. Immortality. There wasn't a way to end the curse without also freeing the genie. The firstborn must be named Wicker, even if the mother claimed a different name through marriage. His own mom, Riti, kept Wicker rather than take his father's surname.

He found nothing concrete regarding the djinn's appearance beyond the constant of yellow eyes and wide metal cuffs around the forearms, whether she appeared as a human or animal.

With more questions than conclusions, Jacoa focused on what he could control. The challenge of his genie's shape-shifting could be solved with a wish. Once she revealed herself, he hoped to gain her trust. She must want the curse to end, something they had in common. A place to start.

Jacoa tossed the top book to the side, then the second. He stopped on the most familiar pages, a telling from 1919. Rafe had terrorized New Orleans and was Jacoa's least favorite ancestor. Riti's interpretation found hope in the horror. This fairytale showed the genie had choices. There were lines she wouldn't cross, sacrificing her own desire to end the curse to protect others.

Jacoa pressed his arched fingertips to the spidery scrawl, the other hand across his mouth as he closed his eyes, recalling his mother's fairytale based on the emotionless journal entry of his ancestor.

$\sim$

Back when the world was black and white, there lived a man saturated in the color red. To the surrounding people, his earthen-colored clothes and hats of casual cream were enough to keep eyes from his red ties and scarlet lips. Supple leather gloves hid the red on his hands.

Of his black, white, and red life, he owned a special sphere of pierced copper and iron that kept a secret as rich as his own.

The truth of the sphere drew him to be bold. He bet on games that cost. He started fights he could not win. He smiled with his red lips, loosening the gloves on his red hands, and took back what was his from the blood of those who crossed him.

The police found the bodies. He did not run. The investigation grew closer. He did not hide. Instead, he held the copper sphere and waited until the clock struck on his eighteenth birthday.

Ghostly smoke rose from the gaps in the brass, though nothing burned inside. Golden eyes blinked awake, sharp as she took in her new master.

"I want my deeds to be legendary," he wished, "and my accountability none."

Fresh from the darkness, the genie granted his wish, freeing him from consequence. But he was not done.

"Let's write a love letter to jazz."

He penned a note from the Axeman, the legend he had become. Told everyone of his passion for music. He demanded an entire city to play brassy tones from every window, for if any were quiet, he'd play his own bloody game.

A wish for the newspapers to spread the warning. A wish for people to believe the lies. A week later, the people danced, lost in the jazzy blues and eyes closed with the love of the music.

And his red hands found their way to the docks, to the darkest house with the quietest windows. Because the person inside knew a melody would not save him if the Axeman came.

A wish for the locks to be free, for entry gained.

A wish for death.

But the genie refused.

So the man rolled up his own sleeves and gripped the sun-reddened neck of his victim. And though no blood spilled, the red on his hands sunk deeper into the skin.

The golden eyes watched from the sphere that dripped a single salty tear.

The smoke never rose again for the red hands. The power within would not answer to a person who did not know the truth of life.

Life is to be lived. Not taken, by hand or by magic.

There would be another firstborn son, one worth the vision of golden eyes. One worth playing the game of eighteen wishes.

Let that son be you.

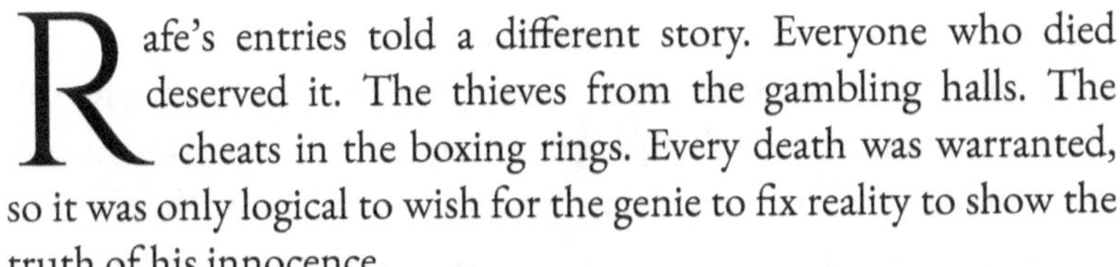

Rafe's entries told a different story. Everyone who died deserved it. The thieves from the gambling halls. The cheats in the boxing rings. Every death was warranted, so it was only logical to wish for the genie to fix reality to show the truth of his innocence.

When she'd stopped granting wishes, it seemed those he'd made faded. Though he wasn't caught for any of his previous crimes, the wishes didn't protect him from future acts of justice. So he'd been forced to move back home and wait for his aging parents to die to gain the only inheritance he cared more about than magic—his fortune.

The fairytale and journal had the same ending, though. His murderous ancestor wrote that he never saw physical proof of the genie again.

Jacoa's eyes shifted over the journals. Each story was a little different. Some ancestors said the genie posed as a friend or mentor. One insisted that after a disastrous first meeting, a black and white cat followed them as if listening for an accidental wish. Another, Gunter, swore she tried to get him infatuated with her, if not in love. Though he alleged he hadn't fallen for the ruse, there was a bitter slant to the handwriting. Jacoa wondered if he'd been more affected than he claimed.

The description of the genie's cuffs remained the same across the ages. She had yellow eyes that tugged at their souls, threatening their sanity. They were always on guard, watching their tongue so they weren't the one who freed the genies.

For each journal was another fairytale, stories his mother told him before he'd learned from his family history that the genie was a monster. He didn't remember them exactly as told, but the resemblance was undeniable. Riti had read these journals and wanted him to learn something else.

His mom had never met the captured djinn. Not only was she not male, but she wasn't the firstborn, either. Her older brother had died before he reached eighteen. One reason Jacoa needed to talk to his genie was to ask her what the connection was. If she might help him put some of his mother's secrets to rest.

Why would Riti have taken these journals and spun fanciful tales that molded Jacoa's opinion of djinn into a softer, more forgiving version? To what lengths would his ancestors have gone to continue the narrative of a cold and manipulative creature?

He held two sets of stories, both obviously biased. Where was the truth?

Not in these pages.

A knock at the sliding glass door pulled his attention from the papers. At the window, a hooded figure stood outlined darker than the night, back-lit by the pale blue lights in the pool. Only familiarity kept Jacoa's features neutral, though his heart raced.

He gestured for his visitor to meet him at the next entryway, out of the mess of documents. The adjacent room boasted a leather topped card table and a wall of cabinets decorated with cloth-bound books and the few art pieces he'd snuck past the interior designer.

Jacoa flipped the lock on the glass door and it slid open. Here stood what he thought was an answer to the genie and Wicker dilemma. The creature approached Jacoa weeks ago with a promise of a wish-less escape from the curse.

Jacoa's original plan had been simple. Don't have children. His mother didn't have any living siblings. Any other family fell far away from the direct line. If he buried the proof with him, the curse would flicker out.

That left the genie trapped, though. Jacoa cringed when he thought of stranding her in the name of ending a situation that had been a significant benefit to his family. If she was the monster from his ancestor's journals, it would be an easier choice.

Then Jacoa met Aali, the draconian who stood before him. The lizard-like man's alternative made sense, a perfect solution. Once he'd agreed, Jacoa wondered if the offer was too good to be true. Had the intimidating person who offered it simply overcome him?

Thick scaled fingers rose to the edge of the hood and pulled it away from a wedged, golden snout. The pale yellow scales on the creature's face shimmered under the electric lights and the wedge flattened into features more akin to human.

Jacoa's heart punched his sternum and he did his best to hide the reaction. Aali was a draconian, and the first magical being Jacoa had met. This creature and his kind hunted the djinn. A monster to kill a monster, yet he offered Jacoa freedom.

He braced himself against the crash of his too-good-to-be-true hopes.

"Aali."

"She is out." The draconian cut straight to the point.

"Yes."

"In what form?"

"Invisible, as far as I can tell." Jacoa scrambled back as Aali's large frame moved further into the room. "She granted one wish for certain. Perhaps two. But I never saw her."

A low grumbling echoed from Aali's throat.

"She is no longer held in the nether by the power of the vessel. That is all that matters. Where is it?"

Jacoa didn't want to turn his back on the draconian. He sidestepped at first, backing away, then hit his thigh on the table. His breath froze against the pain, and he rounded the piece of furniture until he reached the cabinets. Opening one of the upper doors, he pulled out a metal sphere of soft golden color.

The incense burner was a work of art. About the size of a small melon, the molded copper and iron bent into interlocking waves reminiscent of locks of hair wrapping and tangling around one another. As they crossed and parted, gaps were created to allow scented smoke to escape.

It had been a long time since the sphere held anything. The genie didn't live in it, but was bound to it. The same batch of molten metal ores created both the vessel and the bands surrounding the genie's wrists.

Aali closed the distance and reached for the incense burner, exposing his arm from the folds of his dark brown cape. The underside was covered in lighter cream scales, where the back of his hand and along his arm showed stripes of black and white spaced evenly across the gold.

Jacoa sidestepped again, keeping the card table between them as he pursed his lips and held onto the sphere.

"We had an agreement." A hiss accompanied Aali's words, a warning backdrop to the reminder.

"I'm uncertain of the terms," Jacoa admitted.

"I assure you, the curse needs to end. Without magic, your

family should never have kept the trapped djinn from the draconian. There is much you can set right if you just pass me the vessel."

"You're certain this one is your cursed daughter?" Jacoa asked.

Black eyes narrowed. The draconian rose to his full eight-foot height. Jacoa bent his neck at its furthest reach to look up into the sharp teeth of Aali.

"Either way, it is not your issue. I will deal with the genie, false or not."

These were the terms Jacoa was uncomfortable with. He couldn't help that his body trembled with Aali's nearness, or that he swallowed hard against a mouth that was desert dry. His brain still worked.

Perhaps his lack of knowledge was a blessing. Maybe djinn were terrible creatures and deserved the death he saw in the jaws of the predator before him.

Or they might be beautifully misunderstood, unique and brilliant beings trapped and rebelling against that fate. His mother had thought so.

Without meeting the genie, Jacoa couldn't make an informed choice. Jacoa had no problem handing a monster over to a hunter. If she was anything less than evil, he didn't know if he could trust this lizard-creature's parental connection to be enough to save her.

Jacoa would die for the chance to see his mom again. No matter the result of the reunion with Aali and his daughter, Jacoa believed that the parent and child preferred a moment together. He wished he could have spoken to his genie and known for certain, but all he had was his gut feeling.

Jacoa maintained eye contact as he passed the skin-warmed sphere to the draconian.

"What is your daughter's name?"

"It isn't written in your journals?"

It hadn't been, but that wasn't the point.

"If my genie isn't yours, I want her back."

Aali hissed. Clawed fingers wrapped around the orb, digging into Jacoa's hand against the metal.

"Foolish to think our deal can change." The draconian tucked the antique into his cloak. "But brave. When Isra comes, do not tell her the vessel is missing."

"You're confident Isra is this genie." Jacoa rolled the 'r' in her name just as Aali had done, testing the feel and sound of it against the stories in his head. It felt right.

"I have had five hundred years to track her," Aali said. "I do not make mistakes."

The human-like nose extended into its natural wedge. He pulled on his hood and slipped into the desert, disappearing into the shadow of the hill.

CHAPTER 4

Isra

Isra settled against the couch in frustration. Maram hadn't been able to answer half her questions about modern history. The djinn didn't pay much attention to the short lives of humans, though she loved their creation of high fashion and found their 'magical' electronic devices hilarious. The djinn never studied how to live amongst them and found Isra's questions about their lives frustrating.

"What does it matter?" Maram asked. "Just learn as you go."

"At least the first part of the plan is for me to remain invisible to him," Isra grumbled. "It will give me a chance to figure out how to blend in."

"Yes. Great idea. To that end, let's hide these."

Maram's tapered fingernail tapped the copper and iron cuffs around Isra's narrow wrists, her eyes aglow with power. A low assonance filled their alcove and jolts of djinn power pierced through Maram's reality, warning her to keep to herself. Isra covered the spot with her hand, stilling the vibration caused by magical resistance. The cool, time-etched metal was one sensation Isra did not enjoy and would never appreciate.

"No magic will change them," Isra chastised Maram, though

the djinn would know and must have only messed with the cuffs for fun. "I can cover them, though."

Isra used her own ability to weave reality and brought into form long, thin leather ribbons. As they wrapped around the cuffs, she twisted certain pieces, burned the letters of her ancient tongue into the pliant material, and placed a stretch of snakeskin agate beads in line with her thumb.

Maram smiled in approval until she came upon the script. Surprise parted her lips, and she raised her dark gaze to Isra's.

"Why can't I read it?" As djinn, Maram absorbed the meaning of any writing, or the intention for any painted scene. Almost anything.

"It's draconian," Isra replied with a smirk.

"How can you use draconian while djinn?" Maram's shoes gained a sharper heel and a platform toe.

"I'm a genie. I've never been only djinn."

"Jann must enjoy this game. Leaving you with scraps of your old life, forcing you into the worst fate of those you once hunted. But you must not hate it too much since you are dressed in silk and are making out with the couch, enjoying each of your djinn senses. Mmm, it's gorgeous, isn't it?"

Isra flushed and curled her fingers so her nails scraped dark lines into the upholstered velvet.

"If it's so delightful, then why do you need to bother helping me end it?"

"Do you really need a reminder?"

The light flickered around them. With a gentle pop, the walls of Maram's personal reality disappeared to show the interior of the bar. Where it had appeared empty when Isra first entered, each table hosted djinn in their varied forms.

Maram had subdued all other illusions. The rival who'd claimed the top spot earlier was now gone, leaving Maram to play whatever game she pleased by putting the Wicker genie on display.

A few of the djinn stood as they recognized her, some with the cuffs that marked them as cursed. The 'them' Maram likely referred to had a fire in their eyes that demanded answers and insisted on results. They wanted to be freed. Isra had the means. She'd failed for five hundred years.

But that wasn't her worst crime.

Born a draconian, she had trained to hunt and kill djinn. She had been very successful at her job, especially at her young age. Now she served the sorcerer family who designed the curse. Despite their power, no one wanted to risk gaining the First Djinn's ire for interfering with his game.

"Relax friends," Maram said. "Remember, she is the key to your salvation."

"In what lifetime is that freedom coming?" The genie banged his cuffs together and filled the room with an ear-popping din.

"You're helping her complete the contract?" The question came from a now towel-wrapped sauna djinn. "We can support you and end this curse all the faster."

Maram narrowed her eyes at the djinn offering help. Isra stilled and watched the play between the creatures. Djinn were ranked by birth, and the more powerful ones did not appreciate younger djinn challenging them. The first nine were the closest to royalty djinn had, and were very reclusive. Isra had learned of Jann, the First Djinn, but the other eight were a mystery. Unlikely one of them, Maram still gave herself away as being one of the older creations with the level of rancor heating up her aura.

"Do you think I am not enough?"

Isra winced at the force radiating from Maram, her knees weakened and she struggled to stand. The other djinn wilted beneath the weight.

"Of course not," one of the swamp sisters soothed. "We are all eager for the genie to be free."

Maram eased her overall pressure. "Isra had a change of heart. I'm just making sure it doesn't shift back. I don't need help with that."

"Leave her be," said a bull-headed djinn. "When Maram is

ready for playmates, she'll let us know."

Maram's nails dug into Isra's hand on the way to the exit. Isra remained close to the djinn, who was her safest way out of the bar. Once they were outside, Isra jerked away from the djinn's grip.

The marine layer sank onto the surrounding West Coast city, signaling the sun had been down long enough for the mist to fight back. The two-story downtown buildings were silent in these early hours. Even the human-run bars closed in the darkness before dawn, leaving the djinn free to play.

What was Isra thinking, tying her fate to Maram's plan? These creatures never played fair.

But with Maram came djinn power; power Isra needed to escape her curse.

Isra's tension seeped into her hair and the strands moved of their own accord, twisting into braids or curling against each other only to unravel and start again.

"We did not agree on bringing other djinn in." Isra crossed her arms, glaring at Maram.

"Nothing is off the table. It's better that you know now. As long as you are granting wishes, I can hold off that horde."

"Which is why you dragged me out so fast."

"It was time to leave. You would have stayed in there forever playing Twenty Questions."

"I need to blend in so I don't give myself away."

"He was interested in your male form. Change back into that and flirt your way into wishes."

"Why? So a later generation can seek revenge for a grandfather's broken heart?"

"That is the wrong mindset."

"What do you prefer?"

"This is the last Wicker."

"Do you think Jann would let the line die out?"

"This isn't about the Wickers. This is about freeing the djinn!" Maram's stilettos grew taller, the pointed toe wrapped in steel.

Isra played a dangerous game, putting so much trust in a djinn. Especially one willing to play with the edge of death and scare Isra's human master into wishing. Would Maram follow her own rules, or change them as she saw fit?

Isra wrapped her right hand along the braided leather covering of her cuffs on her left forearm, feeling the branded words of an ancient tongue. *My family shall be known*, she'd written. A reminder of her roots. A prayer that her father would find her and end this curse.

She longed for freedom granted by an honorable death. Draconians were impossible for djinn to track. She could find her way to the draconian den. Any of the collective would complete the task, but Isra needed her father. She wanted him to know she'd done her best. That she remembered her family even while making difficult choices.

Her father should have discovered what had happened to her by now. To catch his attention, she needed a bit of rapid-fire magic, something Isra hoped Maram's plan would bring. And though it was generations of her father failing to show that made Isra focus on the next master, Maram was right about her mind-set. This could be - would be - the last one.

"You said this Wicker is different," Isra prompted. Maram's shoes lost a few centimeters of height as she blew out a harsh breath. "You've been watching him?"

"Not obsessively, but yes. He wasn't raised by Isra-hating men. Not to mention, he likes museums and art shows, so he must enjoy old, pretty things."

"How does that help me?"

"I'm not here to do your job. I'm sick of Jann's game and I want it to end."

Isra frowned. "I don't want to get between two djinn."

"Too late." Maram spoke the words against the shell of Isra's ear, then wrapped the genie's arms and torso in a hug before she spun the world around them into a blend of rainbow and starlight.

CHAPTER 5

Jacoa

"Are you sure about coming in?" Jacoa asked Ward. They climbed out of Jacoa's convertible, the canvas top stowed away.

"I'm not going to miss the moment my best friend becomes a gazillionaire."

"That's exactly what's happening. And I'll even give you half of that imaginary number."

Ward swallowed his laughter, though it came out in a snort. Jacoa stopped at the trunk to grab his suit jacket and leather messenger bag, making sure everything was in place before heading inside.

A small parking lot separated the busy street from the unassuming stucco and glass business complex that was situated a few miles off downtown. Large brass letters sparkled in the sun and advertised Humphry's Tower, though the three-story building wasn't a tower, nor did it hold any offices by the name of Humphry.

Desert Skyline Law Firm was on the top floor. Jacoa and Ward headed for the stairs. The ding of the elevator drew his attention, and he changed direction the moment he saw a small, red-haired child peek through the opening.

"Ruby?" Jacoa asked, jogging toward her with Ward right behind him. His six-year-old cousin was holding the open-door button as if she were a professional bellhop. She wore a simple black leotard with a fluffy tutu, her regular costume choice. "What are you doing?"

"Daddy said I could play in the elevator." Ruby stepped out and rushed to hug Ward first, then Jacoa.

"No nanny today?"

"No." Ruby's eyes stared at the red sequence on her shoes. "She let me swim in the pool, but I swallowed too much water and had trouble breathing. She didn't come to help me. Mrs. Nguyen had the window open and heard me. She stopped making dinner to pull me out."

"What was your nanny doing?"

"Um, tanning, I think? With her earphones in. When Mrs. Nguyen yelled at her, she said it was fine. I had a floaty on. And then she got fired."

"Hmm." Irritation gnawed at Jacoa's composure, though he struggled to keep his face calm for Ruby's sake. He exchanged a glance with Ward, who gave a quiet nod.

"Hey, do you want to hang out with me?" Ward asked. "I'm more fun as a babysitter than the elevator."

Not to mention safer, no matter what Uncle Dave thought.

"Jacoa, do you have my pencils?" Ruby asked, twirling to Ward's side and slipping her hand into his. Jacoa dug into his messenger bag and produced a small plastic cylinder of coloring pencils and an old coloring book.

The lobby wasn't much. A huge ficus stood near the window with two plastic chairs pushed against the wall. Simple places for people to wait for their ride. Ward and Jacoa got Ruby set up at the tiny table between the chairs, then Ward sat with her.

The unfortunate truth was they both rescued Ruby from neglectful parents or nannies on a regular basis. While they watched Ruby at Dave's house one day, Jacoa had asked Ward if he minded having a little girl thrust on him so often, but his friend had pushed Jacoa into the pool in response. When Jacoa sputtered to the surface, Ward and Ruby were laughing like partners in crime.

That Ward cared about his cousin was a tremendous relief in these moments. Jacoa spoke his thanks and checked his watch, then gave a quick wave as he took the stairs.

Ruby didn't have any luck with nannies. His aunt and uncle accepted the first available applicant—often without an interview—simply to be done with the job. Jacoa had gotten into the habit of spending as much time with his cousin as possible, struggling to protect her childhood and keep the bright sparkle in her smile.

It seemed nothing had changed since he moved out. That Mrs. Nguyen had been present during the swimming incident was a stroke of luck. She was his aunt and uncle's personal chef and only came a few days a week.

His little cousin's safety would be worth wishing for, if he only knew anything about his genie. With Ruby more than any other, he couldn't risk the chance of a twisted wish from an angry magical being.

He really needed to get a hold of Isra and keep her near.

"Jacoa!"

Startled, Jacoa stopped just inside the frosted glass door of the law office. The sound of Uncle Dave's voice bounced off the glass walls that allowed visitors to view the offices. Across from them, a patriotic mural decorated the long wall and its doors. Portraits and accolades of the firm and its lawyers hung over the bright paint. Each door had a brass plaque that marked where it led.

Jacoa frowned at Dave, who was resisting one of the firm's lawyers. She struggled to direct him into a glass-walled office. His feet planted on the low-pile geometric carpet and he refused to face the door he was meant to step through.

"There he is," the lawyer spoke through clenched teeth and a forced smile. "If you come in here, we can get you settled."

Mr. Mendoza, Jacoa's lawyer, stepped out from the library

doors and took in the scene. With a heavy sigh, he motioned for Jacoa to follow him, then offered his colleague a nod.

"Go on in, Mr. Graph." Mendoza spoke so his voice didn't echo as Dave's had. With Jacoa approaching, Dave tugged his suit jacket and followed the woman. Mendoza let the door swing shut as he passed it, directing Jacoa into the next office.

Jacoa refused to acknowledge the muted shout that came from the next room. He chose a chair at the six-seat meeting table and Mendoza took his place across from him.

Dave was losing his life of exuberance. As far as he knew, Jacoa's fortune was Old Money, and the result of lucrative investments and general luck with the stock market. He considered the funds an endless fountain of wealth.

The first time Dave remembered he wouldn't have access forever was when the house was signed into Jacoa's name a few weeks ago. He'd missed that benchmark, but remained hyper attentive to the others, making every possible objection along the way.

What he couldn't stop was Jacoa's birthday and, as of today, his cushion was gone. Dave wouldn't be poor, but he'd have to start budgeting. Limit the number of cars he bought every year. Maybe go for first class instead of a chartered jet.

No one in the world felt sorry for Dave except for Dave.

"I'm surprised to see him here. Was this planned?" Jacoa asked.

"It's just the latest and last delay," Mendoza said. "Dave has been putting off signing the papers, and only agreed after we threatened to fine him."

"Why is he in the next office?"

"He wanted to ensure you're healthy. He wants to make sure you can take care of yourself, as he hasn't seen you since you moved out a month ago." Mendoza's lips twitched beneath his thick mustache. "So now he's seen you. Thanks for wearing a suit, by the way."

Jacoa couldn't find the same humor as Mendoza. His uncle's

neglect had driven Jacoa into a lot of reckless behaviors. He was getting alcohol poisoning at twelve. Tripping mushrooms at fourteen. House parties were easy when the adults were never home.

A few too many trips to the police station hadn't brought Dave, but they had brought Mendoza. The lawyer had threatened Jacoa. Get his act together, or deal with a longer term with Uncle Dave as guardian. Ruby was getting older and beginning to feel the same sense of abandonment that had led Jacoa down such a destructive path in the first place. She'd need him for support.

So he'd cleaned himself up. Once sober, parties weren't as fun anymore. Random hookups provided temporary companionship, but were easy to let go once they were done. When Mendoza had given him the journals, they reawakened memories of his mother and presented Jacoa a puzzle that became his new obsession: Isra.

Jacoa picked up a pen and passed it back and forth between his hands, studying the shiny black casing with the law firm's gold foil logo shining in the overhead lights.

He was alone with his lawyer in a room that wasn't sound-proof, but close. What range did his genie's powers have? Could she have been far from the party when he'd made his wishes?

"I wish my uncle would be satisfied with his own fortune and accept that his guardianship has ended."

Mendoza snorted over the document he inspected. "As do we all."

The lawyer slid the thick packet over to Jacoa, yellow plastic 'sign here' labels poking out.

"We've already reviewed this in preparation for today. Nothing has changed. Tell me if you have questions or concerns, because once this is signed, it's all yours."

"I'm good," Jacoa assured him. He straightened his spine and twisted the body of the pen.

His heart thumped at the sight of these documents. The pile of pages provided permission to leave Dave behind. A rush of pride expanded his chest. Mendoza would have delayed the process, but Jacoa had done the work. He had turned his life around and with a few signatures, he would be in control of it.

Two-thirds through the contracts, a sharp knock rapped against the glass from the next office.

"Well, I'll be damned," Mendoza muttered. "Go ahead and look, Jacoa. It seems your wish came true. Jones must have talked sense into your uncle, after all."

Jacoa turned to find the lawyer organizing and straightening her own pile of papers, a discarded haystack of signing stickers mounding on the tabletop. She caught Mendoza's eye and shrugged before returning to work.

Dave waited at the window, his ear pressed against his cell. He offered a two-fingered wave and a crooked smile that pulled in his dimple. Tilting his phone from his mouth, his lips exaggerated the shape of a word.

Ruby.

Jacoa nodded to acknowledge the message, unnecessary as it was. Even though he'd moved out, Jacoa still saw his cousin more than Dave did. Jacoa debated getting up to tell his uncle where he could find his daughter, but decided to stay put and not test his luck. Dave would see her with Ward in the lobby. Instead, he sent back a quick wave and Dave took that as his signal to leave, engrossed in whatever business his call contained.

With shaking fingers, Jacoa returned to his own stack of papers. Isra had heard him. He just didn't know how, and he was tired of being one step behind his genie.

A few more signatures later, Jacoa was done with the lawyer. The two men stood and clasped hands.

"Excellent work, Jacoa," Mendoza praised through their matching grins. "I knew you had it in you. Congratulations, and don't spend it all today."

Jacoa left with a bounce in his step and a lightness in his heart. Finally free.

The lobby was empty. Ruby and Dave were nowhere to be

seen, even in the parking lot. Father and daughter must have reunited.

Ward leaned against the side of Jacoa's electric conversion classic Mercedes. The pearlescent sheen of the paint blended with the chrome accents. He popped the trunk and lay his jacket in the shallow well, placing his bag on top.

"Your uncle..." Ward trailed off, shaking his head. Everything had been said before and many times over. The end conclusion: Dave was an ass.

"Yeah," Jacoa agreed. "Thanks for hanging out with Ruby."

"Please. I only hang with you so I get to see her sometimes."

Jacoa laughed as the pair climbed into the car, settling into the tan leather seats.

"Where are we going to spend your new fortune?" Ward asked.

"The Strip, of course."

"Excellent!" Ward drummed against the dash. "Where to start? We can break in the slots or go straight for the—"

"Exhibit."

Ward's chin dropped to his chest and his shoulders deflated.

"Hey, you do whatever you want," Jacoa soothed as he pulled out of the parking lot and into traffic.

"No. I said I'd spend today with you to celebrate. I just didn't realize that meant shopping."

Jacoa ignored him, excitement rushing through his blood and giving him a high. There was little in life he hadn't been able to get either with his generous allowance or with Dave's approval. However, Dave hadn't approved of all of Jacoa's interests and would hold back every once in a while. Even the changes to his house were made on credit, all to be repaid now thanks to today's stack of signatures.

What Jacoa really wanted couldn't be bought with the promise of future payment, and he was tired of being patient. A grin split his face as the car sped toward the Las Vegas Strip to collect his treasure.

CHAPTER 6

Isra

Isra's molecules sped through the city, the gasses that made up the air tickling and energizing her vaporous form. She kept her essence spread over the back of the car, enjoying the aerodynamic rush trying to push her in the opposite direction.

She'd followed Jacoa all morning, hiding in obvious places. While at the lawyer's, she thought she'd been particularly clever, only to discover the consequences of her choice. Her last time in the living realm had been in 1947, and television detectives and their gadgets had amused her, so she'd spun her own take on the recording pen. It proved an interesting experience.

Jacoa had taken her up in his hands and pressed each end of her length between his palms to leave her suspended in the radiating warmth of his skin. Fingertips examined her casing and drew small circles around the logo, catching the variations on the surface. As he'd gripped her, his warmth saturated her core. Vibrational movements caused mini explosions that filled her with frenetic energy. His breath had flown in gentle puffs, scented with the rich earthiness of coffee and caramel.

The shifting of papers and movement of the pen lasted for long, sensitive minutes. Disguised as the wind now, she found herself intensely jealous of the steering wheel that held the full attention of Jacoa's fingers. She caught herself moving further toward him, calculating the magic needed to get back within his reach.

She denied herself. Her flight was precisely what she needed after the intimate sensations brought by his touch. The soothing warmth of the sun, the brilliant sparkle of his car, the light and joy.

Jacoa wished again, but this one differed from the others. It had been for someone else.

He might have wanted the papers already signed. He could have asked that he no longer required his uncle's participation. Instead, he requested his uncle be satisfied and accepting.

Sensing her master's thoughts or emotions wasn't part of her genie or djinn skills. She didn't know him well enough to guess why he made the choice to be considerate. In the world of wishes, semantics were incredibly important. There were selfish ways for Jacoa to get what he wanted. Instead, he chose to be gracious.

Of course, the context of his wishes shouldn't matter as long as he kept making them. Three in two days was a record. She buzzed with how different this outing was already. Maybe she could abandon Maram's plan.

She needed to be careful. Success wasn't guaranteed just because Jacoa was testing the waters. Three wishes, even in rapid succession, weren't enough to gain draconian attention.

Jacoa seemed well contained for eighteen, as if he'd grown up faster than usual in these modern times. It made her wonder what thoughts hid behind these wishes. Mind reading was not one of her skills, though she caught glimpses that accompanied a wish, like when Jacoa wished for a drink and she had a vision of a whiskey sour.

She would stay close and see if he gave anything away.

Jacoa turned onto a road that had widened into multiple broad lanes, and the increased traffic slowed his speed. Deep side-walks provided thousands of people space to wander between street acts and fountains, whether they were on their way somewhere or enjoying the glitz of Vegas.

The buildings sprawled over manicured landscapes and grew until they reached the feathery clouds accenting the translucent blue sky. Chrome-lined windows glinted in the sun. Giant screens danced with alluring imagery to draw people to shows and events. Music filtered into the air from someone with a guitar on the corner, then a small steel band sat half a block up, where a group of show girls paused for a photo, their bright red feathers fluffed and their bodies twisted to frame their tourist marks. Rushing water teased with specks of mist, though it never cut through the powerful desert dryness.

Isra's absorption came to an abrupt end when Jacoa turned his car off the wide road and into a twisty drive that led to a cream building. Under the lit overhang, someone rushed to greet him. Jacoa and his friend hopped out and passed the keys to the valet. Isra drifted away, no longer wanting to remain gaseous in this stagnant air. But what form to take?

Maram announced her presence with a jolt of energy. The broadcast went to all djinn in the area, though she could have kept her essence specific or hidden had she chosen to. Isra noted Jacoa's laughter cut above the noise of human and vehicular traffic. Long, casual steps carried him away from the gold-framed revolving doors that led to the casino entrance with long, casual steps. His jacket was back on and buttoned, hands tucked into his pant pockets. He headed toward the shops, while his friend gestured and begged for just five minutes at the tables and a few drinks.

Isra wouldn't lose him. Their connection was bound by genie contract. She was unable to ignore his presence. Her vessel wasn't required for a summons. The spherical incense burner held her contract and acted as a timepiece, marking when she was free from the nether and required to return. To escape its tyranny, she either needed to grant eighteen wishes, or use just enough magic to call the draconians.

It was her theory that the distance between wishes was why

her father had never found her. There hadn't been a large enough, or long enough, spend of genie magic for him to pinpoint her location.

Which was where Maram's plan came in.

Isra shimmered into form. A desert mirage come to life behind a Grecian-style pillar, nearly invisible in this self-absorbed crowd. She materialized dressed in a soft cotton dress that fell just above her mid-thigh. She lifted her fingers to her collarbone and drew the neckline into a deep V. The neckline grew a lace fringe that knitted into racerback straps. Gladiator sandals wrapped up her calves.

Maram appeared in a red ruffle crop top that wrapped around her upper arms and chest. Her torn jeans left little cloth along her thighs, but solidified past her knees. Her heels were chunky and coffee-toned, signs of a good mood.

"Let's go to the mall," Maram said.

"Why?"

"People watching, of course. And who else to keep you company? Few djinn care for the sun."

"You do?" Isra asked.

"I have skin in this game, too. We will get those wishes together."

Isra studied the pure djinn with a tilt of her head.

"Who is it you want to free?"

"All of them."

Maram's image blurred. Her clothes faded to ebony. Her heels thinned to a needle point, held on with the thinnest strip of black leather, their chrome soles ringing against the granite-tiled sidewalk as she stomped away.

It seemed Isra had struck the wrong chord, but not so dissonant as to make Maram leave. Though she'd never assumed the djinn was helping her out of altruism, her near-constant presence suggested something deeply personal.

Isra wished she knew more about the djinn. She'd only learned how to trap, then kill them. Her current self had only seen glimpses into their world for a combined twelve years over the course of five hundred.

Who were the djinn trapped as genies? How many suffered this curse?

The answers were dangerous and valuable information for a draconian to have. Isra could never ask without bringing the full force of Maram's suspicion on her head. That type of attention was best avoided, as she didn't intend to follow the djinn's plan in its entirety.

Trailing in Maram's heel clicks with her own whispering flats, Isra followed the djinn to the air-conditioned gallery of shops. Isra thickened her hair for warmth and let it caress her arms. She slid her palms over filigreed columns of gold and green. Display windows oozed with rich color. Floral perfumes and spicy cologne bit at her nose. Her lashes fluttered and Maram studied her, a curious smile on her lips.

"Do you ever acclimate to sensation?"

Isra was not going to give the creature more ammunition. Maram could not understand the absolute absence of everything but thought. How first you grieved with the strength of earthquakes and hurricanes, yet never created a ripple. How anger inflamed every waking hour, yet nothing ever burned. Despair fell without rain. Insanity pulsed without accompanying delusions.

And then the minute arrived. The dawn of a new day. The mark of a birth that became your own. Watching the sunrise with fresh eyes. Breathing air with raw lungs. Feeling every nerve tingle into life as the dawn brought the sun, and you knew after endless days, years, decades, that you were alive.

In that moment of distraction, Isra didn't notice Maram's smile shift until too late. The djinn licked her front teeth in anticipation, her eyes focused beyond Isra's shoulder.

Hot breath wove through her hair to excite the skin at her neck. The aura of a warm-blooded body radiated at her back.

"Isra." The rolling sound of her name sent a matching vibration into her lower belly. She filled her hair with the sense of touch, let a few strands cling to his shirtfront to tangle in the smooth buttons.

Why was she so drawn to this master? His sorcerous ancestors betrayed the draconian by harboring a djinn. His many-greats grandfather had cast a wish that ended in her curse.

Yet, it didn't matter with Jacoa. She could die a million deaths from his fingertips and be happy every time.

"I wish for you to remain in my presence, in human form, until our time ends."

Isra's hair uncurled from the buttons and fell flat against her own body.

She took it back.

He was the worst Wicker. Binding her. Locking her into form. Taking her freedom after only a day.

And Maram laughed at it all, having turned invisible to any but Isra's own eyes. She faced the cocky human who thought he was being so clever.

"Wish granted."

CHAPTER 7

Jacoa

His genie was beautiful.

No. Beautiful was too generic for Isra. Her yellow sapphire irises flashed with alien appeal. Inky black hair framed her face, only to burst into a pure white blanket over her shoulders. She embodied the warmth of day and the discomfort of night.

As she stood before him, a brush of red darkened her cheeks. She wasn't happy. That was fine; he was thrilled enough for them both.

"Isra," he spoke again, pride expanding his chest. He'd caught this elusive creature and the revelations could begin.

Until Aali returned. He replaced thoughts of the draconian by flooding his senses with the ecstasy that bloomed while standing before his genie. The consequences of dealing with Isra's father were not part of this moment.

His eyes absorbed every detail—the rich bronze of her skin, the height of her cheekbones, the curve of her brows. Her lines were firm and light, delicate in strength. His heartbeat doubled when she scowled.

So very human, and so very magical.

"Jacoa." Her hair rippled as she stepped back, ripping the halo of her body heat from his.

"It's good to meet you," he said, keeping his voice gentle. "We need to go this way."

Her frown deepened with his instruction, and guilt laced his triumph. He imagined she felt as if he'd destroyed her careful plans. Once they talked, he hoped she realized his way was better.

That would have to come later, though. Jacoa was meeting Victor Rusch, an artist with a short-term lease in the mall. Victor was due to pack up the coming weekend. Jacoa had begged him for weeks to save a particular art piece for him, but no promises were made. He hadn't found out if his prize was still available before he'd spotted a flash of yellow eyes. Not knowing if it had been a trick of the light, Jacoa had taken a gamble by speaking her name. Making a wish.

A risk well worth it. His wins were greater than Ward would collect at the gaming tables he'd snuck off to.

Jacoa checked to make sure Isra followed as he entered the store. Glass display cases sat at different heights and sizes throughout the gallery. Diamond-shaped bulbs illuminated the artwork. One bronze creation melded flowers and vines into the shell of a motorcycle. A clockwork dragon had scales that acted as a combination lock to ease the creature off its pedestal and expose whatever treasure it guarded.

These mass-appeal items designed to draw in customers held no interest for Jacoa, since they were reproducible. He wanted the unique.

"Mr. Wicker," Victor greeted him, though his eyes latched onto Isra as he presented her with a smile that ignored Jacoa. The artist stepped forward, ready to shoulder Jacoa aside for the new entrant.

"She's with me."

Victor stopped in his tracks. He'd always treated Jacoa's visits with veiled impatience. A youngster from money whose rich uncle wouldn't pay for impractical art.

Jacoa didn't find art frivolous. He reveled in the innovative power of it, in awe of the skill and patience required for creation, something he didn't care to cultivate in himself. He loved to collect, though.

"In the back gallery," Victor agreed, eyeing someone on the outside who had their nose pressed against the window with the clockwork dragon. "Stare as long as you wish."

Victor shifted toward the new customer, but Jacoa stepped in front of him, lowering his voice.

"You can chat with them about things they can't afford, or we can discuss my purchase of the wall sculpture today."

"Wh-what?" Victor's eyes widened, his feet rooted to the floor.

"I'm eighteen."

Victor's mouth gaped, then a grin split his face.

"Well, look at that! Happy Birthday! Please, let's go see it, to ensure you're still pleased with it."

Victor practically danced from the front gallery filled with smaller pieces to the back room, where his larger wall art hung. After six months of Jacoa's visits, he knew what that magic number meant for his bottom line.

"You should come," Jacoa called to Isra, who circled a free-standing podium. She didn't spare a glance for him before walking to the next. "Please?"

She never looked up, her black and white hair hugging her back and shoulders.

Well, she couldn't go far after granting his wish. He'd talk to her when he finished here.

Peace filled Jacoa's chest as he went to meet Victor. He'd longed for this artwork and for his genie. To gain both in one day left him walking on cloud nine.

Statement pieces dominated, with plenty of viewing space between each. Three dimensional creations rose smallest to largest within the room, the taller figures encouraging a customer's exploration to continue toward the back. Wall sculptures hung on the walls in a mix of glass, metal, and other light catching elements.

Though the front room items were inventive and intricate, they were reproductions. The larger, abstract pieces that filled this space were one of a kind. Their organic and hypnotic structures were products of heroic effort. The emotions and energy of each piece couldn't be recreated.

The first time Jacoa walked through, he spent hours taking in every detail. Victor liked to alter and twist materials, so each section caught the light differently. Luminance bounced out of the center, or absorbed into the surface, drawing the eye and defying expectation.

Jacoa's prize floated off the back wall. Some might assume this piece was simple compared to the others. Someone might even say it wasn't worth the hefty price tag. But they missed the magic.

What used to be a single, five-foot square steel sheet had been cut into two rectangular pieces and nine smaller squares. The metal warped at different points, then painted with an oil-slick of midnight blue gloss. Victor welded rods between the steel, then made them sparkle. Crushed crystals and tiny diamonds encrusted each strand of connecting metal and shimmered along the outer edges of each piece.

Distorted reflections laced with a shimmering glow spoke to Jacoa of darkness breaking. Divots and pools of the inky paint worked to draw you in, even as the growing strands of diamond kept the trap at bay. The light wasn't at the end of the tunnel. It interlaced the dark.

"You have surprised me yet again, Mr. Wicker," Victor said. "I didn't know if you would ever take this piece home. I'm glad it's you. Not many people recognize the delicate work of balance and strength that goes into artwork like this."

"What do you mean?"

"Others have admired the shiny threads of crystals and diamond that tie the pieces together. Though they say they are interested in how I did it, as I explain, their enthusiasm fades away. They don't want to know the truth of magic. Once they do, it is easy for them to walk away."

"How is it easy to leave the promise of freedom?"

Victor's hand landed with a solid thump on Jacoa's shoulder.

"You assume everyone sees what you do. Be careful with that."

"You see it as something else?"

Victor studied the artwork as if seeing it for the first time.

"I can understand how it means freedom to you. That's what matters, now that it will be yours. Are you ready, then?"

Jacoa thought of the genie waiting for him. His grin was exaggerated in the reflective curve of the warped metal before him.

"Absolutely."

CHAPTER 8

Isra

The ties of Jacoa's wish pulled at Isra as a plan formed in her mind. What an underhanded move, politely asking her to follow him after the command to remain near him. Of course, her answer was no. He'd already taken enough.

He wanted her close, did he? Always in human form? Fine.

Isra set the parameters of 'in my presence' to mean within sight. The wide arch that led to the back room limited her range to the center line of displays. Irritating, yes. But hopefully an emotion Jacoa would share soon.

She wove around the few pieces of art within reach. The pedestals stood like pawns facing off on a chessboard. Prices weren't displayed, giving off a 'if you have to ask, you can't afford it' vibe.

That wasn't Jacoa's problem with his family's wealth. Though he didn't seem interested in gambling any of it away, he was more than happy to spend a fortune on something for the sole purpose of enjoyment. Even Isra knew the back room of any establishment housed the higher priced items.

He liked to collect, she guessed, in part based on the way he looked at her when they met. The triumph of acquiring an amazing prize softened as she faced him. He had hovered, his eyes roaming every inch of her face, breath held as if in awe. No one had ever stared like... like she was a gift.

No. Not a gift. A Wicker would never view her kindly. A prize, then. Something to add to his gallery.

Isra's frustration wasn't only with her new master. Maram's agenda was just as irritating. Isra hoped for more time to listen from the wings. She was sure she could have gotten more from him while invisible. Isra assumed he'd been planning to catch her and make this binding wish.

As Isra wove around the pedestals, she stopped in front of a figurine that left her gasping, its impact visceral. A mechanical dragon worked to shed its man-made clockwork as it struggled toward life. The tail, the darkest part of the lizard, had been created with bands of metal, hexagon rivets driven through and nailing it into form. The metalwork softened along the body, the brass polished in an ombre finish until the glorious golden head scattered the reflected light, its mouth open. A red, pulled-glass tongue peeked from between curved fangs.

On the bottom third of the wings, tendrils of dark gold metal curled up as if trying to hold on to the mechanical form, losing the battle against a brilliant burst of silver lead that supported shards of blue and green. The cool shades shifted within the glass, alighting under the spotlight. Her breath fluttered in response to the joy in the creature's jade eyes and her skin electrified with the power of its transformation. The emergence of the creature both broke and healed her heart.

"It's a bit on the nose, don't you think?" Maram's voice hummed. The soft weight of the other djinn's chin settled onto Isra's shoulder. Maram was leagues away, and the sensations she cast were a reminder of her greater power.

"Always trying to escape, but never succeeding," Maram continued. "It might as well be titled 'Isra'."

"And this would be Maram," Isra replied, turning to a sculpture depicting a glass butterfly, mostly intact. The right wing had scattered pieces pulled away and held by delicate strings of metal in suspended disintegration.

"As if I would ever fall apart."

"Even after I abandon your little plan?"

"You're mad that I tricked you into Jacoa's waiting hands. Fine. But you were going too slow."

"The first stage was to listen. We've had three wishes in two days."

"He was onto you. I've been watching, too. Cute play, by the way, turning into a pen. You would have done just as well being invisible."

Isra's chakra chain stuttered. Maram's point was more accurate than the other djinn could know. That Isra enjoyed every stroke of his fingers was a truth she would never share. Maram didn't need any more ammunition.

"It's time to move on," Maram ordered. "And he's taken your freedom now. You should have plenty of anger to fuel your fire."

"Did you help him with that wish?"

"No, but it was delicious to watch."

Isra spun her chakras counterclockwise to press energy out from her body, a firm push against the consistent pressure on her shoulder. As the younger djinn, Isra couldn't overpower Maram, but she made her point. Maram backed off with a teasing laugh.

"You have a few days for in-person efforts before the next phase. I will be waiting for opportunities to put him in danger, since you can't break the genie rules. When the time comes, delay your instinctive reactions long enough for him to make his wishes."

"I know the plan."

"Yes," Maram agreed. "But see that you remember it when it matters."

Maram withdrew her presence. Isra clenched her fists against the rolling argument within her chest.

Isra did not trust any of the djinn; particularly one who presented her with a plan that included threats of harm. If her own power had attracted the draconian, she would have never entered this agreement.

None of her brethren had come. Her father, the best hunter of them all, hadn't found her.

Aali might not know of her curse, but he knew about the Wicker vessel. The bloodline had once held magic. In fact, some of the greatest sorcerers of history had been Wickers. Jacoa's ancestors had been the ones to invent the cuffs and vessels that bound djinn into genies. They were the very family who had reached back in time and spliced dinosaur and djinn genes to create the magic-resistant draconian race.

Had her disappearance distracted him from acquiring the vessel? Had he looked for her in all the wrong places?

Five hundred years ago, she was supposed to work with her father to go after it. Eliminating the First Djinn would deal a massive blow to the creatures. Isra had heard rumors that the Second Djinn was neutralized, leaving only seven of the ruling class. The draconian had already existed far longer than expected, failing in their mandated task to rid the world of djinn. Jann's vessel could provide a wave of momentum toward victory.

Aali had wanted to wait. She'd been impatient. They were close to her twentieth birthday, when she would have to be presented to the draconian collective. She had to prove she was the best hunter. If she didn't, her status as a female mandated that she'd be locked in the den for the rest of her life.

So Isra had gone in alone. She'd found the vessel tucked into a puzzle box on display in the cigar room of the English estate. The Wicker of the time, Abraham, attacked her with a fireplace poker, catching her unprepared. She turned to throw her body into his and limit the power of his swing, but he'd dodged. They studied each other through the gloom, gauging likely attacks, the darkness not a friend to either of them.

"What do we have here?" Jann appeared from nothing, lounging on the couch. Their blue skin faded into the night-darkened room, their white eyes aglow in contrast.

"Get back to the nether," Abraham ordered without taking his attention from Isra, more cautious of the lizard person than the one who held the power of the universe in their veins.

"Aww, what a very caring master, protecting me from this dangerous hunter. Do you want to wish her away?"

Abraham snorted in derision. Jann released a jaw-cracking yawn.

"Well, if you don't want her gone, why not bound? What's another slave to the latest Wicker heir? Just think, her yin to my yang."

Abraham straightened, his eyes flickering toward the djinn.

"And she wouldn't be able to harm me?"

"That depends on your wish, of course," Jann purred.

Abraham licked his lips, the poker lowering as he deliberated. Isra took a slow step backward, calculating the distance to the door. Her draconian blood protected her against the illusionary magic of the djinn, but wishing magic was a more powerful and dangerous breed. It solidified illusion into reality. She could only hope distance would save her.

"She's sneaking away. Now would be the ideal time to wi—"

"I wish for this draconian to be mine, unable to harm me or my descendants."

"Your wish is my command."

Jann's voice vibrated the room, and a separate laugh filled Isra's ears, both from the djinn's throat. They raised their arms and the copper and iron bands dissolved, the particles racing through the air. Isra sprinted for the door, but she was no match for magic.

"Let her be your genie, then," Jann declared. "But I'd be remiss not to explain the rules of the game. She shall appear to your descendants on their eighteenth birthday, and for only one turn around the sun. To gain her freedom, she must grant eighteen wishes within that year. If she does, all other genie contracts will be void. Let's see how the Wicker line does once those they imprisoned are free."

Jann and Abraham forced Isra from one trap to another. Neither she nor the Wickers planned to complete the contract, but they both intended to use it to their advantage. She needed to grant just enough wishes to call out the draconian. The Wickers desired to secure their fortunes. They should have been able to work together, but that required trust.

Any vulnerability she shared had been used against her, with Wickers using wishes to bind her further in an attempt to keep her from altering their dynamic. The Wickers wanted a genie to be tied to their line. They no longer had magic, so they wanted the power of wishes to help secure their wealth and legacy.

The Wicker secrets passed between generations through journals. Isra imagined the pages contained strict instructions on how to manipulate the rules of her curse. Though they used her power, not one had ever forgotten how many wishes they'd asked. Never did her offerings of friendship move them further.

But this Wicker was different. He did not have the same male-to-male training as his ancestors. Was it a greed, similar to Abraham's, that brought him to this expensive showroom? His home was opulent. He had a car that cost a small fortune.

What could she offer him that he did not have? What was his deepest desire that his money couldn't buy?

Jacoa emerged with the older man, who beamed with delight.

"And you're sure you can deliver it?" Jacoa asked Victor.

"Of course," the artist promised as he moved to his computer. "I need your address before I can tell you the price. With the care the sculpture requires, I only trust my own contacts. It will be expensive. I hope you understand."

"I wouldn't pay so much for something I intended to treat carelessly."

Victor started typing and Jacoa faced Isra. She moved her eyes away, still standing before the morphing dragon.

Maram had pin-pointed her obsession with the sculpture. Isra didn't need Jacoa discovering the same thing. With him in the room, now, she had greater freedom of movement.

Isra drifted over to view the jewelry. The tiny creations were much less interesting than the sculptures, but she studied them as carefully as the more complex pieces.

"Do you like anything?"

Jacoa's voice was uncomfortably close, his lips at the level of her ear. The velvet flow of his warm breath drew a shiver of appreciation from her, nonetheless, reminding her once again that no matter what challenges she had now, it was easier than being in the nether.

"Why, yes." She tried to throw in a little of Maram's throaty purr. It came out more like a growl.

"I'll get it for you."

As if a genie couldn't provide everything for herself. As if he could charm her with a gift. Except for one thing, of course.

"How very generous. I can ask for anything?"

"Name it."

"What do you wish for?"

Jacoa jerked back, his lips thinned and his brow wrinkled with question rather than anger.

"You didn't say there were limits."

"I didn't." Jacoa's shoulders curved down for a moment before he pulled them into proper posture.

"I wish..." His head dipped.

Isra stepped forward, lifting her face toward his. He wasn't much taller than her, so with him leaning in, their noses practically touched.

Whatever she was going to say escaped her tongue when he exhaled. Their breath mingled in Isra's lungs. The unexpected warmth sent her blood rushing to her third eye and her lashes drifted closed. She held on to the air he'd given her, igniting *Manipura*. A low energy buzzed between them. Her flow of magic spun right, then left, not knowing if she should take more of him in, or give him more of herself.

Not a single part of them touched, yet Isra was consumed.

"Nevermind." Jacoa jerked back, breaking the spell as he

looked away. Isra gulped in fresh air and struggled to get her reaction under control before his light green eyes found her again.

"You're taking back your offer?" Somehow she kept her voice level.

"I have an idea, but let's talk about it later."

"You're considering a wish, though?"

"I'm considering a conversation," Jacoa clarified. He lifted his hand and Isra held herself still, watching his face for signs that he felt the same unexplained energy between them.

He gave nothing away, even as he halted his reach toward her cheek and gestured to the door on her right instead.

Isra took the offer of escape. A happy artist stood at the exit, hands gripped in front of his chest. His smile brightened as they came closer.

"I'll have my people call you once your purchases are ready for delivery," Victor said. Jacoa waved and smiled, though his eyes never left Isra as she led them from the shop.

CHAPTER 9

Jacoa

J acoa shook off the odd energy that coated his skin. Standing close to Isra had filled his body to the brim, like a battery fully charged and ready to run. He hadn't been drawn in so much as connected. Somehow, it was her breath in his lungs rather than his own.

He'd torn himself from the sensation, not knowing if she manipulated magic to make him feel that way, or if he was high on her presence after wanting it for so long. Her cheeks had been tinged pink. Was it because she experienced a similar draw, or was she angry over their conversation?

She gave nothing away in how she held herself as she walked. Her feet skimmed the marble floor, her wavy hair shifting in a slow kinetic dance. When she paused and raised a brow at him, he figured she didn't know which way to go and copied her mute example as he took the lead.

He guided Isra through the opulent shopping center until they reached the large, arched opening that led from the relative quiet into the reigning chaos of the casino, where Ward should be. The slot machines were by the doors, their bodies lined in LEDs and their screens flashing a siren's call of winnings to the wide-eyed tourists.

Jacoa passed them without paying attention. Ward rarely spent time here, preferring to squeeze into a space at the crowded roulette, dice, or card tables where a real live person sat at the helm. The sound and lights of the casino pressed against Jacoa in a physical force, and he tuned most of it out, retreating inward.

Offering Isra an artwork from the gallery proved to be a miscalculation. He'd responded to her absorption with the art, which echoed his experience. Jacoa assumed she must want something, just as he had. A small chuckle was lost in the noise around him as he realized Victor's words were coming back to haunt him.

It wasn't the gift itself, but he'd wanted to extend a peace offering. He thought he'd known what she would like, but the way she stared at the jewelry had him second guessing his instinct, and he took the opportunity to ask.

All that interested her were wishes.

He wasn't surprised. Perhaps a little disappointed. A genie so focused on wishes was expected.

Jacoa twisted to glimpse Isra. She appeared to feel the opposite of him in the crowd. Where he ignored the stimulation, her eyes danced on the shifting light. Her head tilted toward a person who let out a frustrated bellow, then she smiled at a group bent in laughter.

The desire to study her as she examined the world gripped him. He wished she walked beside or in front of him. A wry smile twisted his lips. That was all it would take. Just that image spoken out loud, and he'd have exactly what he wanted. Jacoa rejected the temptation.

A floor to ceiling advertisement caught Jacoa's attention. It broke up the crowd of people with a shifting display of blues and reds, advertising an immersive experience of flying through space and walking on other planets. The artistry of the ad called to him, and his adrenalin ignited.

Jacoa loved when creative minds put together grand exhibits like this one. He recognized the work that went into the event, and was in awe at the execution he would never have the patience to recreate. A QR code floated in the corner and Jacoa pulled out his phone to capture it.

"A human interpretation of space," Isra spoke beside him, her voice cutting through the crowd's noise with ease. "Why waste your time on that, when you could see it all for yourself, with a wish."

The desire of addiction sent a tremor through Jacoa's hands, and he lowered his phone. He hadn't felt this intense a need since his partying days. Art was one thing, but to truly be able to see and to know what no one else on Earth could clawed at his soul.

His phone buzzed in his hand, breaking him out of the fierce longing Isra's words had conjured. He shook his head clear and rode the wave of disappointment that he would not be giving in to the promise of adventure that she offered. Part of him was impressed she'd locked onto his interests so quickly. He was more driven to get her someplace they could talk and hopefully get past her need to push him.

Grateful for the distraction of his phone, Jacoa checked the text that had broken through his craving.

Ward: Saw you got a girl and bailed. Good luck with that one. She's gorgeous.

Had Ward seen them walking through the casino? Still, the fact that he'd abandoned the tables was a curious turn of events. Ward wasn't addicted to gaming. Rather, he had the best luck Jacoa had ever seen, and he liked to play. He claimed it was patience, not good fortune, but even the casino gods didn't believe him. Ward had to grab small doses of fun with his gambling passion, leaving before winning too much.

They'd met on Jacoa's sixteenth birthday. His aunt organized an underage casino party and Ward had crashed. Something about their interaction that day had tied Ward to Jacoa's side. Ward started hanging out, always with some new story. With Jacoa working on his best behavior after Mendoza's warning, Ward didn't pressure him to come out on the town. He had plenty of fun poking and prodding Jacoa to find out what made him tick.

Ward's friendship proved peaceful without being boring. His stories were entertaining and varied, since he never lacked for the chance to try something new in Vegas. Then there was Ward's incredible perception, like noticing Jacoa picked up a girl even though he hadn't been nearby.

Jacoa lifted his eyes from his phone to the person in question. She examined the casino with unexpected intensity, taking in whatever floated to the top of the chaos. How she surveyed the world reminded him of how she studied the sculptures. Every detail was important to capture. Did she view everything with the same absorption?

Rather than shout through the noise, Jacoa stepped closer to catch her attention and once he had it, gestured with his hand that they were changing direction.

"No need to be polite now. You ensured I can't get far with your wish."

The cacophony muted to make way for her words. Magic. A flow of energy burst from his feet to the top of his head.

"Can we hear each other because of our connection?" he asked in conversational tones. "Or is it something you did yourself?"

Isra's quick tongue wet her lips, but formed no more words.

Jacoa's skin tightened with goosebumps. He led the way to the valet. His head lightened with excitement. He'd read about this genie's magic many times from the fragile pages of his ancestors' journals. Now he was experiencing it. Jacoa's senses flooded with joyful energy, and his steps sprung from the floor. Even having collected the sculpture from Victor did not match this feeling.

The Mercedes arrived twenty minutes after he ordered it, the top still stowed away. Isra moved toward it before Jacoa, and his lips twitched. The premature movement divulged that she had been with him before he'd caught sight of her.

Once in the car, Isra's fingers caressed the tan leather of his seats, dipping into each seam. Jacoa drove them from the garage and out of downtown. Isra's eyes were in constant motion. She appeared to be interested in everything from towering buildings to the gentle curves of the layered overpasses of the freeway. The city melted into the desert hills, and she marked the transition with a sigh. The wind combed through her hair, and she turned into it as if greeting a beloved friend.

A thrill rippled from Jacoa's heart to his foot, and he accelerated on the empty road. He couldn't wait to get her home and delve into the richness of her magic and secrets. To discern if the legend was a fairytale or a monster.

As his car pulled into the garage, no small talk sprouted between them. She remained silent as he unlocked the door. There were no benign comments about the decor of his home. Though she observed everything, her lips remained still.

Isra refused to answer when Jacoa asked what she would like to eat. She didn't join him at the table for dinner, but stood outside the window and ran her fingers along the curves of the teak-framed outdoor furniture.

The electric rush that sparked between them at the art gallery had thickened into a heavy weight that sat in his chest. He banged the pan into the sink. The dishes crashed into the dishwasher. Anything to break through the quiet in his house.

As the sun set, he joined her on the patio. Her head tilted back as she gazed up at the darkening sky and the newly revealed stars.

How could he learn who she was if they never conversed? He refused to spend a year existing with this exceptional creature, but never untangling how she connected to his mother. His eyes narrowed at the thought of that potential waste. It would be like procuring a stunning artwork, only to leave it in the rain to watch the paint run.

"What will it take for you to talk to me?"

"I suppose a wish would work." Her voice was smooth, though her top lip curled as she glared at him. He shook his head to dislodge the heat that threatened to awaken his full temper.

If he wished for her to be completely honest with him, he might get his answers faster. He disregarded that idea as soon as it formed. Dave, for example, was especially skilled at twisting his words so they were always factual, but not necessarily the whole story. A genie was likely more adept at half-truths.

Today was only their first day. Maybe they needed more time. Jacoa rolled his shoulders to relieve the tension. He debated grabbing a few journals from his office to refresh his memory on some of the genie stories, but decided it was better if they stayed put. If Isra wasn't going to share information, he wouldn't tip her off to where he stored the papers that were his only trump card in this game.

Jacoa turned inside and Isra followed him, so he closed up. Abandoning the main floor, Jacoa took the stairs upward. Three bedroom suites were spread out on this level, two to the left and the master on the right. A sitting room separated them, and another set of accordion glass doors led to the deck.

Isra's gasp drew Jacoa's attention. She'd followed him and stared past the hammock to the evening sky. Her yellow eyes reflected the deep oranges and reds of the fading sunset. Jacoa's lips relaxed into a smile at the sign of hope. If she appreciated beautiful things, surely they could find common ground. He'd try again tomorrow.

"Take either of those two suites," Jacoa offered her. With each step toward his room, his tension faded away. A shower sounded amazing. A book might distract him from the challenge Isra presented. He closed the door, only to spin around when he heard a strangled yelp.

Isra phased in through the wood, chest arched forward as if being pulled by an invisible string. Her yellow eyes glittered and lips thinned.

"What the hell?"

"Don't you dare blame me for the consequences of your wish," Isra snarled.

"You've kept plenty of distance between us all day."

"You were always within sight."

Jacoa sputtered. "But I want a shower."

"Shy boys shouldn't wish for a constant companion. Should I promise to turn my back?"

Isra crossed her arms and her lips curved up, though there was no humor in the motion.

"Where are you going to sleep?"

"The bed. Unless, of course, you wish it otherwise. Then I might take that tiny couch as if I were truly your pet."

Jacoa's cheeks flushed. He turned his head on a cough caused by the constriction in his throat. Her attitude toward him suddenly made sense. She'd known all day how he'd trapped her.

Could he wish his way out of this somehow? Would it be worth it? If his last request backfired in this manner, what would happen if he gave her more freedom? She might take advantage of that space and he'd struggle to be near her again.

For the moment, he appeared stuck. He was too tired to think as carefully as he needed. Surely there was a compromise here.

"What if I keep the door open? Will that work?"

Isra raised a dark brow. "Only one way to find out. Do you wish for me to go deaf, so I don't listen to you splash?"

Jacoa flung his hands out to reject the idea and he stalked toward the bathroom. He eased the door closed out of habit, but threw it wide when Isra drifted in his direction. At least only a sink was visible from the bedroom. He moved into the marble and brass room, eyes locked on the entrance as he fumbled for a rolled towel from the basket.

Isra wasn't dragged in. His shoulders eased away from his neck, and he took a deep breath in thanks for small favors. Jacoa grabbed a robe from where it hung. He'd never used it before, but was thankful for his designer's forethought.

He peeked into the bedroom. Isra had chosen a book from the bedside nightstand. She sprawled out on her stomach, nose deep in the pages, comfortable with the distance and the open door.

When Jacoa turned on the water, he swore he heard a throaty laugh drift in. He couldn't help his own exasperated chuckle, a small part of him finding amusement in his own blunder.

CHAPTER 10

Isra

Isra could have told Jacoa her response to his wish was changeable and creating more space between them was possible. Within the same building could technically count as 'in my presence', if she chose that interpretation. The reason she hadn't done so before was because she'd wanted to be close to him, to watch him much more subtly than he thought he watched her.

But his expression when she'd phased through the door had been too delicious. Out of his room, he'd controlled his emotions. As their conversation continued and he stumbled over words, it was clear his bedroom was his sanctuary, and he did not have the same defenses when inside of it.

There was also a large rush of validation when the full force of understanding hit him. His wish hadn't just kept her from leaving, but trapped her. Why wouldn't she take advantage and make him almost as uncomfortable?

When the lights went out and they lay alongside each other in Jacoa's bed, Isra was caught by an unexpected phenomenon. The dark didn't disguise how little space existed between their bodies on the queen-sized mattress. Isra's chakras sputtered and shifted, struggling to align. She focused on one energy center at a time until the disks connected her body to the earth and the heavens, providing a direct link to the magical forces of the universe.

She spun her chakras clockwise at a steady pace and created a gentle shield within her aura. When those energies brushed against Jacoa's own natural force, she gasped. Her energy struck his body as if it were her own hands exploring the solid length of his form and her eyes fluttered closed on the joy of connection. Every muscle froze as she hyper-focused on the contract. Jacoa's soft sigh jolted her from the sensation, reminding her there were consequences of such contact.

Her chakras recoiled and reversed into herself until she felt the inner pull collecting Jacoa's essence and drawing its edges into her own. The invisible current intertwined like the fingers of two hands giving space for each other, palms pressed together.

Jacoa rolled on his side, closing the gap in the bed. Isra redirected her chakras. The back and forth cycle marked each slow hour that passed in the night.

As a genie, Isra did not need a human's sleep. Yet this ebb and flow left her in limbo between exhaustion and peace. She had never experienced energies blending this way. In fact, she hadn't known it was possible. The djinn were always forceful with their auras, commanding her to retreat. Humans often had a greasy feeling; the type brought on when a being's chakras weren't fully in line with the universe.

Jacoa was different. Isra didn't know if it was due to him or his wish that their life forces matched so well. The sensation was equal parts welcome and unsettling. When the sun lightened the sky, she thought it would bring relief. Instead, it brought her a vision she'd denied herself in the dark.

Jacoa's body sunk into the soft mattress, the comforter drawn to his waist to display the rise and fall of his chest with each breath through a thin t-shirt. Ebony eyelashes curved in gentle crescents, an inky contrast against almond skin a few shades lighter than her own.

Isra recalled when she'd mentioned how his lashes outlined his eyes while posing as a bartender. He'd instantly lost interest in the conversation. It appeared she hadn't been the first to comment on them. A frown sunk her lips. How many others who noticed had seen them as she was doing now - while he slept? Her chakras, so in tune with Jacoa's, sparked. The surge was unexpected, though an interesting result of their intimate energy sharing.

Isra filled her lungs and eased her shoulders from her ears, shifting onto her back to stare at the ceiling fan. Her motion brought an echoing one from Jacoa, who stretched his body and raised his arms to press against the upholstered headboard.

Jacoa blinked a few times before taking a deep breath. He caught her presence out of the corner of his eye, then jerked into a half sitting position, almost falling out of his bed. A laugh bubbled up and burst out of Isra.

"Crap," he croaked, running a palm over his face. His lips were smiling as his hand fell. "I guess I deserved that scare."

"Amongst others," Isra agreed. "You don't wake up to other faces in your bed?"

"Are you asking about my dating habits?"

"I suppose it doesn't matter now, since you're stuck with me. How would you ever explain?"

"I know a few who would welcome it." Jacoa winked.

Isra startled at his teasing, but wasn't about to let him win.

"How many people are we allowed to invite to this sleepover?"

"I said my friends would like it. I didn't say I'm willing to share."

Jacoa lowered himself onto an elbow as he spoke, their chakras mingling as if last night's experience had changed their very nature. Isra's chest warmed, and a blush threatened her skin at the nature of their conversation. She didn't assume Jacoa was serious, but couldn't help where his words took her thoughts.

Draconians didn't have a biological drive to have sex. As a djinn, she found human, non-master partners only for the sensation of physical connection. Isra recalled a couple wrapping their arms around Jacoa at his party, lips brushing his cheeks and tickling his ears with unknown whispers, though their seeking fingers on his chest and hips gave their meaning away. Even though he hadn't encouraged more of the contact, Jacoa had appeared relaxed with their attention, indicating that his own experience was more varied than hers.

Would he mind her dual nature in the moments she liked to be male? When a curious tickle struck her belly, Isra decided it was time to get out of bed. Her thoughts were not where she wanted them when she should be focused on her mission. She hopped to her feet and sent a pulse of magic through her body to refresh her appearance.

"That looks far easier than a shower," Jacoa said.

"A single wish and it, too, can be yours."

"You weren't too fond of my last one."

"Neither were you last night."

Jacoa threw the blankets off and stepped out of bed, dressed in a t-shirt and cotton pants.

"I wish..."

Isra stared at him across the expanse of jumbled comforter and sheets. Dawn filtered in through the windows at his back, a soft halo of glowing light, an effect that provided him with a more powerful presence than he held otherwise.

"But perhaps not," he finished with a smile.

Isra released her pent-up breath as Jacoa rounded the bed and passed her to enter the walk-in closet. His tease of a wish and then its retraction left her fidgeting with her hair.

Was he done wishing now that he had her? That wouldn't settle well with Maram. Isra hoped to keep up a steady enough stream of wishes so that the djinn would hold off on the next phase of her plan. Another surge of magic would certainly alert her father, especially with the desert where the draconian lived so close. Death Valley had the scorching sands and empty spaces preferred by their kind, and Jacoa's home was only a few hours away.

Lucky for her. Hopefully.

First, Jacoa needed to ask for more wishes. Isra had to figure out what appealed to him.

Jacoa emerged from his closet, having changed into a fitted pair of jeans and a dark orange button-down shirt that had faded at his elbows and collar. He rolled up the cuffs and studied her with a lowered brow line, as if debating something worth considerable thought.

"If I ask questions, will you answer them?"

"That depends." Tension coiled in Isra, leaving her distrustful of Jacoa's chosen approach. What did he want?

"Would you tell the truth?"

"Probably."

"Without twisting it?"

"Doesn't everyone twist the truth in one way or another?"

"I've waited for you for a long time, Isra. I'd like to play as few games as possible."

"As a Wicker, I assume you know the nature of the djinn."

"I only know what I've read."

"First-person accounts, from what I understand. Did each of your male ancestors pass down a journal, or only the ones who met me?"

"Most of the ones that met you. Some of the others, depending on how angry you made them."

"Most?"

"I don't have the records from when you were attached to the Wickers."

Isra shook her head. Of course it would be Abraham, the feeble-brained idiot. If he had kept a diary, he probably destroyed it to avoid having his mistake recorded.

Jacoa studied Isra as if waiting for her to provide information to a question he hadn't yet asked. She kept quiet about Abraham, not wanting to bring her own complicated history to his attention. Jacoa didn't need to know she hadn't been born a djinn. If his ancestors had mentioned the draconian in their journals, she didn't want him to realize her connection to them in case he might wish that the draconian wouldn't find them. That would destroy her goal of escaping this curse with minimal cost.

"There are things I need to know," Jacoa said. "I want to trust your answers, but that can't blind me. My ancestors' secrets cannot fall into the hands of the djinn. I hope you understand my need for this wish, even though it's another one that binds you."

Isra backed away from Jacoa, hitting the bed after one step. Her fingers curled into claws, dreading the words that would bind her to the honesty he'd been requesting from her.

"I'm going to show you my ancestors' journals. I wish for you to keep their secrets as your own, only able to discuss what you discover with me, but only if you choose to do so."

Wish magic differed from the powers she controlled otherwise. Djinn magic was another sense extended, an invisible set of hands. In essence, it was her power pressing out. Wish energy sunk in and flooded Isra's chakras, given by the universe in answer to the contract between master and genie.

Wickers were trained in wishing. Even though a male ancestor hadn't raised Jacoa, he understood the importance of semantics. The guidance must have come from the records he offered her. What else did the pages hide? The information inside them could prove invaluable to the draconian. Maybe they offered leverage to use against the djinn.

Yet, the journals weren't the most compelling part of his wish. This confusing man before her warmed every inch of her body by presenting her with one of her greatest desires. He'd given her a choice.

CHAPTER 11

Jacoa

Jacoa wondered if Isra made time stop, or if the world naturally slowed with her presence. Just now, he had frozen in place with his wish. Last night, he almost accused her of extending the seconds, which felt as if they'd stretched to the length of an hour.

As they'd gone to bed last night, he'd been hyper-focused on how her breath filled his usually silent room. Yet, after a few minutes, his tension drained on her inhale and peace seeped in with each of her exhales. It was as if an external energy ebbed and flowed around him, a gentle wave that relaxed every muscle in his body and let him drift to sleep despite the strangeness of having someone else in his bed.

He hadn't slept well since his mother passed away. That he'd done so with the object of her fairytales had Jacoa waking up to a world saturated with possibility.

The enveloping comfort had not followed him into the morning. He brainstormed ways to keep yesterday from repeating itself, where his genie avoided and ignored him.

Their unexpected banter opened a small door to hope. A little light flirting had to mean she wasn't as mad at him as she appeared. He'd even surprised himself by staking a claim. Jacoa knew himself well enough to realize his attention was difficult to hold, and, being eighteen, he didn't feel any pressure to settle into a long-term relationship.

So after revealing he didn't want to share, he'd clamped on his tongue to keep it from disclosing any other unexamined thoughts. Isra seemed uncomfortable, too, since she was quickly out of bed after his statement.

As he got dressed, he distracted himself with planning. He wanted Isra's trust and doubted she had much reason to have faith in a Wicker. A gift was still his best idea, but there was only one thing to give her that his genie couldn't provide for herself.

It was a huge gamble to show Isra the journals. She might twist his wish in a number of ways. He didn't know if she valued the content enough for it to make a difference between them.

Offering his family records could open avenues of conversation he was desperate to explore. The documents were not going to be one hundred percent accurate. Jacoa studied enough history to know the victors were in charge of the retelling. They tended to represent themselves as heroic rather than as the invading thieves they'd been.

Would she be amused by the tales of struggle? Angry at how she was portrayed? If Isra agreed to discuss the differences, maybe it would lead to talking about his mom.

Jacoa shifted from foot to foot, raising a hand to massage his neck as he debated snatching back his words. The air between them had gone stagnant. Isra herself had adopted such an intense level of stillness she might have transformed into a statue.

"Okay." Isra's answer was light and airy, though her accompanying nod was firm.

"Um, okay?"

"You have your wish."

"That's it? You don't have to say 'wish granted?'"

"I tend to reserve that for the irritating wishes."

Jacoa smiled at the freely offered insight. Perhaps his gamble would pay off after all.

"I'll do my best to limit those, then."

Isra snorted, seemingly not convinced he'd be successful. He silently promised to try.

Jacoa lead the way to the lowest level. His fingers shook as he reached for the knob. A chill ran down his spine when he opened the door. Surely his ancestors were turning in their graves and sending him curses from beyond.

He hadn't cleaned up from when he'd had the journals and accompanying files spread out two nights ago. Isra picked her way into the room, her bright yellow eyes wide as she took in the clutter.

"So this is where you hide your mess," she said.

"Figuratively and literally," he agreed with a sharp laugh. "Most of these are archival documents. Some were passed down, and I found more in the public records. You're welcome to go through it all, but I imagine you're more interested in their actual words."

Two piles of journals rested on Jacoa's glass-top desk, which sat in the center of the room. A floor-to-ceiling bookcase was built into the wall behind it. Across the way was a small cocktail table placed between a set of plush chairs angled inward. Isra lingered a few steps from the doorway, her hands gripping a few twisted locks of her hair. How did she feel, about to dive into his ancestors' recorded thoughts of her?

It wasn't a question he could ask, so he chose a different one.

"Is there a particular order you'd prefer to read them in?"

"No."

"Do you want the entire stack?" Jacoa asked as she sat, curling her legs up under her.

"I can get them." The topmost journal flew from the pile, opened in mid-air and settled into Isra's waiting hands.

Sparks flashed between her palms and the binding. The book dropped to the floor as she hissed with pain at the contact. Isra's features darkened and her fingers curled into fists at the same slow pace she closed her eyes.

Jacoa sprung across the room. He stepped over the splayed pages, his concern laying with Isra's hands. He reached for her, but she jerked away, and his stomach sank, certain her recoil meant she was hurt.

"Is it bad?"

"That depends. Did you know they were spelled against djinn power?"

"No, but never mind. How are you?" He grabbed for her wrist, but she twisted away.

"Not amused."

"Damn it, Isra, are you hurt or not?"

"Jacoa." Isra opened her hands, palm up, the skin perfectly formed and intact. "I'm a genie. It takes more than that to injure me."

With a deep breath of relief, Jacoa eased away from Isra, frowning at the journal on the floor. He picked it up and smoothed the few creased pages, then closed it.

"Should I hold it for you?"

"Or..."

Isra's unspoken words hung between them.

"A wish can overcome whatever spell is on these?"

"I guess these journals haven't told you everything about djinn and genie magic. The short answer is yes. Any wish I grant for you will change reality to be as you ask."

Jacoa's stomach flipped with the thrill of being on an amusement ride. Isra didn't elaborate on how his education was lacking, but she was talking to him now rather than sticking to the silent treatment from yesterday. What was another wish? How she manipulated it would reveal as much as her words, if not more.

"I wish that the spell keeping djinn from accessing the Wicker journals no longer affects you, and only you, of all the djinn and genies."

"Very well phrased," Isra murmured, curling up into the chair once again. The book slid from Jacoa's hands. He flinched in preparation for another backlash, but none came.

A grin lit Jacoa's face as Isra devoured the text, turning pages with her magic. She hadn't said 'wish granted.' He must have gotten it right, at least in her eyes.

"Are you going to stand there and watch me read?" Isra asked.

"Oh. I can make breakfast. What would you like?"

"Space, but a particular wish has eliminated that choice."

Jacoa shifted between his feet, a frown on his lips. "Do you want me to wait until you're..."

Isra stood, then gestured toward the hallway while keeping her eyes on the pages. So he hadn't gotten his wish about proximity correct, but he already knew that. He could only move forward.

Jacoa found his way into the kitchen and opened the fridge. He turned to offer Isra something. She read while waiting for the glass door, which was stacking itself open by magic.

The refrigerator dinged at him for keeping the door open too long. He reluctantly turned his back on Isra, not sure if presenting so much vulnerability would gain her trust, or end in heartbreaking loss.

CHAPTER 12

Isra

Jacoa cut laps through the pool, the water heated enough that a light mist rose from its surface. The medium parted for his steady strokes and flowed into a liquid coating that reflected dancing will-o'-wisps caused by the blue lights spaced along the tiles inset below the waterline.

Isra stretched out on a navy cushioned chaise, which had become an early morning recurrence in the last three days since Jacoa gave her access to his family records. Her master didn't stay still for very long. Though she had hours to read the journals, and could have simply absorbed their meaning in a moment, she found herself taking her time, and indulging in distraction.

Jacoa tried to give her time to read at whatever pace she desired. She made it a game to list the ways he entertained himself. He never returned to the same thing twice in her four days with him, except for his morning swims. Jacoa had played three different video games, none for more than two hours. Two days ago he made pretzels. Once, while she read on the patio, he even took on climbing the steep hill behind his house, making it halfway up before the slope became too much and he slid down, a devilish grin on his face.

Yesterday, he'd clearly had enough and talked her into going out. She wasn't sure what to expect, though, when he pulled a canvas cover off a four-wheeler in his garage. Her own energy matched his in excitement.

For hours, they drove into the desert. This late in the year, the temperatures were comfortable during the day. While on the road, Jacoa was cautious. Once on the trails, he let loose. He cornered with deep twists of his torso and took hills with a speed far above what was recommended, standing on the machine as they flew through the sky.

Isra sat on the back of the ATV. She didn't need to hold on, and simply enjoyed the battle of physics. This was how it felt to become the wind itself, feeling the rush and sudden turn of gusts while gravity tried to ground you. She closed her eyes, forgetting that she was stuck in human form, her spirit flying right along with Jacoa and his reckless driving.

He stopped at one point to ask how she was doing. She caught his dusty, contagious smile, unable to fight the rise of her own.

The moment broke when she realized how far they'd driven. There were no signs of civilization beyond the rough trails created by outdoor enthusiasts. The empty space gave the impression they were alone in the desert. Isra knew better.

Death Valley was hours away, but the draconian weren't limited to those sands or the climate. Three days prior, Isra would have searched the horizon for a shadow that didn't belong, hoping to be found. Yesterday, her chest tightened and breath shortened, and she wanted to avoid any chance of running into her people, for this moment to be interrupted with something as final as her death. She laced the breeze with the scent of the yeasty, caramelized pretzels Jacoa baked earlier. On cue, Jacoa's stomach growled, and they headed back to his house.

They started their fourth day together the same way as always. Despite that, Isra didn't know what would come next. She enjoyed that about Jacoa, the not knowing. He was up for every-thing, capable of anything, and excited to explore.

The lowest level of the patio didn't get sunlight in the morning hours. She indulged in the autumn vibe, keeping warm with thick black leggings and a loose knitted sweater whose green color might match a certain pair of eyes.

Isra was used to fully focusing on whatever she chose. Becoming distracted was a new experience. Another djinn would have devoured and destroyed the Wicker journals by now. Instead, Isra found her eyes invariably leaving the words on the page. She hadn't even opened the journal in her hands. They weren't half as exciting as guessing what Jacoa's need to move might drive him to next.

She had discovered little within the pages of these books, beyond the fact that the djinn overvalued them. Mostly they read as angry autobiographies where all faults in the author's life stemmed from their one year with a genie, as if they had no true accountability of their own.

"I don't know what your strategy is, but it sucks. Much like your fashion." Maram appeared on the chaise next to Isra's, dressed in a barely-there bikini and large sunglasses as if they were under the tropical sun.

"What are you doing here?" Isra checked on Jacoa to make sure he was still swimming, even though she knew Maram kept her presence hidden from him. The thought of Jacoa looking up and seeing the djinn's mostly-bare form compared to her covered one sent twisted lines through Isra's restless hair. Braids wound and unwound, curls tightened and eased. From her comfortable position, Maram watched it all with a crooked smile.

"Ah, I get it. You're playing the domestic game."

Isra kept one ear on the sound of Jacoa moving through the water and both eyes on Maram.

"We have a year. I think it's worth exploring options."

"You have had half a millennia, you false djinn. The time for exploration is over. We want results."

"We?" Isra asked. "Who else have you brought into this?"

"No one. Yet."

"Why would you even consider bringing in other djinn when we haven't moved onto the next phase?"

"Very good point, Isra, dear." Maram sat up and stretched her arms overhead. "All right, you've convinced me. We'll try it your way before I declare open season."

Isra straightened in her chair, realizing where Maram's maze of words had led her.

"Unless I get more wishes from him first."

"Which hasn't happened for three days. No. It sounds like your master needs a little inspiration, and I can definitely help with that. No backing out now, Isra."

Maram disappeared, removing her presence along with the current threat, though the reprieve wouldn't last long. Isra was relying on her proximity to Jacoa and their wish magic to stop the djinn from going too far, but she hadn't anticipated that Maram would be so insistent on a fast timeline. Isra needed to draw the magic out to attract the draconian, not move at a lightning pace.

Isra glared at the hill behind Jacoa's house, her anger punching through it and traveling across the desert to where the draconian had built their dens under the heated sand. If they'd only come sooner, she wouldn't be in this position.

Yesterday, she'd discovered her dedication had changed when she urged Jacoa to cut their off-roading trip short. She argued with herself she'd drawn him away from a possible draconian interaction because she didn't want him to be part of her death. He'd been a kind master mostly, if a little misguided. He shouldn't see what would happen.

Maram's visit made it clear the draconian were a distant worry at this point. Her honorable out appeared less of a worry than her struggle with Maram. Isra hadn't realized how fast the djinn wanted to move. She'd assumed she had more time.

Isra would have to remain alert. Maram intended to attack Jacoa and force wishes. Her threat to bring in others wasn't idle. The casual words hadn't only brought about the next phase, but acted as a warning. Isra wasn't allowed to quit this game.

They weren't entirely at the djinn's mercy. This part of Maram's plan meant an increased use of djinn magic and had to draw in her father, or even another draconian. Their presence repelled the djinn, since they never traveled without the means to capture or kill. If they ended Isra's life and her curse, then Jacoa would be free.

No matter Isra's impulse to drag Jacoa from the desert yesterday, she could not lose sight of the big picture.

Tears pricked her eyes. She blinked them away, glaring at the frayed cloth cover in her lap. For the first time, regret accompanied the thought of dying. She pressed up the sleeve on her sweater, her hand gripping the leather bands covering the metal cuffs.

My family shall be known.

Isra had never wanted to become a djinn. Though she'd made an excellent draconian, as a female her future there was no less of a trap than the copper and iron wrapping her wrists.

The water shifted and Isra welcomed the distraction. In a rush of contrasting forces, Jacoa thrust himself from the pool. He grabbed his towel from the neighboring chaise and threw it over his head, scrubbing at his hair until his cell phone chimed.

He grasped for the small device as if he'd been waiting for its musical call all morning.

"Today's schedule is going to be tight," Jacoa informed her after checking the screen. The skin around his eyes narrowed in apology. "Crap. I need to shower."

Isra rose since she was obligated to follow him. Jacoa didn't head up right away, his attention snagged on her face as if he saw something he couldn't quite make out.

"You don't look happy. Is it a bad portrayal?"

"What?" Isra startled.

"The journal. Whose is it?"

"It's Gunter's."

"Oh. Did he tell it wrong?"

Isra placed her palm flat on the top page and sent her energy out on an exhale, flooding the book. On the inhale, she pulled the magic back in, bringing with it all the meaning written within. She flipped the end with a slow turning of pages, using her hand to move each one in an effort to delay reaching the entries composed after she'd disappeared from Gunter's life.

"No. He told it exactly right."

The answer was only a partial lie. As far as she knew, this was Gunter's truth. It hadn't been hers. What it provided, though, was invaluable. She'd thought her time with Gunter was special. He only saw her as a genie.

As Jacoa headed upstairs, Isra kept her distance. She plopped on the bed and opened Gunter's journal once she was alone, a strange sense of déjà vu floating up from the pages.

Gunter had been her tenth master. She'd seen them as friends. So much so that she'd worked with him disguised as of one of his employees.

Seventeen wishes had come and gone in the space of ten months. Her father had not appeared. Then Gunter started talking about the last wish, granting her the freedom he thought she wanted.

Isra couldn't allow it, not with the fate of all other genies tied to hers. Gunter had told her he didn't believe she should suffer at the expense of keeping the genie curse. She didn't agree. Most of Isra's life had been spent tracking djinn and genies. Killing them to protect the world from their powerful illusions. They caused famine. Wars. Panic. Death.

She had wanted freedom, yes, but not the type Gunter offered. So she'd disappeared before Gunter could act.

The journal told a different tale. He omitted wanting to free her, and had written that she'd tried to seduce him, though that had never been her intention. Each harsh slant in his penmanship added another weight to the ache in her chest and created a juxtaposition of her memories against his retelling. She closed the book with a snap.

Jacoa's bare feet on the tile drew her attention to the open door of the bathroom. He'd dressed in jeans and a simple gray t-shirt, staring at his phone. The heaviness in her chest eased with the very sight of him, and Isra wanted nothing more than to let him erase all her past troubles.

"I was afraid we'd be double booked today, but luckily the delivery has come early."

Jacoa's eyes rose from his phone to take her in. His energy shifted into an outpouring of excitement, wanting to share this moment with her, giving her the gift of an easier breath. His addiction to movement and adventure called to her, drawing her mind away from the journal she tossed across the mattress. Isra's chakras responded to the high frequency of his, desperate to replace her thoughts of Gunter with Jacoa's compelling presence. She didn't know if he was conscious of this connection between them, closed off to magic as he was, but he reacted to it either way.

Isra absorbed what he offered until the dark energy in her chest dissolved in the light of his. She rose from the bed. Jacoa drifted to her, their essences tangling. It wasn't magnetism, but two spools connected by the same thread, each taking and giving in equal measure until they stood inches apart.

The doorbell rang. Jacoa jerked up as if noticing for the first time that he'd lowered his mouth toward hers. Isra took a smooth step away, locking her hands behind her back to hide the tremors in them. Jacoa tried to speak but had to clear his throat before sound emerged.

"Um. We have to get that."

Jacoa skipped stairs in his hurry. Her mandate to stay close meant she had to follow even as she worked on getting her jumbled thoughts back in order.

Whatever was happening between them was not normal. As much as she wanted to fear their connection, she couldn't. Instead, she waited to see how often the exchange might happen. How many times could they mesh before her year was up or her father found her? If she experienced everything possible with Jacoa, perhaps her fate would be easier to face.

Jacoa reached the entry and threw one of the doors open, then worked to unlock the second panel.

"Thank you for waiting. Please come through here."

Two delivery men lifted a canvas-wrapped package as tall as Isra into the house. Jacoa walked backwards, his eyes never leaving his treasure. Just past the stairs was a large, empty wall where he wanted the sculpture to hang.

Ah. It must be his artwork from Victor.

The men placed the wrapped parcel in the living room and produced drills and mounting anchors. Where the tools didn't look dangerous, remembering Maram's recent threat caused Isra's throat to tighten. She made her way to Jacoa's side. Each strand of hair locked in place so they didn't brush the back of his hand, no matter how the ebb and flow of energy between them tempted her.

"There's an easier way," she murmured as one man pulled out a nasty looking drill bit. "You can ensure your masterpiece will be perfect and safe. Secure."

Jacoa shook his head and though he flashed her a frown, it didn't last long in the rush of his excitement. Isra wet her lips with the tip of her tongue, frustration a low burn at the base of her spine. Maybe she should tell him this wasn't like her first push for wishes. He'd ask why, and Maram would discover Isra gave away the game. Then there'd be no phase three, and Maram would call in djinn reinforcements.

The brackets were secured without any accidents. The men returned to the artwork, loosening the ties before pulling on white gloves. As the movers turned the piece so the front was visible, Isra shuddered at the reflective, inky darkness.

The mirrored finish on the two large pieces and nine smaller satellites was not quite black, but too dark to be blue. The warped metal created swirls of isolation. Convex rises caught halos of light that shimmered in gentle echoes from the brilliant lines of diamond and crystal, which surrounded and connected each of the components.

The effect drew her in and trapped her in the deep tones. In her chest, *Anahata* struggled in its revolution, wanting to spin opposite the other chakras to push this feeling away. Tears pricked her eyes and she held her breath to keep it all in.

"I thought you would like it." Jacoa's quiet voice tickled her eardrum. His body pressed behind her, close but not touching. She pulled his energy into her, latching onto their connection as if he were an anchor. His excitement was tempered and was replaced by worry, as if he was upset that this artwork wasn't as powerful for her as it was for him.

In truth, it was so much more for her. The inky swirls wanted to swallow her, to drag her into the emptiness of the nether. She yearned for physical contact. To grab Jacoa's hand and remember that she was still with him. But she stood still.

"It's triumph, don't you see?" Jacoa asked. "Everyone has darkness in them. Whether they came from it or it found them doesn't matter. It's there, but it can be broken. We can escape from it and turn it into something beautiful."

He was looking at it backwards. He focused on the space in between and the brilliance of light. All she saw was the void piecing itself back together.

Isra's resolve cracked and her hair drifted to brush the soft fabric of his t-shirt. Individual strands found the hand he held casually at his side, barely brushing his skin. What a silly reaction, attaching to a human. When the time came, his grounding presence wouldn't be able save her. He couldn't wish her out or keep her in this realm.

Static electricity snapped between them and Isra ripped herself from both Jacoa and the artwork, only to stop in her tracks when she saw what else had been installed.

They had placed a black block of a pedestal in the large entryway on prominent display. Gloved hands lowered a crystal-clear cloche over a creature that echoed Jacoa's words and was breaking away. In Isra's periphery, Jacoa had a brief conversation with the delivery men, slipped them a tip, and walked them out. He returned to Isra's side, where she remained as frozen as the clockwork dragon.

"I noticed you studied this for a while. I think I can see why it speaks to you. The stories between my sculpture and your dragon are similar, aren't they? I suppose that makes sense, since they come from the same artist. The same human experience."

"I'm not human."

The words flowed from Isra, breaking the spell. With a sigh, Jacoa eased away and checked his watch, though he couldn't hide the slack features of someone who had been denied something important.

"We're running out of time."

"Where are we going?" she asked.

"The city. Can you be ready in a few minutes?"

Isra raised a brow at him, though in truth his distraction was welcome. Her sweater shimmered, reworking itself into a cold shoulder peasant's blouse, the three-quarter sleeves stopping just before her leather wrist wraps. Bedazzled jeans replaced the leggings and gladiator sandals wrapped around her feet.

Jacoa's lips twitched. "One day you'll have to tell me how much magic you can work outside of wishes."

"There's another way to see more magic," she reminded him, but not to encourage wishes. Jacoa didn't like being reminded of their contract, and she needed the space her words would bring.

Jacoa didn't disappoint. He refused to answer her and turned away to run upstairs for a pair of socks. As Isra was pulled along with him, she debated extending their range, but decided against it. For the moment, this particular deceit was beneficial, especially with Maram biding her time.

CHAPTER 13

Jacoa

Jacoa's phone rang on the way into Las Vegas. His car didn't have Bluetooth, so he pulled off the highway. Any other day he would have waited, but today he was meeting Ruby. He didn't want to miss any messages from her nanny or from Ward, who usually joined them.

The call hadn't been from Ruby, but Mendoza. Jacoa hit the button to return the call and checked on Isra. She had acted strange earlier, but appeared settled now. She'd produced a pair of sunglasses and stared out the window at whatever image entranced her at the moment. He let her have the space she seemed to crave. Maybe as she became more comfortable with him, she'd confide more.

"Hey, Mr. Mendoza," he greeted once transferred through.

"Jacoa, good. Are you planning on coming into the city soon?"

"I'm nearly there. Was there something wrong with the paperwork?"

"Ah, no, not that. As we reviewed everything, we discovered an envelope that should have been given to you after you signed. I'm terribly sorry. It had gotten lost amongst the rest of the estate documents. I'm happy to hand it off as soon as you can make it in."

"Yeah, not a problem." Jacoa checked his watch. It was only ten in the morning. He had time for the quick stop.

The outer city held little of the glitz and glamor of the strip. Many of the one- and two-story buildings were covered in stucco. The neighborhood surrounding Desert Skyline Law Firm was occupied by glass buildings and oversized office complexes, where white-collar workers reigned. The law firm was one of the smaller buildings, though in a prime spot on the corner of a major road and a residential side street leading toward modest apartment homes.

The receptionist waved Jacoa past her small desk and barely glanced at Isra. He smiled at the truth of his secret. To the outside world, the oddest part of Isra must be her bi-colored hair. Even her use of sunglasses inside wasn't odd for a visitor in an office made of glass, with the low morning sunlight pouring in. If they only knew.

Mendoza greeted Jacoa with a relieved smile once he knocked on his door.

"Jacoa, thank you for coming in on such short notice. Really, I'm sorry about this."

"Not a problem," he assured the lawyer, returning the firm handshake.

"Here's your envelope." Mendoza offered the manilla legal-sized package. Jacoa felt the dimensions of a standard sized book. Wondering if it was another journal, he ripped the top open and peeked inside.

This book wasn't old. In fact, it was a perfect-bound paper-back. He bowed the stiff paper to see the cover. When the title came into view, he froze. Jacoa's throat tightened around a thick lump and he struggled to swallow.

The Genie Curse, by Riti Wicker.

Not a journal. A book of fairytales. A gift from a mother to her son.

It was the most valuable thing he'd inherited. Jacoa smoothed the envelope around his prize and tucked it under his arm.

"Thank you." It was all he could manage before his voice threatened to break.

"Glad we got that sorted," Mendoza said. "What plans do you have in the city today?"

"I have a date," Jacoa answered. Mendoza's eyes flickered to Isra, but he kept his counsel.

Jacoa's watch buzzed, and he checked the screen. Ruby was ready for him. The message came from an unknown number, so she must have a new nanny. He pulled out his phone to let Ward know where to meet them, just off the main Strip.

"Speaking of, we have to get going. Thanks again, Mr. Mendoza. I appreciate everything you've done."

At his car, Jacoa grabbed a messenger bag from the trunk, then locked it. Their destination wasn't far, and he didn't want to bother with a valet. The law office wouldn't mind if he parked for the day. Dropping his mother's book into the bag, he settled the strap on his shoulder before leading Isra to the edge of the street. A cab stopped at the curb to drop off a fare, and Jacoa waved to the driver who nodded back, securing their ride.

"You left your convertible for this." Isra gestured to the worn material lining the seats after they'd both settled in. "Your date won't be as impressed."

"I doubt she'll care, as long as I show up."

Isra scowled and redirected her attention out the window. She'd been upset with him most of the morning, but she'd still been present. This time, she took her warmth as she turned away. Jacoa shifted in the seat, surprised by the need to reach out and touch her despite her clear hands-off stance. What had they been talking about? His car?

"It's not always convenient to park on the Strip, but we can go somewhere later. We'll drive with the top down so you can feel the wind. We need a plan, though. It's been modified with an electric engine, and we need charging stations."

"It can go as far as you wish," Isra countered.

Today's return to the old tactics caused Jacoa to clench his teeth. He'd thought offering the journals had softened her need to manipulate. Their interactions over the last few days led him to believe trust was developing. Yet she once again returned to talk of wishing. Would this be the pattern for them? Every conversation just another opportunity for her to ask him for a wish?

The weight of his mother's book rested in Jacoa's lap, hidden in his leather bag. There had to be more than this. He wanted there to be more. He'd handed over her vessel in an effort to be free of the curse and give them a chance at a different life.

Except that wasn't all of it.

With the fairytales in his hands, fanciful thoughts flickered. He rubbed his knuckles against his sternum, the fluttering inside causing an odd ache he tried to massage away. He'd thought being patient was the answer with Isra. That she suggested wishing again told him there was probably no perfect time. He might as well get his question out.

"Is there any reason my mother would have known you?"

The inquiry claimed Isra's attention. Her brow wrinkled.

"I was in the netherworld while she was alive."

"Did you leave anything behind, by chance? Something she could have gotten from the boxes that I haven't seen?"

"No. Jacoa, what is this about?"

"Nothing, not really. She said something that made me wonder." He shrugged. Like he hadn't waited years before posing the question. Like it didn't matter the connection he longed for was nonexistent.

Isra's eyes fixed on Jacoa's. He waited for her to dig deeper, to ask what his mother said to pique his curiosity. Instead, she offered a small nod, then turned back toward the window. He stared at her clasped hands, but didn't see anything as he tucked away hope and accepted reality. A reality where a strand of Isra's hair curled around her arm.

Jacoa blinked to test his vision. She held herself stiffly, her hands threaded together in her lap. Only her eyes moved as she took in the city. They'd left the local streets behind and merged onto the wider boulevard of the Strip, which was lined with the façade of eras past meant to enchant tourists and lure them into the dark, timeless rooms where they would forget how much money they spent.

Yet, the sights didn't relax Isra as they had last time he'd driven through. Her hair appeared to Jacoa as if it moved in calming patterns. A gentle wave caressed the skin on her cheek. Strands wrapped around her fingers looped together. At her back there was a constant, comforting sway.

Now that was interesting. How had he missed this? Perhaps he'd been too distracted by the way she opened doors or caused books to fly across the house. This was subtle.

Or maybe she hadn't allowed him to see it before. That was surely progress.

Screeching cut through the noise of traffic as they pulled into one of Vegas' massive intersections. A high-powered sports car wove between cars on the cross street, the driver showing no sign of caring that they headed toward a red light.

Isra sucked in a deep breath, her focus on the oncoming vehicle, her hands fisted around her seatbelt.

"Isra." Whether he shouted or not, Jacoa didn't know. He couldn't hear his own voice over the honking of horns and revving of engines or their own driver's rapid cursing. Isra heard, though, her yellow eyes jumping to his, her lips flattening.

She didn't look surprised. Had she caused this? There wasn't time to ask before the hood of the sports car crashed into the front passenger side of their taxi. Their top-heavy SUV flipped and rolled over the aerodynamic frame of the offending vehicle.

Jacoa had seen crashes on film. He'd read about the crunching of metal and the sound of glass breaking. He experienced none of that. Eyes squeezed shut, breath held, he drew his knees up and curled as far as the seatbelt allowed, hanging tight to his messenger bag, waiting for it to be over.

They landed with his side of the vehicle down. He rested against the door. Heat on his face suggested a cut somewhere. His breathing was restricted, but not painful, so hopefully his ribs were intact.

Jacoa opened his eyes. Isra remained in her same spot. The car crumpled around her, the glass-shattered window open to a cloudless sky. His genie sat perfectly balanced, as if they were still upright. Only the long strands of her hair fell down to brush against his cheek.

"Was this you?" The words croaked from his throat, his jaw cracking with the movement.

"Are you okay?" Isra slid across the seat toward him, moving outside the law of gravity.

The pain in his body exploded into his consciousness. His vision blurred against the strength of it, teeth clenched against an involuntary grunt.

"No."

"I'm so sorry."

"Why weren't you surprised?" Jacoa coughed, wincing at the burn radiating through his injuries.

Jacoa pictured the thin line of Isra's lips, the way she held onto the buckle and braced herself on the door. She had seen this coming. The journals said she twisted wishes, refused some, or disappeared when she'd been needed. There was not one mention of her threatening her master to gain a wish.

Of course, she could always shift tactics as she had this morning, returning to a subtle demand for more wishes. Had she been upset over the car change because she knew an SUV would be better protection in a crash than his little electric car?

The physical pain in Jacoa's body heated his anger. Darkness ate at the edges of his thoughts, making it difficult to think past the fact that he was hurt and Isra was unsurprised.

If she wanted wishes, so be it. He'd wish it all away and bring peace back into his life.

"I wish for you to go—"

CHAPTER 14

Isra

Isra stopped time.

This spell was not an illusion. Her genie power convinced the universe the pause was necessary to Jacoa's life. She would check his injuries and look for danger so she could react and ensure their contract remained intact.

Jacoa had looked at her with rage, not in fear. The heat in his eyes did not bode well for his next words. He wasn't far off, thinking she'd caused the crash. Though it hadn't been her magic, it had been her fault for getting involved with a djinn.

Maram had pulled no punches with this one. There had been no starting small. Whatever illusion the djinn cast on the driver of the sports car caused horrifying circumstances.

She checked over Jacoa's body, satisfying part of the agreement with the universe. His bones weren't broken. There was minor bruising on the inside, heavier on the outside. His head was cut in front of his ear, either from the glass or from banging against the car's frame. When she resumed time, he would survive, so she focused on her next task. Observing the environment for any additional surprises.

Isra reached for the open window above her and pulled herself up and through, balancing on the door of the tipped car. Her eyes widened at the extent of the destruction. The sports car's roof had been crushed, and the frame was bent. It had slid through the intersection and collided with the line of cars waiting at the stoplight, creating a string of vehicular casualties.

People watched from the sidewalks, mouths agape. A backdrop of dramatic buildings and water blasted from fountains suspended in time offset the horror and fear twisting their features. The pedestrians crossing the street were mid-leap as they attempted to dive to safety. A child's face was bright red and compressed into a silent cry, tears frozen on his cheeks.

Isra tested the spell stopping time, recognized it had not affected the djinn who were not as bound to its limitations as humans.

"Maram! What have you done?"

"Only what we agreed." The djinn appeared in the intersection, glass crunching beneath the narrow toes of her stilettos. "Fancy trick you pulled here. It's interesting to see that you are well-versed in the capabilities of genies, but you still can't close your contract. And here I am, presenting you with the perfect opportunity, but you pause time and stop his wish."

Maram's voice whipped through the air, and Isra flinched at the contact.

"It won't do us any good if he wishes me away because he thinks I'm a part of this!"

Maram hesitated with a scowl, then shrugged. "There are other ways to encourage wishes."

"So we can choose a different tactic? He has a particular love for unique—"

"Of course not," Maram interrupted. "Fear is the best driving force there is."

"I assure you, he is more pissed than afraid. That is why I stopped time!"

"And you will restart it and he will wish for what he wishes. If it's to send you away, so be it! I'll keep coming after him until he wishes for you to return."

Isra hopped from the car, landing in front of the djinn. She wanted to be bigger, to assert her presence and demand to be heard. Shoulders widened, hips narrowed. Biceps expanded, her clothing conforming to her new dimensions.

Maram rolled her eyes and held out her palm. Isra's form slammed into the undercarriage of the car. Steam attacked her skin. Heated metal burned through her clothes. Isra struggled to escape the vehicle, but Maram didn't release her hold. The older djinn had the upper hand, inflicting her own version of reality over Isra's, forcing the young genie to endure.

"Your way did not work." Maram spoke through her teeth. She lowered her extended arm and Isra stumbled away from the car. "He's not dead. Whatever he wishes will not be the end of this, I can promise you. Pretend that you are worth the great honor handed to you. That Jann didn't allow you a taste of the awesome power of the djinn just for you to squander it."

Isra healed herself as she settled back into her smaller body. Her retreat did not mean she was giving in. She decided to regroup, and to ease Maram's temper. If she collected a wish from Jacoa now, perhaps the djinn would give them space. Isra needed time to find a loophole in her deal with Maram.

She only had to keep Jacoa from wishing her away.

"I will get this wish," Isra agreed. "But I hope, in the future, that you include fewer humans."

Isra gestured to the crowd. Maram looked at the crying child, her features flat and unmoved.

"Grant the right wish, and they'll never remember." Then the pure djinn was gone.

Isra took a deep breath and turned back toward the car. With a light jump, she vaulted to the top and dropped through the window. Adjusting gravity, she sat on the bench seat and returned to the same place she'd taken up as Jacoa began his wish.

Isra raised a hand to cover his mouth, but stopped when she felt the soft buzz that flared to life between them, always present, and intensifying the closer they became. She would have to resort to magic so she could keep her distance, and hope for the best as she pulled him into the timeless space.

Jacoa's jaw moved, but his lips did not open. His brows contracted and those inky black lashes shadowed stormy green eyes.

"I know," she whispered, easing the magic that kept him from speaking. "But you must be careful with your wishes, Jacoa."

"You're angry that I tied you to me. Why wouldn't you want me to reverse that?"

"Is that all you were going to do?"

Jacoa looked away. He worked the tension from his jaw without a sound, his attention drawn to the front of the cab where the driver hung upside down, held in place only by the lap portion of his seatbelt.

"Is he dead?" Jacoa asked.

"No. I stopped time. Everything and everyone is frozen."

"How many people were caught in this accident?"

"A lot."

"God, Isra. Why?"

She flinched, aware that by not explaining herself, she was damning herself. She wasn't sure how much she could share without invoking Maram's ire, or confirming to Jacoa that she had a part in it. She certainly didn't want to explain her alternative plan to him. Her past experience taught her masters were generous and dangerous with their wishes when their connection to a genie was threatened. With Jacoa angry, wishing her to be locked away somewhere wasn't out of the realm of possibility.

This was only Maram's first attempt, and Isra hadn't been ready. She had been obsessing over who his date might be, and what he expected her to do during it, since she was practically tied to his side.

Maram had chosen her moment well. Isra wouldn't give her another chance now that she'd seen how much damage the djinn caused in the name of a wish. First, she had to clean up this mess and hope Jacoa would help her.

"You don't have to wish. It would be helpful if you do. A lot of people's bad day can be erased."

"Bad day." Jacoa's harsh laugh blended into a series of deep coughs. He placed a hand on his ribs and Isra winced with him. Even though his life wasn't in danger, he was hurt. Maram had gone too far.

"Why would I wish when that's what this was for? What's stopping it from happening again?"

"I can't account for every accident," Isra answered carefully. Though his assumption was correct, it was only a guess right now, unless she slipped and confirmed his suspicion. "But yes. Let's erase the bad day. Even yours. You were heading to meet someone before this."

"Ruby." Jacoa closed his eyes, resting his head on the ground. "Fine. You want me to wish carefully. But damn it, Isra. Be honest with me first. Did you cause this?"

"No."

Jacoa squinted at her, seeming to sense there was more to the story but choosing to accept her answer.

"I wish this car accident hadn't happened, and that we do not repeat it."

Isra let go of her tension through a heavy exhale. Her shoulders relaxed and her eyes closed, accepting the flood of power that came from her master's wish. With his words and her magic, they erased the effect Maram's game had caused, setting their car upright on its wheels, rewinding the time flow to a point in the past where they had been safe.

Jacoa and Isra sat as far apart as possible on the bench seat of the SUV as they approached the intersection. Their driver slammed on the brakes just as a blue sports car ran the red light from the perpendicular direction.

"I am so sorry," the cab driver gushed. "Is everyone okay?"

"Yes, of course," Jacoa said, his gaze locked with Isra's. "Thank you for being so quick to react. That could have been much worse."

Isra lowered her eyes to her lap, then looked out her window. People walked along the sidewalk. Some stood in awe at the incredible height of the waterspouts from a dancing fountain. A small child tugged at his dad's hand as they crossed the street toward a cart with helium-filled balloons, pushed by a clown.

Everything was as it should be, colorful and full of life. Moving.

None of it could distract her from the knot in her stomach.

CHAPTER 15

Jacoa

The casino hotel where they were meeting Ruby was on the outer edge of the Strip. It didn't have the posh veneer of the fancier locations. This was his cousin's favorite, though, painted in red and yellow stripes with colorful murals depicting dancers and acrobats along the stucco walls.

The cab turned into the curved driveway in front of the casino. The wide pavement allowed for three cars to drive side by side. Jacoa stopped the driver before he got trapped in the grid of vehicles under the Edison bulb lined awning to give him the chance to U-turn his way out. He paid twice the fare and assured the shocked driver he deserved it for avoiding the accident.

Isra waited at the brass-edged double doors, not able to go in without him. Jacoa jogged to catch up. Together, they wove through the large entry lobby and passed the hallway that led to the elevators and rooms. The crowd thickened here, half heading straight into the casino. The other group merged right toward a blockade of ticket booths and steel turnstiles. Jacoa nearly stumbled on Isra when she stopped in the gap left between the branching pathways.

"Jacoa, I—"

"We're going to the right."

Jacoa didn't want to talk about the accident now. For the moment, he wanted to ignore what she'd erased. Once again Isra reset time, and he remembered both versions. His birthday party hadn't been risky, but keeping his memories of the accident meant more. He retained the image of her lack of surprise. He recalled every word of their conversation where she answered just enough to give nothing away. And she let him keep it all, even though it meant he'd remember his shaken trust.

Isra claimed she hadn't caused the crash. He wanted to believe her, but had to admit how little he knew her. The journals were biased, but how much so?

She'd said Gunter hadn't lied about her attempted seduction. He wouldn't say she'd tried that tactic on him, but Jacoa couldn't deny the powerful draw that formed between them, or the small moments of flirting they sometimes fell into.

That had all seemed so natural, though. Or was she tricking him into feeling connected?

The questions would have to wait for now, since Ruby wouldn't. Jacoa cut through the crowd. The carnival style entry separated the hotel's amusement park, where his cousin liked to spend her time. There were seven separate ticket booths, but Jacoa ignored the lines in front of each. He pulled a card from his wallet and flashed it at the person manning the last box to gain instant entry.

Ruby was here so often, Dave had used some of Jacoa's inheritance to secure daily entrance for the girl and her caretakers. Instead of collecting disposable wristbands, they'd been given cards to use. With these, they bypassed the lines and could partake in entertainment included with any paid entry. Rides and food cost, but Ruby wasn't interested in any of that. She preferred the shows.

The stages were situated at the back of the indoor amusement park. The loud voices and overpowering machine noise wasn't out of place on the Strip, though the occasional whoosh of air brought by a carnival ride was unique. Jacoa usually blocked it all out. This time, he searched for things to appreciate in the mess, trying to see what Isra found so engrossing. When a sudden gust blew past them, the movement of her hair pulled at his attention, and joy fluttered.

The strands floated deliberately, as if embracing the air instead of passively riding it. He remembered how the length had hung in the car, the only part of her body that appeared to honor the laws of gravity. The only part of her that touched him. Had it been on purpose? A way to check his wellbeing? His fingers itched to reach out and touch the floating wisps, to see how it would respond and if Isra would notice.

"Jacoa!"

A whirlwind of leotard and tutu threw herself at him. Jacoa caught her little body against his waist, then juggled her wiggling form until he held her in a tight hug.

"Hello, Ru-boo. Who are you escaping today?"

Ruby's face dug into Jacoa's neck, her arms wrapped tighter until she nearly choked him with the strength of her hold.

This was not her usual excitement. Tension wound from her body into his, and Jacoa's gaze narrowed into the crowd until he found a person marching straight for them. Dressed in a summer tunic over brightly-patterned exercise tights, the woman looked the part of a nanny. The way she scowled and her fists knotted suggested she needed to take on a profession that required less patience.

"Isra." Despite his low tone, his genie stepped closer, her eyes curious. Jacoa wasn't sure what was happening, but he wanted his small group close.

Ruby trembled, and Jacoa felt a damp heat against his skin. He rubbed her back and shifted so the girl was suspended between Isra and himself, his shoulder directed toward the angry woman.

"You must be her cousin." The woman's lips were thin as they quivered, her fingers curled into her palms.

"I'm Jacoa."

"It's about time you got here. I quit."

"What did you do to her? I've never seen her so upset."

"Me? She is the child!"

"Exactly. The adult is supposed to control themself around a six-year-old."

The woman jerked upright, all the color of her face concentrating into two red spots on her cheeks. Her neck sucked in on a deep inhale, then she gripped the strap of her brown leather satchel and stepped past them.

Jacoa turned his attention to his cousin. Isra had taken his cue and completed the watchful sphere around Ruby. The strands of white seemed to caress Ruby's bare calves in soothing waves. Though he wasn't certain, he would bet Isra used her hair for touch. That his genie became instantly protective of the little girl softened the edges of his distrust, and he couldn't look away from the movement, almost missing the commotion behind them until he recognized Ward's deep drawl.

"You should watch where you're going in a crowd like this."

"M-me?"

The ex-nanny had fallen to the floor, the contents of her satchel spread out on the matted blue carpet. His eyes narrowed on something that sparkled from the opening. Ward was already on it. He bent and snatched the delicate tiara from the bag. From what had spilled, he singled out the small plastic entry card that matched Jacoa's.

"I'll just return these for you. I suggest you leave before someone thinks to accuse you of theft." Ward's offer was a warning the nanny took very seriously based on how quickly she swept her things into her bag. She hurried out the door with a hand pressed against her tailbone.

Ruby peeked out from where she hid against Jacoa's neck. Her tremors had calmed, and her breathing normalized. When Ward was within reaching distance, she leapt from Jacoa's arms toward the man with her tiara and kissed him on the cheek.

"Thank you! She said I was a spoiled brat, and that I didn't deserve it."

Ward snorted, fitting the sparkling headpiece onto Ruby's tangled hair. "That's what every wicked witch tells the princess."

A soft tickling sensation brushed the back of Jacoa's hand. Isra had moved closer to watch Ruby's excitement and her hair caressed his skin. A warmth filled his chest. There was more to Isra than her first impression implied. His mother had that right, at least.

"What time is it?" Ruby asked.

"Just past eleven," Jacoa answered. Ruby squirmed in Ward's arms and he put her down at the non-verbal request. She grabbed Ward's hand, then reached for Jacoa's with the other, looking at Isra through her eyelashes.

"Who is she?"

"This is Isra," Jacoa said.

"Is she your girlfriend?"

At that, Isra smiled. "I'm his genie."

Jacoa stiffened at the announcement. Ward's choked bit of laughter assured him Isra's statement would be taken as a joke, yet he was still surprised she chose that tactic with his cousin. Isra lowered in a narrow squat and straightened the tiara on the girl's head. As Isra's hands swept along Ruby's hair, the tangles eased into gentle curls.

"Really?" Ruby asked.

"Really," Isra said.

"You're going to free her with your last wish, aren't you?" Ruby demanded of Jacoa.

"I haven't figured out if she's a good genie or not."

Isra's eyes flew to Jacoa's as she rushed to her feet. Instead of their usual bright yellow, they were a warm fawn. Jacoa's stomach clenched and fluttered, an odd combination. He hated that some of her genie self had been hidden, yet he was fascinated by her ability to change so easily.

Ruby's cheek pressed into Jacoa's thigh, and he cursed himself when he saw the trembling on her lips. Isra's chat about genies had calmed the girl down, and he'd carelessly taken it away. Ruby had met her fair share of people out to take advantage of her and her family, today's experience was only the newest. He didn't want his own challenges with Isra to dim any of Ruby's sparkle.

"Hey, she seems pretty okay so far. Would I bring her to meet you otherwise?"

Ruby shook her head slowly, then squared her shoulders and faced Isra with the unique confidence only six-year-olds had.

"You will be a good genie."

"Unless the genie can magic us to the tent, we should get going. The circus is about to start." Ward's crooked smile showed he didn't believe a word, but would play along for Ruby's sake. With the reminder of the show, the little girl heaved her small body forward, dragging both grown men behind her.

Jacoa lost sight of Isra as the crowd flowed between them. She stood frozen, her hair long and straight. He tried to let go of his cousin's hand, but Ruby's grip wouldn't release him.

A half-smile curled his lips, and he shook his head. Somehow, the crash was all but forgotten amid the mess with Ruby and how Isra had handled it. Whether his genie was good or bad was something he could joke about, ill-timed as it was. Then, when she slipped from sight, he was tempted to abandon his cousin to Ward's care and find her again.

Jacoa soothed himself with the fact that Isra couldn't go far. He could see her whenever he wished.

His gut twisted. She wanted him to wish more, the faster the better. Were wishes really all that bound them together? Would her desire for them prove his mother wrong, and reveal that Isra was a monster at heart?

His patience wore to a thin mask over his features. He was willing to play a longer game for a happy ending, but the promise of that dimmed and an ache pressed against his ribs. No. He needed to know now. He would ask her what the hell was going on before he gave in to any more hope, or spoke any more wishes.

CHAPTER 16

Isra

Isra trailed behind Jacoa's group without paying much attention. His wish kept her close on its own, and she moved on autopilot. Sensations roared around her and for once, she didn't revel in every shift of light or let the layered sound of music and laughter fill her. Instead, she was stuck on one thought.

Be good.

Being good got her into this problem.

Being kind. Being nice. Not wanting to kill humans. Allowing months to go by without mentioning wishes.

Being a good draconian. And when she matured into her sex at fourteen years old, she doubled down on becoming the best hunter. All draconian children were born sexless and were expected to return to the collective for inspection when they reached eighteen. The stated reason was for census, but really, it was to reclaim the females.

She and her father hadn't wanted the fate that befell other draconian females - being locked into the brood den and forced to one task only: procreation. So they kept to themselves, constantly tracking and hunting to hone her skills. Their goal was to make her so valuable as a hunter the collective would delay or bypass her as a potential mother.

Aali's particular skill proved useful in aiding her successful training. He had a knack for locating vessels, but he had to be close. So whenever someone came into unexpected wealth or shot miraculously into stardom, he investigated in case wishes were involved.

With her father's guidance, she became the best at extracting vessels. She'd also been overconfident. Not only had she been caught by Abraham, but they'd released Jann and tied her spirit to the vessel.

Now the curse had brought her Jacoa.

Isra zeroed in on Jacoa through the crowd. He was bent over to hear whatever Ruby was trying to yell at him, then he shook his head and laughed in response. As if on cue, he and Ward swung the little girl, letting her kick her legs out as soon as a rare pocket of space opened up. Ruby squealed in delight, perfectly confident that both men held her tight and would keep her safe.

Just as it was Isra's job to keep Jacoa safe. That did not include entering into agreements with violent djinn.

Nervous energy spun her hair into a thin braid against her temple, and her fingers curled until sharp nails bit into her palms.

If Isra could grant her own wishes, she would want to have met Jacoa before giving into Maram. Changing the past was not one of her powers, though. Her mind had been saturated with hate for the nether. She'd been deeply disappointed in her father. Isra made the wrong decision, and almost paid for it.

Jacoa had wanted to send her away because of the car crash. She'd stopped his words, but the heat in his eyes had branded her with his anger. Jacoa thought Isra had been the source of that incredible disaster. He'd confirmed his intent when he said the almost-wish would have negated his command that she stay close.

Any other master and she wouldn't care. Isra could have willingly left Abraham or any of his other descendants behind, including Gunter.

But not Jacoa. His fourth wish had taken some of her freedom, but he'd given her choices with the others. Even though he was uncertain about her, he trusted her enough to call her to his side when his cousin needed protection from that horrid nanny. She was addicted to the ebb and flow of energy between them. Assuming there was no wish binding them together, Isra wasn't confident she could leave him for long.

An odd stutter caught *Anahata* in her chest as she realized she didn't hate being stuck with Jacoa. In fact, she might choose it on her own...

He couldn't wish her away. Whether or not she was bound by contract, Isra craved these hours with Jacoa. She enjoyed being part of his erratic energy and seeing where his need to move led them. The quiet mornings where he swam and she read were something she looked forward to. She wanted to watch the sunsets from his large windows and laugh as he tried to get her to eat.

Isra's life didn't offer many happy choices. She found some satisfaction in observing, but what if she allowed herself more? The big picture shouldn't stop her from experiencing joy for herself. Events like the car crash threatened the easy way of being that she shared with Jacoa.

Why was she trying to pacify the djinn, anyway? The genie contract would help her protect her master. There had to be a way out. There was always a loophole.

"Maram, we can't do this." Isra only guessed that she had Maram's attention, but was rewarded with a quick reply.

"I'd call you yellow-bellied, but I suppose that's a compliment for a draconian," Maram snarled, her voice distinct and her presence hidden.

Isra shifted her way through the crowd, searching for Jacoa's dark hair beside Ward's curls. She tried to redirect the mass of people aside and urged them to clear a path for her, but met the resistance of djinn magic. It was as if she pushed against a glass wall that would not budge or allow her ease of movement.

"Maram," Isra growled, knowing the warning was useless. Isra needed to be faster.

She must remain in Jacoa's presence, per his wish, and the djinn couldn't negate that. Isra was able to adjust the semantics based on her belief. She had wanted a bit of separation after Ruby's declaration and had expanded that reach, but now she required it to mean within touching distance.

Tension drew her closer to her master, and she dodged human bodies. She grit her teeth when she phased through a few of them to satisfy the new boundaries of the wish, the humans blind to the magic happening right in front of them. Jacoa had become part of the group assembled around a raised circus stage. Most seats were filled as families gathered for the day's first show. Ward helped Ruby onto Jacoa's shoulders, then balanced on his toes to try to see over the crowd.

"Do you need a box?" Jacoa teased his friend, unaware of the tension that drew Isra to his side. She wouldn't catch Maram if the djinn didn't want her to, but she knew the plan. She simply had to remain diligent.

The lights above flickered on the broad oval circus sign surrounded by naked bulbs. The thick, coated wires that held it to the ceiling eroded before her eyes. As before, it wasn't only Jacoa who stood in the danger zone, but others that included his fragile, six-year-old cousin.

An echoed memory of when she failed her father darkened the edges of Isra's mind and she shoved the shadowed halo away. She was a genie. This would be easier than breathing.

The light above them creaked, the sound so faint the human ears around her missed it in the surrounding noise. Isra stepped next to Jacoa, and he swayed toward her as the connection between their chakras flowed. A warm wave washed off the last of her doubt. Maram's games hadn't broken them yet.

Isra focused on the chain above and commanded it to repair itself, to cease the threat against her master. Realities clashed. Two invisible forces connected in a silent discord that drove the air from Isra's lungs. Her consciousness pushed against the weight of Maram's. Magic challenged her right to overpower the older djinn.

Genies had to keep their masters alive. Interpretations varied. Choose a synonym and go.

So Isra would keep Jacoa unharmed and safe, even against someone stronger than her.

Djinn magic popped like a soap bubble. Isra's power took its place, repairing the sign while those below were unaware of the averted crisis.

Maram hadn't made a sound after losing the battle. Isra wouldn't make the mistake of assuming the djinn had backed off politely. She eased toward Jacoa until the edges of her hair brushed him and the little girl while looking natural.

"Isra?" Jacoa whispered her name. Isra shook her head and glanced at Ruby. She wasn't sure what to say. How much would she have to confess until he understood? How would he judge her?

"She's being a good genie," Ruby decided from her high perch. Isra's startled gaze met the six-year-old's big hazel eyes. "Aren't you?"

"I don't know if there is such a thing."

Caught in the child's innocence, Isra found herself speaking the truth.

How could one be 'good' when it meant heading toward an unwelcome fate?

The child patted the top of Isra's head as if she understood the genie's dilemma. Ruby appeared to hold onto the faith that everything would turn out right. When the stage curtain opened, the excitable girl returned. She squeezed and bounced when a tumbling contortionist started the show.

Jacoa nudged Ward, who turned to take Ruby, settling her weight on his shoulders instead. With his cousin settled, Jacoa guided Isra toward one of the large pillars that separated the walkway from the stages. He leaned a shoulder against the stone, the pillar wide enough for them to stand beside it and remain out of the flow of foot traffic.

"What are we doing?" she asked.

"You were saying something to me when we first arrived, but I cut you off. I'm sorry. What was it?"

Isra thought back to when they'd entered the casino. She hadn't had words at the time, just a feeling that she needed to ensure he wouldn't send her away. Jacoa frowned as she searched for an answer. He stepped close and their energy reached for each other, but struggled to mesh.

Isra steadied her chakras and sent her energy toward him, hoping he would accept it and allow her to encourage his own alignment. His eyes widened and a rush of breath pushed from his lungs, blending with her involuntary gasp. They moved opposite, his inhale reversing the flow and completing the cycle, only for it to begin anew. The effect locked them into place. Reality narrowed. The passersby would only notice two people talking quietly, unable to overhear. To Isra and Jacoa, their auras blended into a milky cocoon that muted their surroundings.

"What is this?" Jacoa's fingers phased through the foggy shell and he retracted his hand. "Are you doing this?"

Isra took a deep breath, her hands laced in front of her. She struggled to subdue her hair to keep some semblance of normal in Jacoa's life as she worked to explain a magic even she didn't understand.

"We are. I'm not sure how. This isn't djinn."

"But it's happened before?"

Isra shook her head. "Not like this. You would have noticed."

"No, I meant with your other mast—the other Wickers."

"No."

"Just me? Why? How?"

"I don't know."

Jacoa lowered his face for a moment as if taking in her words and deciding what to do with them.

"We really need to talk," he said when he brought his attention back up. Isra flinched.

"Wow. Even I've heard that's not the best way to start a conversation. Are you sure we should do this here?"

"I would have liked to have figured this out before, but you've clearly been hiding things."

"What do you want to know?"

"What's going on?" Jacoa asked. "What really happened with the car crash? And you've been acting strange for the last few minutes. What puts a genie on edge?"

"It's not something I can talk about right now."

"What if I need you to?"

A tight wheeze squeezed out with Jacoa's question. Isra took in the small lines between his eyes and the way his lips pressed together in a slight tremor.

The honesty in his reaction stopped her automatic denial. It was rare that Isra dealt with someone as open and vulnerable as Jacoa was right now. She responded to the intensity of his need. But protecting him meant keeping him from knowing that he, and these people around him, were in danger. Maram would retaliate if he knew, and step up her timeline even more.

Jacoa rubbed his palm on his face.

"What is your hesitation with having a conversation? Or is it truly all about wishes with you?"

"No, not wishes." Isra's breath caught, but she was unable to draw the words back in. Jacoa looked up at the ceiling, the line of his shoulders softening.

"Look. I realize I screwed up with the wish to keep you close. But I can't regret it." He met her gaze, no longer hesitating. "I need to understand you, Isra. I choose to believe that you didn't cause the car crash. I want to know you."

Air pushed from Jacoa's mouth as if he'd meant to say more, but the words refused to follow. The tight lines around his eyes smoothed out and his lips lost their tremors as he studied her, though she had no idea what he saw in her that relaxed him. Jacoa lifted one of his hands toward her, his fingertips so close to the strands of her hair, but staying an infuriatingly small distance away.

"You won't send me away, then." She couldn't pose it as a question, unsure she wanted to hear the answer.

"Will you be more open with me?"

Isra licked her lips, thinking of all the secrets she'd kept from him so far. Why couldn't he be content spending time together and enjoy each moment? Opening up might mean they both learn truths they didn't want to discover.

"These aren't simple things you're asking. I don't think I can be what you want. Have conversations. Be a good genie."

"Ruby asked you that last one, not me." Jacoa caught a twist of white strands and caressed it. With the weight of his stare on her face, Isra worked to hide a shiver. Her hair ached against the desire to wrap his finger like a present. "I don't actually agree."

"What?"

"I don't need you to be good, Isra. I want you to be in this with me. To be mine."

Isra spent her entire life fighting against those who would make her theirs. First the draconian, then the Wicker descendants who held her vessel. But the way Jacoa said the word 'mine' didn't send images of cages into her thoughts. In fact, it felt as if he asked permission.

"I don't know what that means," Isra admitted. "Your what? And I thought you had a date?"

"Yeah, with Ruby." Jacoa's brows bent for a moment before a smile bloomed and lightened his eyes. "Wait. Did you think I meant a romantic date? Is that why you weren't talking to me in the taxi?"

Isra pursed her lips against a struggling smile.

"I only knew you were dragging me someplace." She crossed her arms to hide the way her breath kicked up into quick bursts.

"Are you sure she isn't your girlfriend?"

The cocoon of energy released once Jacoa's attention was

called outside of it. He blinked as if the sudden intrusion of the world startled him. Isra breathed through her nose, working to stop the rise of color on her cheeks.

"I guess we weren't as hidden as I thought," he murmured, raising a brow at Isra.

"We didn't turn invisible." She lightened her voice so it would appear to Ward and Ruby as if she teased him, but hoped Jacoa would understand she was offering an explanation.

It was strange, though, how he noticed their separation from the crowd. He descended from sorcerers, but their line had been blocked from access to magic ages ago. How could he be so in tune with the universe? With her?

To distract herself, she turned to Ruby and summoned a smile for the child.

"What's more likely?" Isra asked. "That I'm his genie or his girlfriend?"

"Why not both?" Ruby presented Isra with a dimpled grin. "Daddy says I can be whatever I want to be."

"And have you decided?"

"A ballerina and a princess," Ruby informed Isra as if it were common knowledge. With the tiara and the tutu, Isra should have guessed.

"Either way, the show is over," Jacoa said. Isra startled, thinking he referred to what was going on between them. As the crowd thickened with people drifting away from the stage, Isra released the tension at her scalp, realizing he likely meant the circus show. "Why don't you choose where to go for lunch, and then I call your dad and tell him about the latest wicked witch?"

Isra frowned at Jacoa. "The latest?"

"Let's just say it's difficult to find trustworthy help these days. Come on, Ru-boo. You pick the place."

Jacoa swung Ruby into his arms so she was at his level as she chatted away, listing places she didn't want to go and why. They were so comfortable together, relaxed in their trust. Isra was glad she'd kept the truth about Maram from Jacoa so that he would have this moment with his cousin without worry or fear.

"Isra."

Ward fell into step beside her and Isra looked away to hide her flinch. She preferred to stay close to Jacoa, but she didn't want to inspire curiosity in his friend. Ward's quick ability to sense a drink at Jacoa's party and his swift hands when he reclaimed Ruby's things from the nanny's bag were just strange enough that she didn't trust him.

"How long have you known Jacoa?" Isra groaned inwardly at his casual question. But surely he was just a friend checking in; nothing nefarious at all.

"A few days."

"Oh. You're not from around here, right? I don't really recognize you, and your hair is kind of a dead giveaway."

"And you know everyone in Vegas?"

Ward's crooked grin didn't make it to his eyes. "I've been here for a while. The local crowd isn't as big as you think and tends to be tight-knit."

"Ah." Isra didn't know how else to respond.

"Anyway, that was nice what you did for Ruby, saying you're a genie and all. If you haven't noticed, she likes the shows around here. You should have Jacoa take you to a couple of the magic acts, see if you can pick up a few things to impress her with next time."

Ward couldn't know she hadn't been lying, but she had the definite feeling he was poking fun at her somehow, or trying to rile her up. Isra bristled. She did not need tips or tricks from some human illusionist. There was something different about Ward, though. She couldn't put her finger on it, and with Maram floating around, Isra didn't have the luxury of time to explore her instinctive reaction.

She really needed to speak to the djinn before—

Ruby screamed. Ward sprinted past Isra, throwing the front doors open in his haste. Isra stopped in her tracks. Too many people were entering, exiting, or waiting for valet to have a direct line of sight. She focused on magic to figure out if something had happened to Jacoa. She felt a wave of djinn power, but nothing that threatened her connection to her master.

The image of a little boy in the middle of the street popped into her mind, tears frozen in time on his face.

Oh, no. Maram wouldn't have gone after Jacoa's cousin for a wish? Would she?

Isra cursed her human form as she ran forward through the chaotic crowd. Trusting a djinn was proving to be a miserable mistake.

CHAPTER 17

Jacoa

Ruby babbled on a 'remember when' tangent about all the places she'd ever eaten after attending the circus performance. Rambling was her version of coming to a decision, so Jacoa listened for a few keywords while he analyzed the quiet interaction with Isra.

He'd noticed something was off when Isra touched Ruby and him with her hair in front of the stage. The only other time he remembered her actively reach out was during the car crash. Jacoa stopped her from speaking before, so it was up to him to restart the conversation. He had taken her to the side, knowing it was his only chance to get her to talk openly.

Jacoa's imagination was limited by what he knew. He liked facts and experimentation over creation. Follow the recipe and make perfect pretzels. Push the accelerator harder and discover how far his ATV can lean while banking. He had a minimal concept of magic before meeting Isra. His collection of evidence pointed at the results, but his ancestors failed to explain how it felt to be engulfed in power.

Being around Isra was intoxicating. Seeing her phase through the door their first night. Discovering her hair might be an active part of her. The way the world appeared to fade during their conversation. It echoed the times they'd connected at his house, but was far more profound and powerful when surrounded by people. And she'd only experienced it with him.

Isra hadn't reacted when he'd touched her hair, but the very stillness she'd adopted made him think it was on purpose. She was still hiding herself from him. He'd been naïve to believe sharing the journals would be enough to form an instant accord.

Their conversation gave him hope, though. He wasn't a gambler like Ward, but he'd bet half his fortune on her withdrawal in the taxi being because of jealousy. Jacoa fought against the grin that wanted to break free. Perhaps this morning's impromptu declaration of not wanting to share wasn't one sided.

He'd happily be patient for progress like that. Unfortunately, he didn't know how much time he had. When he handed her vessel over to Aali, he'd been hedging his bets. Nothing went as he'd hoped. In his mind's eye, Isra would appear at his party and they'd have a chance to talk. She'd hear his proposal and fill in any gaps. They could make a decision together.

Of course, he hadn't understood all the challenges. Isra wasn't starting fresh with him. Aali had hundreds of years to practice his vessel pitch on previous Wickers.

The draconian began stalking Jacoa months ago. Rather, he started letting Jacoa catch glimpses of him at the end of June, just after graduation. Likely, Aali had monitored the Wicker family for much longer. Jacoa thought the shadowy figure was an image brought by the strange change of preparing to live on his own.

With Dave pissed that Jacoa was reclaiming his estate, Jacoa spent more time at the house he'd inherited once the renters moved out. He pulled his parents' furniture out of storage, keeping what he liked and selling off other pieces. With Mendoza's help, he opened lines of credit that allowed him to furnish the house. The day his patio furniture had been delivered, Jacoa headed over after school. Waiting for him as if pre-determined, a tall figure wrapped in a cloak sat on his new outdoor sectional.

"Who are you?" Jacoa asked.

"I'm Aali. I'm sorry to appear in such an odd way, but I would like to discuss something with you."

"The house isn't for sale." He'd received other offers since taking possession, but none had been so bold as to show up on his patio.

"I'm only interested in one thing inside of it. You recently retrieved your parents' items from storage. Have you gone through them all yet?"

Jacoa hesitated in his answer, taking half a step back toward the open door of the house. The request was more personal than he'd expected. How would this person know what was inside the box?

"Were you a friend of theirs?"

"We shared similar interests."

Jacoa winced, aware that he didn't remember enough about his parents to know what their interests might have been.

"I've been through most of their things," he answered cautiously. "But I've sold a few of the pieces."

Aali lifted a gloved hand in a dismissive wave.

"You wouldn't let this go. A package of journals and a particularly decorative antique sphere hinged through the center."

Jacoa stilled. This box hadn't come from his parents' storage. Mendoza had released it when Jacoa turned sixteen, a year and a half ago. Since it wasn't money, Dave hadn't paid any attention to the dusty contents.

"Why are you interested in that old stuff?"

Jacoa's thick voice must have given him away.

"So you've read them. Good. Do any mention an offer they received when they were seventeen?"

"N-no." Jacoa stumbled over the answer to the oddly specific question. Just how close had this stranger been to his parents?

"Ah. It turns out the draconian is never as interesting as the djinn." Aali reached up and lowered his hood. He wore a human face, though it was covered in beige scales. Black, white and tan stripes alternated around his head. From a distance, he might even pass as a real human.

His eyes destroyed the illusion. The pupil took up most of the space between folds of skin. A thick ring of ocher filled where the white of a human's eye would be.

The sight was horrifying, but Jacoa couldn't run away. He couldn't feel his legs, frozen in place where they were. He took in the sharp lines of the beings face that were slightly softened by the overlapping armor of scales. An objective corner of Jacoa's brain noted the beauty of the creature, and how amazing it was to see something no one else had.

Clearly, his self-preservation instincts were stunted.

"Do you believe the stories in those books?"

Five minutes ago, Jacoa would have had a different answer. Raised on fairytales of a genie, he'd always wondered at the reliability of the journals. Perhaps writing this story was a family legacy—decades of Wickers reimagining what this creature would accomplish in their own lives. Part of him hoped it was real, though he'd never seen magic before. Wouldn't he have noticed if the world was being terrorized by djinn?

With Aali before him, the doubt shed like an old skin. The odd combination of fear and awe held him captive, but his fear of what the creature would do if he didn't answer won out. Jacoa offered a shaky nod.

"Then you know what the vessel holds."

His full belief might be brand new, but his mother's tales had shaped how he would react at this moment.

"She's mine." Jacoa's fingers clenched around tremors, the shell of emotion that held him in place cracked. No matter his stunted instincts, Jacoa likely wouldn't get far if this creature decided to attack, though so far he seemed content to talk. It was worth putting up some form of a fight to see where it would take him.

Aali narrowed the skin around his massive pupils. "She is stolen."

"And you want to steal her in return?"

"Your ancestors are the cause of her entrapment," Aali said.

"Because they invented the means to trap djinn."

"A few journals haven't made you an expert. The sorcerers quickly discovered what a disastrous plan that had been. Forging contracts with the universe is too dangerous. So they created my kind to eliminate that danger."

Jacoa drew back, taking in Aali's features anew. His ancestors had a hand in creating this creature and others like him? So that was why the djinn had attacked his family and blocked their access to magic.

"I see understanding dawn in your eyes. At least the Wicker intelligence has some good qualities. Perhaps you'll be willing to hear me out?"

The genie and the fairytales were all Jacoa had of his mother, Riti. He wouldn't consider giving them to a stranger, but couldn't bring himself to refuse the lizard-man outright.

Aali took his silence as permission to continue.

"I'm requesting the vessel, but not now." The last three words were spoken loudly over Jacoa's nonverbal objection. "It is useless to me while the genie is still trapped by it. I would ask for it when she has been released."

"She won't notice it's missing?"

Aali shook his head. "She won't care to lay eyes on it while she is free."

"What if it's not who you think?"

"Then there will be one less djinn after they come looking for it." Aali's stiff lips curled away from a mouth full of pointed teeth. Jacoa shuddered at the added proof he was not speaking to a human. He gripped the back of the chair beside him, tilting as his vision darkened and he searched for thoughts in the blur. Was this a genuine offer? Or was this paranormal being giving him the illusion of a choice?

"And if it is who you are looking for?" Jacoa asked.

"It will be more complicated. But there's a chance I can free her."

"You would want to free a genie?"

"This genie was not born djinn. She was cursed against her will and birthright, thanks to one of your many-great grandfather's wishes."

"Oh."

"This would free you as well."

"So, no more wishes?"

Aali stiffened. "I hope your ancestors' records have taught you the danger of them. Besides, you already have a tremendous amount of wealth. I'm sure you and your progeny will be fine."

"What are you asking me?"

"It is your possession of these journals that convinces me I have found the right genie. None of your forefathers have taken me up on my offer. Will you be the one?"

Jacoa flinched in the face of words that closely echoed his mother's.

"All I need is the vessel," Aali said.

"I still don't understand why."

"She is my daughter."

Jacoa lost his grip on the chair in front of him and fumbled his way into the seat. He pictured his younger self, tucked neatly into bed. His mother was tinted blue from the nightlight, spinning tales until his eyes fell heavy and she kissed him good night. Would she go to the same lengths as this draconian if she could find him?

Yes.

He slouched against the cushion and covered his face.

"Okay. I'll help you."

Over time, he'd come to regret the speedy response. Just because they were father and daughter didn't mean Aali was someone Jacoa should listen to. Had he already given up his chance at being a worthy Wicker by agreeing to the draconian's deal?

Ruby jostled in Jacoa's arms, returning him to the present as they passed through a large door to the outside. He glanced behind to see Isra about to step through after him, and a frown flickered. How would she react to the truth? As he demanded more from her, he would need to give the same. He was suddenly uncertain he should have pushed the issue.

A high-pitched scream attacked Jacoa's eardrum and Ruby was pulled from his arms. He lost the battle of tug of war in his efforts to keep the six-year-old from falling to the concrete. Her kidnapper scrambled back, out from under the awning and away from the parked cars. She increased the distance between Jacoa and Ruby, backing into the flowerbed that marked the edge of the sidewalk.

The red-rimmed eyes he met were not of a stranger. The ex-nanny had one hand gripped around the tiara in Ruby's hair, the other arm wrapped under Ruby's armpits for purchase as she caged the child against her chest. Fat tears wove through his cousin's fear-twisted features.

"What the hell do you think you're doing?" Jacoa demanded, taking slow steps forward.

"I'm not going to walk away without being paid for watching this brat!"

"Whatever, fine. I'll pay you. Let Ruby go."

The woman's lips rounded as if she hadn't expected him to give in so easily.

"Show me!"

Jacoa lifted both hands before using his right to reach into his pants pocket for his wallet. He opened it and moved closer to the pair to show her the fanned-out bills.

Tires screeched beside them. Jacoa jumped at the sound. Ruby cried harder as the woman holding her gripped tighter.

"Let that baby go!" A woman hollered from the passenger side of a giant white pickup truck. Jacoa stopped breathing when a handgun was pulled from the glove compartment.

"No! I have it handled! Don't point that at my cousin."

The woman aimed the barrel at the ex-nanny despite Jacoa's plea.

"Don't worry. I've got a steady hand."

"Put the gun down, ma'am!" A new voice. Jacoa waved the security guard back. The man ignored his directions, a hand on his holster. This was way out of control.

An explosion burst from the truck, and Jacoa whipped around. He caught the wide-eyed open-mouth horror of the woman in the car as she reacted to the gun's kickback.

When he faced the nanny and Ruby, sparkles of plastic gems and bright drops of red glittered in the sunlight as they raced toward the ground.

"Isra!"

CHAPTER 18

Isra

Isra halted next to Ward who had stopped his sprint, his fists clenched as if ready for a fight. Her breath pulsing at the same rapid rate as her heart. They hadn't passed the grid of cars yet.

Jacoa approached the haggard ex-nanny where the sidewalk curved from the casino toward the street. He had cleared the awning out of the crush of vehicle and foot traffic. Ruby was no longer in his arms, but struggled in the nanny's grip whose hand twisted in the little girl's hair.

Isra's stomach dropped. Was this Maram, or simply a crazy human? Djinn magic was present. Isra forced herself to ignore the horrifying scene and focus on the flow of power.

The presence Isra discovered pressed their aura into hers, swatting her away like an irritating insect. This was djinn all right, but it wasn't Maram.

A lifted, white pickup swung in through the exit lane of the wide drive and screeched its tires in a U-turn, placing the passenger side facing the nanny. The pressure of djinn magic built as the barrel of the woman's gun appeared through the open window.

A second, new surge of djinn power wrapped the truck.

Isra's breath stopped, and she squinted, trying to reach past the thick surface to judge the age of who might be in control of the colliding realities. As the forces rubbed against one another, they seemed evenly matched.

"Maram?" Isra was careful to keep the word wrapped in power and away from Ward's ears.

Maram's laughter mixed with triumph and frustration.

"It seems our plan got out earlier than expected and other djinn want to help." Maram answered from a distance.

"So you're not going to stop this? You said you would handle them."

"If you'd granted all the wishes by now, they wouldn't be interfering. If you played by the rules, I might have stopped them. As it is, we extended the invitation, and it's rude to cancel in the middle of the party. Well, unless you can wish."

Isra clenched her jaw, lips curled away from her teeth. The damn djinn club. Maram's game had more layers than expected.

The explosion of the gun snapped Isra's eyes open. Jacoa spun back toward Ruby and the nanny.

Isra's magic reached for the projectile, secure in the knowledge that she would protect her master.

She could not change the trajectory. The bullet was not aimed at Jacoa.

Ward twisted from the scene before him and turned to Isra. The power that swirled in his eyes left her gasping. The weight of it weakened her knees. She fell to the ground, her chin tilted up as she could not look away.

Time slowed, but did not stop. Every second became the length of an hour.

"They have lost all faith in you," Ward growled. "A djinn who cannot do her job is not to be trusted."

Isra gulped past the fear in her throat.

"You're djinn," she gasped.

He snorted. "If I was, this would be over. I cannot protect them as you can."

"I already tried. Jacoa is not in danger."

Ward bared clenched teeth and, as he looked at his friends, lines etched into the skin on his forehead and around his mouth. All signs of emotion disappeared when he turned back to her.

"There is one very small thing I can do. The djinn powers are competing against each other. One is trying to get the nanny to break the girl's neck. The other wants their bullet to win. The space between can be used."

How did he gauge the intent? Isra struggled to look toward the frightful scene of humans and the patterns of magic, but it was impossible to move her attention from the overwhelming figure Ward had become.

"I can redirect the shot into the seam between these powers," Ward said. "It will be close, but it should miss Ruby and strike the nanny instead. The djinn will try again. Make your master wish, and quickly."

Isra's *Vishuddha* contracted in her throat, reacting to how her demand for this wish would affect how Jacoa saw her truth. "He'll think I did this."

Ward shrugged. "He'll do it anyway, and you can work it out later. Be ready."

Time resumed. Sound returned at an unbearable level. Screams intermingled with the resonating boom of the gun. The bullet struck and caused a firework of blood and bright tiara pieces.

"Isra!" Jacoa called through it all, falling to his knees.

Ward released her from his compulsion, and she was at Jacoa's side in an instant, both kneeling on the ground. Her hair fluttered against the breeze, but no one paid attention to her in the chaos.

"Wish," she begged him as they watched the nanny wedge her hand against her hunched and bloody abdomen. Ruby curled into a ball on the pavement, hysterical screams ripping her throat as Ward sprinted to her side. "I can only protect you without a wish. Ruby isn't injured. There isn't much time before they try again."

"They?"

"These are djinn attacks."

Jacoa's voice produced a sound between a growl and a moan, and his fists against his thighs. His bloodshot eyes never left his cousin. Ward was on the ground, gathering Ruby into his lap. The shooter opened the truck's door with quaking hands, crying out apologies and demanding to know if the child was okay.

"I wish the shooting never hap—"

Isra slammed her magic on Jacoa's mouth before the last bit of sound died, shaking her head.

"Careful! That's not the right wish. We will stop this shooting, but not the next or the next."

Jacoa narrowed his eyes. That she worked to limit his wishes from quantity to quality was not lost between them. Isra only hoped it was enough to convince him the danger to Ruby was not her doing.

"What the hell am I supposed to wish for, then?"

Isra glanced at Ward. He sat on the sidewalk with his legs folded to help cradle the girl in his arms. The djinn power had faded with the gunshot, but started gathering strength once more. On impulse, she pressed her lips against Jacoa's ear. From that small touch, the energy at *Sahasrara* flared behind each of their eyes. Whether they were pulling or pushing, she could no longer say beyond the flood of it passing through her body. Jacoa stiffened at the contact, his own gasp suggesting he experienced the same.

Isra struggled against the need to ignore everything except for this ethereal connection, using their unique affinity to block the sound of her voice from any djinn or other creature in case they worked to stop the wish from happening.

"Protect her from djinn magic."

Jacoa's eyes shot to hers, latching on as if she were his calm in the storm. Competing willpowers grappled with each other. There was no time to explain further.

"Wish."

"I wish for Ruby to be safe from djinn magic and manipulations for the rest of her life."

Isra opened herself to the power of the universe, urging it to rush through her feet from *Vasundhara* without pausing to enjoy the flow. The magic swirled within her chest, rising through her throat and pooling at the top of her head until it burst through to *Sutara*. She turned her gaze to Ruby and let it go.

Powered by the genie contract, magic threaded a new cord into the weave of creation. The power wrapped around Ruby, sinking into her skin. Ward didn't react to the stream or appear to notice the glow that surrounded the girl. Ruby's body absorbed the light, her entire anatomy changing beneath the spell. Neurons shifted, her blood flow reinforced.

Now this small human was immune to djinn influence. The aura around Ruby became an impenetrable shield. The shell expanded from her body, destroying not only the illusions directed at her and their consequences. Never again could a djinn convince someone to pick up a weapon and aim it at this child.

"It worked," Isra said.

Jacoa rushed to Ruby's side as the pandemonium of humanity took over. A security guard held the woman with the gun back. She struggled against his hold, tearfully trying to reach the scene of the fallen nanny and Ruby.

"Not the girl. I'm a good shot, I swear. Tell me it didn't hit the girl."

The security guard constrained the shooter and spoke to the driver through the window. Another guard had sped to the nanny's side. His head tilted toward the radio on his shoulder, informing someone on the inside of the building to call the police. Based on the snatches of frightened conversation and the distant wail of a siren, Isra assumed multiple people within the crowd had used their cell phones to beat the security team to the punch.

This was the problem with djinn. This was a painful example of what draconians prevented by eliminating these creatures.

Ward passed Ruby to Jacoa and stood, dusting off his jeans.

He strode to where Isra knelt, exactly where she'd coached her master through his last wish.

"You can stand up now," Ward said.

Isra felt as if someone suddenly untied her legs. She scrambled to her feet.

"What are you?" she asked. Ward's fiery glance scolded her for her impertinence.

"Ruby is protected, but Jacoa is still a target. The djinn are tired of Jann's game and have given up waiting for you to embrace being a genie."

"They can wait an eternity."

"We don't have that kind of time. You need a plan."

"I have one," Isra countered, thinking of her father.

"One that amounts to more than a 'wait-and-see' attitude."

Isra flinched. Had he truly guessed her strategy, or simply surmised it was a long game based on her history?

"Start with this," Ward said. "Take Jacoa to Death Valley."

"No." Isra's answer was a reflexive act of self-preservation.

The draconian lived in that desert. Maybe even her father. She was no longer looking forward to meeting him, especially not with Jacoa at her side. Ward did not appear to care.

"You have been lucky so far, but the djinn will adapt their strategies. Death Valley is the safest place now that the djinn have decided to force his hand."

"And mine."

"No," Ward countered. "I am the one commanding you."

Isra's knees buckled. She set her resolve against his strength, but it did no good. One knee fell, and then the other. She fought to keep her body high, but he forced her to sit on her heels.

"How are you doing this to me?"

"Consider it one of the many perks of being a sorcerer."

So that's what Ward was. Isra stopped fighting his power, her hands limp in her lap. He nodded, as if acknowledging her reaction as the correct choice.

"Take him to the desert. Lay low until I contact you. There's a lot more going on than you know, Isra Almasi."

Isra didn't feel the immediate need to obey, but the way Ward's commands weighed against her choices told her the move to Death Valley was inevitable. Perhaps it was a blessing in disguise. If they were quiet enough, their trespass might not be discovered by the draconian, and they would be safe from the djinn.

Jacoa finished talking to security and gestured toward Ward and Isra. He held Ruby, who had her arms and legs squeezing around him. The guard gave him leave to move across the parking lot as long as he stayed to speak with the police.

"Pull yourself together," Ward murmured. Instantly, Isra was able to rise and a wave of warmth shimmered, much like a desert mirage. When it cleared, her clothes and face were refreshed. Jacoa blinked, curiosity lighting his eyes at the change, a small tick on his lips showing he didn't know whether to smile or frown.

For her part, Isra frowned. Though it had been her power that caused the transformation, it had come at Ward's command. His control of her was irritating, the forced use of magic uncomfortable. But he'd helped her rescue Ruby and wanted to protect Jacoa, so he couldn't be an enemy.

Isra knew very little about sorcerers. Though they'd created the draconian race, Ward was the first one she'd met. Could they all control her like that? How many more were there?

A shiver ran along her spine, and though she distantly processed Jacoa explaining that the guard was attempting to reach Dave, she wasn't truly listening.

A sorcerer was here, still alive. He'd somehow escaped the curse of the djinn when the creatures had stripped human mages of their powers. And Isra, it seemed, was his unwilling puppet.

CHAPTER 19

Jacoa

Jacoa's shoulders sank forward, his spine weighted into a curve. Gravity was not his friend when his feet dragged like lead. He'd given his story three separate times and shared his contact information with four different people. Dave had arrived hours ago and took Ruby home with a detective who would question them there. The nanny was police-escorted to the hospital, and the shooter taken to the police station. Jacoa had been stuck with the witnesses. They'd been corralled to the side parking lot to allow customers access to the casino and amusement park.

They'd finally given him permission to leave. He regretted not wishing his way out of this one. That would only put him up to nine. What harm were nine little wishes? It was only halfway.

His genie rested against the front of the building, waiting for him to return. As he rounded the corner, he noticed her usually observant eyes were closed, her head supported by the brick as if she shared his exhaustion. The soft lines of her cheeks appeared drawn, her chin tense, and he swore she looked sad.

Jacoa leaned on the wall next to her, deliberately pulling in a deep flow of air as a tingling caressed his body, and then on an exhale he cultivated the image of his own energy tangling with hers.

Did it look like it felt, he wondered, this give and take between them? Their energies made room for each other. A set of hands pressed together, fingers falling one after the other as they intertwined.

"I'm not sure I can drive," he said.

"There's a lot going on."

"I want an explanation. I'll wish it from you if I have to. It would mean more to both of us if you choose to give it." He no longer had the energy to tiptoe around her. After today, he didn't think he had the time, either.

Isra looked to where their hands hung inches apart, then met his eyes.

"Not here."

The only reason Jacoa didn't fall was because Isra's magic supported him as the wall disappeared. The surrounding air became dryer between one breath and the next. Sunshine beat directly on their heads without the benefit of massive buildings to block its full force.

Jacoa gasped when he looked beyond Isra. They stood in the middle of a flat, rocky desert. Skeletal bushes lined the unbroken landscape with the silhouette of hills on the horizon. He turned around, searching for signs of a road or track. Other than the small shadow of a bird of prey circling high in the cloudless sky, nothing moved.

This was Death Valley. He was saved from turning into a sweaty, saturated mess because of the moderate November temperatures, but that didn't mean there weren't other dangers in the barren, waterless landscape.

His heartbeat raced and filled his brain with heated blood that darkened the edges of his vision. He launched from Isra, gripping the strap on his messenger bag as he backed away. There was nothing large enough to create shade in this death trap.

"What the hell, Isra? Is this part of your plan? Freak me

out, exhaust me, make me think you're on my side, and then leave me in the desert until you have your damned wishes? But the absolutely last straw is that you brought Ruby into it. I wish..."

But he didn't know what he wanted. For today to be over. To return to when the sculptures were delivered, and she'd let him forget what she erased. That he hadn't worked so damned hard at gaining her trust when she hadn't reciprocated. For her to have never entered his life. That his mother had never spun fairy tales for a monster.

Each and every one of those fiery desires flared, then died. None of them were strong enough to make it to his tongue. He didn't have the energy to fight this fury, though it drained him deeper than his bones. A heavy sigh burst from behind his ribs. Jacoa lowered himself to the ground, knees raised to support his forearms while his head hung limp. Isra followed, but kept a few feet of buffer space between them.

"It wasn't me," Isra said. Jacoa couldn't hold back a bitter laugh. "It was djinn, but not me."

"What is going on, Isra? I hadn't seen any evidence of magic my entire life before you came into it. And believe me, I looked. Why are the djinn coming after me?"

"Not you, exactly. It's your wishes."

"Because if I make them, all genies will be free? If I do that, will they leave me alone?"

"Do not do that," Isra snapped, drawing Jacoa's attention. "There are genies who need to stay locked up. Destroyed, even."

"You don't."

Isra shifted her feet and stared at the sky, her fingers interlocked. Her hair caught a breeze that wasn't there, tangling into knots. He looked away.

"I did not cause the car accident or Ruby's kidnapping."

"But," Jacoa added, because there was clearly one of those hidden in the tremors of her voice.

"I might have agreed to it."

"Might have." Jacoa's fists clenched in an effort to hold on to his shredded patience.

"Djinn are tricky creatures," Isra answered slowly. "I haven't been successful in ending this curse, as you can tell. This djinn, Maram, made a very good argument. I thought I had more time before she pressed the matter. Or that I could back out if she proved too insistent. I had no idea how it would escalate."

"I don't understand. You agreed to work with her, but just now you told me not to ask all my wishes."

Isra's shadow fell over Jacoa, but he kept his eyes low, counting the tiny rocks as he listened to how his genie had plotted against him.

"The netherworld is a dead place. Nothing exists there except for thought, and then it's only my own. There's nothing to hear or touch or see. When I return to the living realm... She caught me at my weakest."

"So you were willing to put me in danger? To put other people in danger?"

Jacoa rose to his feet. He walked away from Isra, putting one foot in front of the other to increase the space between them. But he couldn't leave her behind. He had considered himself so clever when he'd caught her at the mall, binding her to his side.

At least Aali had the vessel.

He stopped as his stomach dropped and his head pounded with an inner heat that had nothing to do with the desert. He found a relatively flat spot and sat down, eyes closed, wanting his mind to go blank.

Isra lowered herself beside him and remained silent. When he peeked at her, she lay back, supported by her forearms, body lengthened, ankles crossed. The waves of her hair pooled on the ground between her arms, but the lines were too perfect and not quite soft enough to sell the mood. She rested, as if knowing he only needed a moment of quiet before his temper would calm.

Magic or just run-of-the-mill intuition? Either way, Jacoa was tired of dancing around Isra. But diving right in threatened to rekindle the anger marinating in his chest.

"I thought djinn didn't like the sun."

"It's more that they prefer space," Isra corrected. "There's more of it visible at night with stars reaching across the universe. Since I'm a genie, it doesn't bother me as much. Freedom is freedom, no matter the time of day."

Jacoa hadn't expected her to answer. Would she say more?

"Your hair moves on its own," he said, starting small. As if on cue, the strands swirled in a circular motion. The length rested in a loose coil of brilliant white.

"I dislike being around humans for long because I have to control it. It's as much an extension of me as my arms. As touch sensitive as my skin."

"Can you read my thoughts?"

"Only the ones you show on your face. But sometimes your wishes provide me with a flash, like when you asked for a drink."

Jacoa's laugh was a harsh bubble of sound that popped the tension in his chest. His canceled birthday party felt like so long ago, back when he'd give anything for a glimpse of his genie.

"How close to me do you actually have to be?" he asked. "You weren't within line-of-sight while I talked to the police."

"It depends on how I define 'your presence'," she admitted as a braid twisted together at her temple. "In the same room? As long as I can see you? Perhaps only as far as I can hear your loudest shout."

"So you haven't needed to sleep in my bed." Jacoa's lips twitched into a smile when more of Isra's hair coiled.

"You bound me to this form after a single day of being free. It wasn't fair that I was the only uncomfortable one."

Her answer brought his thoughts to her confession, and he ran out of neutral questions. Jacoa tried on Isra's perspective of being stuck in a place of emptiness. She always had her face to the sun or tilted toward a pleasing sound. Her eyes never stopped moving, taking everything in.

"You don't want to go back."

She didn't have to ask what he meant. "No."

"Isra." Her name was all he could muster. Thoughts squirmed around his brain, slippery things he couldn't grip. In the mess, he found one recurring thought.

"I would have liked to talk first."

"I had no way of knowing what type of person you would be. Some of my masters..." She shuddered and Jacoa nodded. He'd read the journals.

"If I could wish you free, all by yourself, I want you to know that I would."

Isra dug her hands into the ground, the hard sand piling under curled fingers. Was she upset at his non-promise?

"There may be a different way," he offered, thinking of his deal with Aali. Isra's bitter laugh filled the air and was swallowed by the arid desert.

"I'm far ahead of you."

"What?"

"There is no curse if there is no genie."

"Wait. Are you talking about dying? No. That is not what I meant."

"Gunter thought like you." Isra's voice fell flat. "He tried many variations of a wish to set me free. He would spend months working out the words, asking me questions about loopholes. He studied every tome he found on magic, sorcery, and the djinn. Each wish failed. The contract that holds me was stronger than Gunter's carefully constructed workarounds."

"You said his journal told the truth. That's not what he wrote."

"I assume it was as he saw it. A matter of perspective."

"How do you remember your time with him?"

The question seemed to go further than Isra wanted to share. Her lips thinned, and she rested her chin on raised knees while she drew swirls in the dust with her fingernails.

Jacoa dug into his messenger bag and pulled out the manilla

envelope. He clutched it between his hands, wondering how many kinds of a fool he would be if he acted on these small gifts by trading access to his most prized possession.

Nothing given, nothing gained, and this felt like the right gesture. With gentle fingers, Jacoa extracted the paperback. Tucking the envelope away, he checked for a table of contents, located the title he needed, and read the tale featuring Gunter.

"It came to be that the genie found herself in the care of a kind master. He enjoyed mathematics and puzzles, and to him, his genie was the greatest puzzle of all."

The book flew from his hands. Isra caught it and leaned into the open chapter. She skimmed with incredible speed, pages finished on each of Jacoa's breaths. She completed the story with Gunter, then moved on to the next. She fanned the paper, scanned a few sections, then flipped her way to the beginning. When she extracted herself from the fairy tales, her rounded eyes were framed by gentle curls tangling around her cheeks.

"Where did this come from?" she asked.

"My mother, Riti."

"But how did she know?"

"I don't know. These stories are why I asked you if she might have gotten ahold of something of yours that I haven't seen. She died without telling me. So, are these true?"

"They're not much further from the truth than the journals. It's impossible. I never even met her."

Jacoa's heart broke a little. If Isra couldn't explain the stories, then there must be no connection beyond the journals and his mother's beautiful imagination. Jacoa accepted the book from Isra, closing it to show the basic black cover with white scripted font.

"This morning is the first time I've seen this book, or known she titled it *The Genie Curse*. She told me the stories at bedtime as if she made them up. It wasn't until I turned sixteen and got the journals that I realized she must have read them. I don't know why she changed the details. Except..."

"Except that she wanted you to be worthy." Isra referred to the last line of every fairy tale. "One thing is certain. She understood the curse well."

"What do you mean?"

"*The Genie Curse*. Not the cursed genie, or the cursed Wickers. We're both caught up in this."

Jacoa lifted the book, a silent offering to Isra if she wanted it back. When she shook her head, he tucked the paperback into his bag and placed it to the side before facing Isra. Her eyes met his, and they were her exquisite genie yellow.

Something about their sunny depths warmed his spirit. She was hundreds of years old, but had lived so few of those because of this curse. They both searched for an escape, just doing their best.

"Every moment we've been together, I've been trying to answer a question that has plagued me for two years. Are you the Isra of my mother's fairy tales, or the monster of my ancestors?"

"Jacoa." Isra's voice was thick and gritty. "I've never been a princess."

"I'm not looking for a princess," he countered. "Between bedtime stories, journals, and this week, you have been with me for longer than any person or thing I've had in my life. Since you appeared, it's been clear I have been asking the wrong question. I don't care if you're a fairytale or a monster. If you're good or bad."

A rush of Isra's energy flowed into him. He accepted it on an inhale, then let it go on his exhale, sending some of himself along with it. Her pupils dilated as their breath synchronized in balance. Their bodies swayed toward each other, shortening the distance of the exchange.

"Just be mine."

Jacoa didn't elaborate, not wanting to spook her with the depth of that desire. He didn't want her for a wish, or a day, or a year. He wanted her forever.

For now, though, he risked a single touch. He reached for the braid at her cheek. Nearly there, he paused, waiting, his green eyes locked on her yellow.

The braid eased forward and slid over his fingertips on its own. Her shudder vibrated into his skin. He closed the distance between them, pausing once again just before touching, fighting against the flow of energy tightening around them with each heartbeat. Jacoa needed her passivity to shift toward action. He couldn't be the only one giving or taking.

Isra's shaken breath brushed him a moment before trembling lips met his. Their kiss was an exchange of gentle pressure. An inner light flared behind Jacoa's forehead. The airiness of his joy mingled with hers, and his eyes widened with surprise. He started to pull away, to ask her what it meant, but Isra pushed into the kiss and Jacoa surrendered to her will. She never broke the simple contact as she climbed into his lap. The silken strands of her hair wrapped around him, binding them chest to chest.

The same flare brightened his chest, his lower ribs, and his pelvis. Each point that touched Isra flowed into her, and hers into him. Jacoa dove into the sensation, wondering if this was how Isra experienced life. Joy at touch. Excited by friction. Drawn to the vibration of sound.

Jacoa's palms skimmed Isra's thighs, pressed through the thin cotton of her shirt. As he moved across her ribs, Isra stiffened and wrapped her arms around Jacoa's neck. He lifted his hands toward her face, surprised when her hair billowed, entangling his fingers, tightening and directing his touch back to her body.

She broke the kiss, pressing that bright point of their foreheads together, her nails scraping along his jawline.

"Don't stop touching." She spoke in a breathy whisper. Jacoa found his fingertips placed on Isra's collarbone against the ruffled elastic neckline of her shirt. She planted one of her own hands over his and curled both their fingers around the edge of the cloth, dragging it down.

"I won't," he promised.

CHAPTER 20

Isra

Jacoa kept his promise for a long, long time. Eventually, his fingertips slipped away, but Isra forgave him. The stress of the day had caught up to her master and his eyes drifted shut, his lips tucked into a gentle smile.

Isra ran her hand along the hard dirt beside Jacoa, softening it into sand around them, sending it deep to cushion him. He'd fallen asleep during the sunset and, as the temperature dipped, goosebumps rose on his naked flesh. Isra heated the sand and eased him deeper.

No wishes asked in exchange for her power. Simply a genie caring for her master of her own free will.

His touch had been a gift she never expected. When she'd confessed to her part in Maram's plan, she was sure he'd wish her gone in his next breath. She'd expected a fight, at least. Instead, he chose to get to know her. Worked to understand her.

Jacoa had asked if she could read his thoughts. She wished for the ability in this moment. She wanted to know what changed his mind, how he had calmed himself down. What did she say that flipped the switch from distrust to connection?

Perhaps it was the simple fact that she'd said anything at all. That she laid it all out for his judgment. Whatever the reason, she didn't know what she had done to deserve this young, wise Wicker in her life. She wouldn't let herself hope she would get to keep him.

As the moon rose, Isra continued to watch Jacoa sleep. She'd fallen into the habit since he'd tied her to his side. She didn't need sleep or food. Both could be ignored or treated as luxuries for the djinn, who gained sustenance from the world around them as easy as breathing.

This ability to self-sustain was part of what made djinn so dangerous. There wasn't much that weakened them. The sorcerer-made cuffs were one of the few things that could bind them. Isra's had even held Jann, the most powerful djinn of them all, and only the power of a wish freed them.

Invoking the First Djinn only led to more confusion. Isra had expected more interference from Jann to get all the wishes completed, yet they seemed content to watch their game play out. Isra considered Maram, the one djinn she'd spent the most time with. Maram was angry with the First Djinn, and had gone so far as to tell Isra to rush the last few wishes before Jann interfered.

Was Jann that dedicated to their game, or was there a deeper motive from the oldest magical being? With the djinn, it could be both. Their sense of time was warped—one of the main reasons they believed humans, shorter lived beings, weren't worth consideration. But what could the First Djinn possibly gain by keeping their brethren trapped as genies?

If only she'd been wiser when going after Jann's vessel. But then, Jacoa...

Isra rested her palm on Jacoa's chest and focused on the rise and fall of his breath. She hated being a genie. That hadn't changed. But now, she wasn't ready for it to end yet.

She would have to get out of her deal with Maram and change tactics. Isra was no longer eager to use her powers, especially in this desert. Djinn magic drew the draconian in, and she brought Jacoa right on their doorstep thanks to Ward's insistence. That they hadn't found her with any other master didn't matter. This release from the nether differed from the start. And she didn't want to lose this Wicker.

Jacoa slept soundly as they passed through midnight. Every bit of tension in his body drained into the earth. Isra lifted a finger above his torso and focused on moving the grains of sand working as a blanket. Thoughts and questions jumbled through her mind, swirling much like the small spiral she drew.

Isra directed a strand of the spiral to ignore the rules of gravity and rise until it stood on its own, a transparent needle of glass. As she stared at the sharp point, she calmed the chaos inside by focusing on a single thought.

She'd slept with Jacoa. She could say the day's excitement swept her away, but that wasn't true. Regret was not one of Isra's tangled emotions. At least, not about this. She'd been desperate to experience every brush from the fingertips she'd obsessed over. He'd given her no reason for disappointment. It was as if, through their battle of wills, all they'd been waiting for was a little give. A little trust.

Jacoa had no regrets, either. She could say that with certainty, because he'd used the flow of energy between them. As she shifted thoughts, she pulled another trail of sand-turned glass to wrap the original needle. Somehow their chakras aligned with each other, his energy circling with her as hers curled into him, creating endless infinity loops.

What did such a connection mean? How could Jacoa actively use it as well? She twisted a third stream of sand around the other two. This one extended in a perpendicular, wavy line from the top of the spire. More tendrils joined it as she manipulated the thought in her head. Her training as a draconian had looked at chakras from the viewpoint of blocking a djinn's access to make them easier to trap. What she'd learned as a genie had been self-taught, and therefore limited. As she searched for possibilities, each strand of glass pulled away from the base in a different direction.

She had heard tales of chakras aligning, but only one at a time.

A meeting of the minds interwove at *Anja*. People meant to challenge each other would meet at *Anahata*. Those who had reached balance with the universe met at *Vasundhara* or *Sutara*. These connections were brief and rare, not even repeatable between those who experienced them.

Yet her energy still tangled in Jacoa's with her body so close to his. It no longer tightened around them, demanding proximity, but it didn't dwindle away as it had in previous days. It was as if their intimate connection had settled the force between them. None of her guesses solidified in her mind as truth. She couldn't work out this puzzle on her own.

"Is it a tree?" Jacoa's slow, patterned breath hadn't shifted to alert her to his awakened state. Even as he spoke, he kept his core as steady as possible so as not to disturb the glass sculpture. A small smile hooked her lips.

"It can be."

"For a wish?" His words were quiet, testing. So he wasn't confident in their relationship, either. Isra took a deep breath and thickened the base with one wavy strand after another. Most stopped at the bottom of the branches. Some continued on to reinforce the delicate shoots, then sprouted tiny, vein-marked leaves.

It made sense that he'd be confused about her attitude toward wishes. She hadn't explained herself well, especially as her own desires were shifting. What would he think if he knew why she'd requested some, but not all his wishes? How would he take it if she told him that now, she didn't want him wishing at all?

The words she'd burned into the twists of her leather bands were invisible in the dark, but their presence was forefront in her mind. Her father should have ended her curse when she'd wanted. If he showed up now, Isra would burn the universe down to stay with her master.

Jacoa's touch to Isra's long hair was butterfly soft, yet it sent a shock through her system. His low chuckle at her response drew her attention from the spun glass, up his chest and over his face.

As he took in her bracketed lips and the crease between her eyes, he lowered his hand.

Strands of her hair wrapped around his fingers, pulling them back in.

"A promise is practically a wish," she whispered, invoking his vow to keep touching her.

The glass formation vibrated, letting off a soft bell tone as he tensed to sit. Jacoa relaxed into the sand, using the hair he held to guide her against his side so their faces were level.

"It's a rather inconvenient piece of art."

"I can get rid of it," Isra offered. Jacoa's free hand wrapped around the trunk to hold it steady.

"You know how I feel about extraordinary things." He lowered his face to hers, eyes open as if he watched for any sign of withdrawal. She let him ease in until his lips gently brushed hers.

"Then it's yours," she said.

The tree disappeared. Along with the glass, Isra sent away Jacoa's mother's book for safety as well. Jacoa didn't protest or demand an explanation. He took advantage of his freedom, reaching around Isra's waist.

Isra's stomach growled. She jerked from Jacoa, who laughed at the sound until Isra stood to scan the landscape. Hunger twisted her gut, her body expressing that she hadn't eaten anything for five hundred years. Her connection to djinn magic was fading. She was under attack.

"What's wrong?"

Isra ignored the question. She focused on her chakras to learn where she was cut off. *Sutara* was sluggish, not completely stopped, but no longer receptive. The rest worked, but not for long.

With her Soul Star blocked, Isra wouldn't be able to create anything, but she could still shift what was already in existence. She collected her clothes and Jacoa's and got them both dressed just before *Sahasrara* locked down, severely limiting her innate protections.

A hiss slid through the desert night, and Isra twisted toward it. Jacoa followed more slowly and took her hand, understanding the sound for the warning it was.

The draconian surrounded them. A djinn had stupidly come into their territory, and they wouldn't miss the opportunity to capture and kill it. Isra knew exactly how they were trapped. They planted artifacts of djinn bone in the sand. Each one connected to a chakra, and was activated in order. The first, a djinn skullcap, had ignited with the touch of starlight and blocked *Sutara*. For the second, a poisoned lotus was ground together with bone dust for *Sahasrara*. They would be working on the third now, meant to block *Anja*.

"What do we do?" Jacoa asked. "Can we fight?"

"No. We run."

She would take Jacoa the one direction the draconian wouldn't expect; a place no djinn dared to trespass.

Isra was not djinn.

"Hold on to me," she said. With her powers weakening, her control would be questionable. She needed him to take care of himself.

Jacoa knelt behind her, his arms slipping around her torso. The sand bubbled and their bodies lowered. Jacoa's face pressed into her neck and Isra wrapped him in the strands even as she burrowed them deep into the Death Valley sands.

CHAPTER 21

Jacoa

Jacoa kept his face hidden in Isra's slithering hair as she buried them alive in the sands. He wanted to remind her he would need to breathe, yet his words caught between his fear of her intentions and his desire to trust.

Isra's body pressed against his as she worked to sit up. He quickly unwrapped his arms and sucked in a staccato breath, surprised to find the air perfectly suitable, if a tad stale and sandy. His stomach twisted against his ribs and he longed to wrap a strand of hair into his fist, but he stopped himself, afraid that it would appear as if he used the length as a leash.

"Now what?" he asked, unable to see in the dark.

"A little light," Isra said.

A dance of small flickers had Jacoa wincing from the strobe effect until the illumination steadied. He blinked against the blurred vision brought on by his pupils' delayed response to the sudden brightness.

They sat on the floor of a long rectangular chamber. Four hospital beds lined either side of the otherwise empty room, three of them occupied by humanesque lizards. Each mirrored the other, laying on their backs, perfectly still. Their scales were such a pale cream that they were nearly white, as if they hadn't seen the sun in a very long time.

Jacoa stood slowly with Isra, his breath coming in gasps.

"Will they wake up?"

"No." Isra's voice was flat in her answer. Where Jacoa couldn't look away from the draconian, Isra stared at the smooth sandstone floor, her hair falling like blinders on either side of her face to block an accidental view of the beds and their supine occupants.

"What is this place?"

"The brood den. Draconian don't reproduce easily, and females are rare. When they reach breeding age, they're brought here."

"I don't understand?"

Isra let out a rough sigh and swept her arm toward the room she refused to see.

"They're trapped here for the rest of their lives, forced to be living incubators. It takes ten years for a draconian infant to gestate. Most of them don't make it. Most of the ones who do are male. If they have a live birth, these females are allowed a few months of life. Otherwise, what you see is what they get."

"I-isra." Jacoa wanted to say more, but his throat constricted on the words. That empty bed. Had they prepared it for Isra? Was being cursed as a genie the only reason she'd escaped this fate?

Was Isra's mother here? Jacoa winced at the thought, not wanting her to be. But then, wouldn't that mean she was dead? Would that be worse?

He raised both hands and pressed his palms to his temples, threading his fingers in his hair to give it a light tug.

He'd been so angry that she hadn't told him about Maram, and now he realized he had a secret just as big. He needed to tell her he knew about her draconian roots. That Jacoa had met her father, who convinced him to pass along her vessel. But confessing to her in this brood den didn't seem appropriate. He'd have to wait and hope the delay wouldn't cost him the trust he'd worked so hard to build between them.

"I'm sorry, this must be a shock. You've probably never heard of a draconian, since your ancestors hadn't mentioned them."

"They didn't," Jacoa chose his words carefully. "But I heard something about them. I just didn't realize... They hunt genies, right? So it was them on the surface?"

Isra nodded stiffly. "And now you know where they live."

"Why did you bring us here? Out of all the places in the world, you brought me to the one that is most dangerous for you."

"The djinn were getting too close in Vegas. This is the safest place for you."

"We need to find somewhere safe for us," Jacoa insisted. "How do we get out of here?"

"They have blocked my powers," Isra admitted. "They have djinn bone artifacts. When mixed with certain elements, they block our chakras and our connection to magic. The draconian are extremely knowledgeable of djinn weaknesses and can exploit them like no other."

The image of Aali's taloned hands around his own brought a tsunami of conflicted emotions. Had he done the right thing?

No matter what he had put into motion, Jacoa would make the draconian explain every detail of his scheme the next time they met. If needed, he could ensure Isra was never accessible to her father. All it would take was a simple wish.

"Is there a plan?" he asked.

"There's an idea." Isra's lips curled as if she smiled, but there was no emotion behind the flat movement. "I happen to know the way out."

"Provided we don't get caught."

"Exactly, but we have the advantage. The draconian would never assume that a djinn would enter their stronghold."

"Or that the genie knows her way around?"

Isra's lips thinned. "You want to know how I know."

Jacoa swayed on his feet as a light dizziness filled his head. His question had backfired. He sucked in a deep breath, but Isra hadn't noticed his response behind her curtain of hair.

"That will have to be a discussion for another time," Isra said, saving Jacoa from sharing his own secrets. "Right now, let's make our way out."

She walked toward one of the brood den's narrower walls, bringing Jacoa's attention away from the motionless females.

There weren't any paintings or decorations in this chamber. The bedding was the same color as the stone. The medical grade equipment broke up the tan shades, but it only made everything appear colder.

There was a simple rope handle anchored into the sandstone wall. Isra pulled on it, and a vertical rectangle moved into the room, then slid off to the right on a track carved into the floor. She peered into the space beyond, then gestured for Jacoa to follow.

They entered a corridor so long, Jacoa couldn't see the other end. The rough stone walls rose to nine feet, then gently curved into an arched ceiling. Dome-shaped devices flickered into red-tinted illumination with their movement, the door sliding shut behind them.

"The hallways are empty, too."

"What do you mean?" Isra asked.

"There's no decoration. No art or paint. It's all so plain."

"The draconian are very utilitarian. Think, the exact opposite of djinn who prefer to surround themselves with sensation."

"Not even in their personal space?"

"Decorated only with the clothing they wear and the weapons they use."

"Tall ceilings or not, that's a very claustrophobic thought."

Isra's lips ticked up, and though she didn't smile, her eyes softened. After studying the hall devoid of any markings, she chose a direction, jerking her body into the turn with more vigor than necessary. Her hair swayed with the movement, as if it enjoyed the pull of the centrifugal force. She defied the bleak nature of this place. Even being trapped in a dangerous situation must be better than the nether, because she could still enjoy her senses.

To distract himself from their current circumstances, Jacoa filled himself with thoughts of appreciation for how she immersed herself. How she'd infused him with that ability during the intimacy they'd shared on the sand. Isra not only insisted that there always be contact, but she'd guided him to places she needed to be touched, not willing to deny either of them the pleasure.

Jacoa had never seen such visceral abandonment. The amazing flow of energy between them had heightened his own ability to experience sensation. He didn't care how or why that connection existed, he was happily addicted. His nerves tingled with the memory, and he itched to reach out to feel her again. To ask her to share that love of life, even in this dire situation. To bring him into that high he would never get enough of.

To remind her she was no longer destined to be stuck in the brood den.

Jacoa recalled the alluring warmth he experienced when they were close, the total alignment when their bodies pressed at certain points. He exhaled mindfully, imagining that the small puff of air carried his hope with it.

Isra's hair relaxed into a gentle wave, a few of the twists drifting toward him. Jacoa brushed his hand over the feathery tips. Isra's smile was more heartfelt this time. She slowed her pace, so he walked next to her instead of behind.

At a point in the endless hall, Isra stopped at one of the inline doors. She moved the slab, peeking beyond before she committed to opening it all the way and gestured him through. It eased shut on its own power, blocking an easy retreat.

The chamber was a large, cylindrical space with a circular opening at the top that revealed a pink dawn sky. The distant skylight did nothing to alleviate the brutal heat of the room that brought an instant bead of sweat to Jacoa's brow. A narrow stucco dome blocked their view of the entire room. A staircase matched the curve, providing a way out through the naked skylight. Isra slid along the outer wall, making her way toward the exit. Jacoa followed her, both of them freezing when they heard a clanging echo against the stone walls.

The rhythmic pounding gave the impression of a blacksmith at work. The egg-shaped kiln blocked whoever stood on the other side. Jacoa calculated how far they could get up the stairs before they were seen.

Isra concentrated on the center of the room as if she tried to see through the oven. Jacoa skimmed her arm to remind her he was there. She blinked from her statuesque state, then nodded with firm lips and indicated the skylight.

So they would try the staircase anyway. This must be the best way out.

Jacoa kept his footsteps as silent as possible. A hissing, wet sound was accompanied by a thick pillar of steam that rose toward the open ceiling. A moment later, a deep whine twisted Jacoa's ears, then released.

The heat increased with the noise. Isra didn't tilt her head toward it as she'd done with the human laughter in Vegas. Her focus seemed to be glued to her feet as she timidly placed her weight onto the woven metal staircase, beginning their ascent.

They rounded the stove as they rose into the room. Isra alternated between keeping their exit in sight and marking when the unknown draconian come into view.

Jacoa didn't know if he stopped first, or Isra, when Aali's face appeared. Jacoa tried to tell himself it could be any draconian. Isra's fingers curved into fists as the draconian glanced up, then startled when he recognized two people who did not belong.

"Isra! What are you doing here?" The rage in the draconian's voice competed with the heat of the forge beside him. He abandoned his work on a simple dagger and rounded the oven to check the closed door.

"Father. Good to know you recognize me. I'd wondered."

Isra's tone was hollow. Despite the warmth in the room,

Jacoa's spine prickled with an icy sharpness, the hair on the back of his neck rising.

"You are far from where you should be," Aali hissed.

"Do you mean caught in the circle? I'm surprised you weren't part of the group that tried to bind me."

"Had I been, you wouldn't have escaped."

"It seems we're both a disappointment."

The folds of the draconian's eyelids bent into a narrow oval over dark pupils as he glared at Isra.

"Assumptions got you into this trouble. You should not compound them." Aali moved his black eyes to Jacoa. "Wish yourself out of here."

"How do you know my master?"

"I've known all of them. Just as I've known all your faces."

"All." Isra's hair fell straight, slick and shiny like a piece of steel. She focused on the nearly completed dagger, only needing a sharpened edge to become a usable weapon. "So close and yet so far, it seems."

Jacoa felt caught between the two in a conversation he didn't understand. He reverted to the last sentence that made sense.

"They blocked Isra's magic. I can't wish."

"We're at eight wishes" Isra glowered at Aali. "Where use of my magic never brought you or my brethren to find me, if we go much further, we will certainly gain the attention of Jann."

Aali stiffened at the name Jacoa wasn't familiar with, but it appeared to be someone who caused both Isra and her father to pause.

"They have let you go beyond before," the male draconian said, his decision made. "You are trapped. Your master holds a contract that cannot be broken while you live. Even the draconian cannot interfere."

Jacoa studied Isra, her eyes fixed on a spot just behind Aali. She examined the dagger with the same intensity she had watched the desert fly by on their drives. The ice wrapping his spine rose and squeezed his throat. His secret would not remain one for long. His unguided decision was coming back to haunt him. Before he could apologize, they had to escape.

"I wish for you to take us to my house right now."

Isra's next words told him exactly how much trouble he was in.

"Wish granted."

CHAPTER 22

Isra

The pair appeared in front of the shattered void sculpture, installed just the morning before. Isra took in her reflections. Some were distorted into swirls and bends. Others were cut off and sliced through with a gorgeous sparkling line of diamond.

"Show me my vessel."

Jacoa's only movement was breath. All she had to do was flick her eyes to be able to see his own morphed reflection, yet she kept her gaze securely on hers.

"I'm sorry," he said.

Isra thrummed with vibration. Jacoa's wish had taken her outside the reach of the draconian's trap, and she focused on each of her chakras, turning them toward the left. Grounding herself with *Vasundhara*. Aligning each of the seven points in her body and connecting to *Sutara* above her head. With this power in her hands, she could bend the reality she lived in, and her master's, if she so wished.

The shape of her vessel didn't matter to the curse. As long as the metal remained, the genie contract held firm and Jacoa could ask his wishes. Those wishes would still be stronger than anything a djinn threw at them.

But now Aali had finally completed the task she'd waited centuries for. He'd taken her vessel and created a weapon. Because the dagger was composed of the same material as her cuffs, it could kill her.

This had been her plan. She'd been right to guess it was her father's. Yet, the tears she held back were sharp and hot.

"You gave it to him?" She tried to hold her body strong, but her voice broke.

"After the party." At least he didn't lie. "Did you see it with him?"

"So did you. He turned it into a knife."

"What? Why?" Air surrounded Jacoa's words, as if each was forced out with the thrust of a punch to his gut.

But she was not angry with Jacoa.

Of course, Aali acted now. He would have used Jacoa's unique education to convince the naïve Wicker to help free his daughter. Of course, he would be smithing it into a dagger, even as she stood next to the one master she didn't want to leave.

The vibrations within Isra expanded from her body. A thick slashing sound scratched at the windows. Jacoa glanced outside in surprise, but this storm would not come from beyond the glass. A sheet of dust and wind coated the ceiling and spun around the room. More sand crawled in through the cracks of the entries and from beneath the baseboards, concentrated gusts kicking it up into the air.

"Isra." Jacoa reached for her, but stopped when she directed a flow of power his way, leaving every hair standing on end. This was not their usual exchange of energy. This was her keeping him from getting too close. She couldn't afford their connection, or his need for conversations that only drew her further in. Her father was on the move, and he was the best.

Jacoa lifted his hands, palms up in supplication. "Isra, what did I do? He said if you were his daughter, he was going to free you."

The wind picked up, rushing from the closed front door to

sweep past them and swirl inside the kitchen. Table decorations rattled. Sand cut into the paint on the walls, etched into glassware. Something crashed in the dining room. Jacoa never took his eyes off her. He wasn't asking her to stop, only to explain.

The tempest died, leaving Jacoa's hair a twisted, knotted mess. Golden grains hung suspended in the air, drifting to the floor in a thick mat of tiny dunes. Isra had spared herself and Jacoa, and the new art. She hadn't been able to bring herself to scar any of those things.

"I get I should have waited to meet you before agreeing to your dad's plan. Just like you and Maram, right? But you've been upset before and never called a sandstorm. Why do you need all this?" He gestured to the mini desert that now filled his house.

"You're not fun to fight with," she grumbled. Jacoa's huff was part laughter, part disbelief as he ran a hand through his hair, only to wince when he caught a knot.

"Is that what we're doing?"

"Generally, the other person is supposed to be pig-headed and defend themselves," she snapped.

"Give me another chance. Tell me what's going on. Once I catch up, maybe we can fight about it. Then again," he muttered, looking around at the dusty mess. "I think I may be out of my weight class."

Isra shed her shoes and buried her feet in the warm sand, moving the scratchy particles between her toes. She left the broken void sculpture behind and approached the dragon.

Atop the cloche, the glass tree she'd spun had rooted and stood tall, its delicate branches sparkling as sunrise poured through the large dining room window. The morning light caught the golden motes of sand floating in the air. The stained-glass wings glowed, ready to take flight if only it could shed the last few bolts reinforcing its metal form.

Jacoa's leather shoes created tiny drifts through the sand. Isra closed her eyes to the rhythmic sound, a soft smile on her lips as she felt the gentle vibrations through the grains. She focused on the outer sensations so the interior noise faded away. So the pain screaming inside found only gentleness.

"If I controlled my reality, do you know what I would choose?"

"Will you tell me?" Jacoa asked.

"I assume since you met my father, you know I was born draconian?"

Compassion filled Isra's chest, a flow of emotion that didn't come from her body, but Jacoa's. He stood centimeters away from her back, using their connection with purpose. And with it, he answered her question without words.

"We aren't a prolific species. We are meant to die out once we eliminate the djinn. It has taken much, much longer than expected. To continue the race... You saw the brood den."

Jacoa waited in silence while Isra sorted through the thoughts in her head, discarding most of them for this conversation.

"My father and I had a plan to keep me from becoming a brood female. I trained to be the best of the hunters. My father is unsurpassed when it comes to discovering sleeping vessels—those with genies, but whose masters rarely wish. We found an incredible prize. The First Djinn's vessel. He wanted to wait and be cautious, but there was one area I excelled in over him. Retrieval. I was smaller. Quicker. So I didn't listen; I went for the vessel without his knowledge and paid for it with my freedom."

Jacoa studied the dragon in front of him, then shook his head.

"It seems more like a trade, doesn't it?" he asked.

"Yes." Isra's whisper fogged the glass cloche.

"But you enjoy being a genie more than a draconian?"

"What a horrible thing to say," Isra choked. "But maybe. It doesn't matter. Vessels can't be destroyed, but in a draconian's hands, they can be changed. Draconians can suspend part of the spell and reshape it into a weapon. Aali's done that. I've been waiting half a millennium for him to end this curse. I only wish he'd completed it before I met you."

"Kill?" Jacoa's body shook, and he looked like he would call his own sandstorm if he only had the power. "He said it was to free you."

"If he kills me, I will be free of the curse. That's all he meant."

"He only spoke of killing a djinn who was not you. Are you absolutely certain?"

"The dagger is only deadly to the djinn who wears the matching cuffs." Isra raised her wrists, though the metal was hidden behind leather.

"No." Jacoa gripped one of her hands and turned her to face him. His free fingertips traced her eyebrow, pressing a spiral curl away from her cheek. "There must be another way."

"Undiscovered by the draconians who cancel out magic, or the djinn who bend reality, or the sorcerers who caused the trouble in the first place? It has been thousands of years, Jacoa, if there was an answer—"

"Isra." Jacoa's voice found its strength. His fingertips at her brow drew velvet lines over her cheek, then settled on her lips to stop her deluge of words.

"I wish for that dragon to be free of its shell," he ordered, gesturing with a small jerk of his head. "I want to see the remnants of its mechanical self scattered underneath it, only one foot left on the ground as the glass wings help it forsake gravity."

Neither watched the sculpture transform in time with Jacoa's wish, though it happened right next to them. Jacoa's energy flowed into Isra, rising with a force that flooded her chakras. Each power center of her body flared with magic and desire. Never in her life had words lit her spirit on fire. Jacoa couldn't free her with a wish, but he could show her he meant to with one.

"When my mom told me those fairytales, I didn't know you were real." Jacoa placed his palms on Isra's cheeks, slowly combing his hands into her hair, curling his fingers around her head to draw her in. "Then the journals arrived. For two years, I hunted for more proof of you. It wasn't until your father came that I really believed."

Jacoa pressed his forehead to Isra's, and their *Anjas* warmed in a soft glow.

"He gave you to me, Isra. Whether he knows it or not, when Aali showed up on my patio, he made you real. And I will be damned if he takes you away."

Jacoa's mouth caressed Isra's. She returned his exact strength, wrapping her arms around his chest. He backed her into the dining room until her hips hit the tabletop. She lengthened her height so she could easily sit on its edge, and widened her legs to let Jacoa in. Isra felt too far from him and shifted further. Her body flattened and shoulders widened as she worked to match each of Jacoa's inches for each of hers with her male body.

"So, you were the bartender," Jacoa murmured against Isra's cheek. "Are you 'he' now?"

Isra's breath caught as Jacoa's fingers massaged her thighs.

"Male," she offered. "Always she. You don't mind?"

"You're gorgeous in every form. Just give me a warning if you shift again. I don't want to hurt you."

Isra laughed, wrapping her arms and legs around this wonderful human. "You just told me a few minutes ago that I was out of your weight class."

"Oh, this is where we fight." Jacoa nipped at Isra's shoulder, then pulled back only long enough to rid her of the peasant's blouse. "I can absolutely take you if I have to."

"I have the power of the universe," she reminded him with a smirk.

"I can trump that with a single wish."

Isra's next laugh was one of surrender. She let go of the day, released her fears and doubts, and immersed herself in the present. All she wanted was to share every part of herself with Jacoa. She might even let him think he was the winner.

CHAPTER 23

Jacoa

"Do you want something to eat?" Jacoa asked against Isra's shoulder. They sprawled on the surface of the walnut dining table. His genie had reverted to her female form, her hair touching him more in this state than when she'd been male. Her preference seemed to center on what kind of contact she sought, and possibly what size she wanted to be. He could ask, but for now preferred to observe.

Isra shook her head and twisted to lie on her side. "I haven't accepted once, yet you still offer."

"I have no idea how you eat," he said. "And I recall a devastating stomach growl in the desert."

"Only after the draconian cut off my access to magic." Isra lifted a hand toward his hair, and Jacoa prepared for the tugs and pulls in the knotted mess caused by her indoor storm. Instead, a soft tingling soothed his scalp with each gentle pass until the top length fell perfectly against his forehead.

"Powers you clearly have back."

"What gave me away? Your hair, or the fact that your house is covered in sand dunes?"

"No grumbling stomach."

Isra's laughter was interrupted by the double chime of the doorbell. Jacoa ran his fingertips along her sternum.

"Make whoever it is leave." He rounded his eyes in a puppy dog pout and pressed a kiss to her collarbone.

Isra's rosy lips parted, a glint of mischief in her smile that extinguished as she sat up and glared at the door.

"I can't," she sneered.

"Draconian?"

"Worse."

The strands of Isra's hair twisted upon each other and piled onto the top of her head. Jacoa's stomach sank. Other than her time as a bartender, he'd never seen her hair anything but loose and free. The clothing that rippled into existence around her skin was subdued. Though the asymmetrical dress was short in the front and long in the back, the cloth itself was a plain cream. No lace. No rhinestones.

What was worse than a draconian? A djinn? Why would one of them bother with the doorbell?

"Isra?"

"What would you like to wear?" she asked, her focus remaining on the door.

"Who is it?"

"Your friend."

Isra's answer should have calmed him, but the way her teeth bit into the words did not imply the person was friendly. Who did he know who caused such a reaction in his genie?

"Jeans and a black button down," he suggested. In the next instant, Jacoa felt fresh from the shower, shirt untucked, and his cologne was even at the concentration he preferred. Obviously, Isra had been studying him as he studied her. He'd think about what he could do to show what he'd learned, too. Unfortunately, he had to deal with the visitor first.

Jacoa approached the door with caution. When he saw Ward's face through the peephole, he sent Isra a confused look and opened the entry.

"Ward, how are you—"

Ward stormed into the house, glowering at Isra, who lifted her chin. He took only a few steps before he lost his balance on the soft floor. Wide eyes replaced a furrowed brow as he raised a sand-covered shoe.

"What happened in here?"

"There was a particularly strong dust storm." Jacoa closed the door, then made his way to Isra's side, reading the emotional undercurrent. Before her outburst, he'd buzzed with the threat of electricity. Now he stood in the awkward tension that built between two people who detested each other.

"What's going on?" Jacoa asked.

"Isra has ignored my request," Ward said.

"If that's what you want to call it." She spoke through her teeth. "Your idea was no better than Maram's."

"If you had kept your head down, it would have been fine."

"They found us in only a few hours," Isra argued. "The draconian might not expect a djinn to enter their lands, but they are certainly prepared for the possibility."

Ward's arm rose, his finger pointing toward the glass tree atop the dragon's cloche.

"What did you think would happen, using djinn powers within their borders?"

"And how close were you spying, exactly?"

Jacoa's head hurt going back and forth between their shouts. He didn't understand what Ward had to do with them ending up in the desert, but his friend needed to calm down. The pressure in his house had increased, and tiny bursts of wind circled above the sand. Jacoa wasn't certain his main floor would survive another of Isra's rages. He held his hands up in supplication, one hovering just out of contact with Isra, the other facing Ward.

"Ward, you need to back off—"

Ward swatted at Jacoa's extended hand and took a threatening step toward Isra. Though she could defend herself, Jacoa wasn't going to tolerate his friends' unexpected aggressive behavior and stepped between them.

Ward's brown eyes shot to Jacoa's, his brows clashing at his forehead. Jacoa gasped when he saw the swirl of light within Ward's pupils. His ribcage tightened at the evidence of magic in his friend. Heat burst from Jacoa's heart, igniting a flame in his own mind as he used his greater height against Ward. The smaller man's hand rested on Jacoa's chest and though his fingers applied no pressure, a different force extended from Ward's palm.

"Not in my home." Jacoa's voice dropped an octave over words as instinctive as his heartbeat. Isra could call in a sandstorm or a hurricane for all he cared, but this hidden power of Ward's would not be allowed within Jacoa's walls.

A flash blinded everyone in the room. The gentle contact of Ward's hand disappeared, along with the greater threat of his magic. When the light flickered to normal, Isra remained at Jacoa's side, but Ward was no longer before them. He'd been knocked off his feet and rested with wide, dazed eyes.

Isra giggled and her hair eased from containment to ripple down her back. Jacoa's ears buzzed, and his jaw hurt from clenching.

"I... magic? What?"

"Kind of." Isra answered his broken question. "It's not much different from when you and I share energy. Ward should have remembered, but it's probably been a long time since he's been in another sorcerer's house."

She stepped through the sand as easily as if it were water as she approached Ward.

"Another sorcerer?" Jacoa asked, trying to grasp the conversation's direction.

"Mmm," Isra agreed, kneeling next to Ward, who closed his eyes when her face blocked his view of the entryway's pendant light. "He'll be fine. It's likely just his pride that's the most wounded."

"Great." Jacoa took a deep breath and ran stiff fingers through his hair, then stopped and looked at his palms. "Am I going to have out-of-control powers exploding from my body?"

"No." Isra appeared at his side, though whether by magic or movement, he didn't know. Her hands curled around his arm, and she shifted so it was her eyes he saw instead of the lines in his palm. Her gentle touch was calming, the soft smile apologetic.

"I don't want it. I finally have control of my life. Things are weird, but I already have everything I want."

He placed the pads of his fingers against Isra's cheek and her lashes fluttered. She had a particular fondness for his fingertips above all else. Though he wasn't sure why, it wasn't beneath him to use the knowledge to his benefit. In this instance, he used her reaction to ground him, to pull him back to the space of confidence.

"Your powers are dormant," Ward grumbled. Sand shifted as he sat up, supporting his rise with one hand planted. "This shouldn't have happened."

Isra chuckled darkly. "The laws are the laws. A sorcerer may not practice magic in another sorcerer's home without permission."

"Wait. Ward, you're a sorcerer? Who can work magic?"

"And one who can control me. He's the reason we ended up in the desert." Isra's lips curled, exposing her teeth as if they were still as dangerous as a draconian's.

"You controlled Isra?" Jacoa demanded.

"Of all the things, that's what you're worried about?" Ward asked.

Jacoa ignored him, going back through the earlier conversation, connecting the dots now that he had more information.

"You put us in danger from the draconians! Isra had her powers blocked and we couldn't get away."

"It seems you've done fine," Ward said.

"Because of a wish!"

Ward stiffened, then cursed and shook his head. "You should really stop doing that."

"That was the plan. It's difficult not to when surrounded by djinn, draconian, and sorcerers manipulating the crap out of us." Jacoa took a breath. His brow wrinkled over the spot of pain blooming behind his forehead.

"Isra, would you mind getting rid of this sand?" Jacoa asked. "I'm going to make some food."

He felt the ache in his jaw that told him he'd locked his teeth together again. He massaged his temples, effectively creating blinders to the rest of the room.

The sand disintegrated into nothing, and the change of texture on the tile set him off balance. A swirl of dizziness hit him when he reached the kitchen. Groping for the island, he missed his first few attempts before his hand landed hard on the polished white quartz. The slight rumble of an earthquake weakened Jacoa's hold on his knees. The bright countertop refused to move as he fell and his skull crashed against its unforgiving edge, a sickening crack drowning him in a pain that did not let him rise again.

CHAPTER 24

Isra

Isra transferred to Jacoa's side the moment his head struck the counter. Her power had reached out to stop his fall, but had slammed against Maram's greater will. The most she could do was catch him before his collapse to the floor inflicted more damage.

"Maram!"

"Oh, he's fine." The djinn appeared lounging on her stomach in a backless jumpsuit on top of the island, peering over the edge to where Isra knelt next to Jacoa. "I'm getting the hang of slipping between the cracks of realities. This one was an outstanding teacher."

Maram's hand flipped toward Ward. When Ward had snaked between the magic fighting over Ruby and the nanny, Maram must have had a front-row seat.

Jacoa's eyes were wide, his pupils dilated, but equal in size. His breath rose in a series of jerks, then expelled like a punctured balloon. Maram had threaded the needle well this time. Jacoa was technically conscious but trapped by the pain. He wasn't bleeding, though a goose egg grew on his forehead, splitting the skin with narrow fissures.

Isra worked to calm her heavy emotions so they would stop

blocking her chakras. *Anahata* struggled the most, vacillating in its revolutions as if it couldn't decide whether to give her energy to Jacoa or pull his in to help mute the pain.

Starting at the beginning, she gave her fear and concern to *Vasundhara*, drawing on the stability below her feet. She let the flow of one chakra support the next until each was in motion at a steady counterclockwise turn, all circulating with the energy of universal magic.

Her power was not enough. Jacoa's life was not in danger. Maram's reality had enforced itself over Isra's, slipping around her attempted adjustments. Maram's definitions trumped Isra's own, and she struggled to find a context that would tap into the genie-master contract. Her hand trembled where it rested on Jacoa's sternum as she measured his breathing, which was almost as erratic as it had been after the car crash.

Of course. Isra couldn't focus on Jacoa's current health. She needed the big picture this time. Isra pulled forth every conversation with Maram where the djinn threatened Jacoa's well-being and recalled the massive amount of destruction Maram was comfortable causing—and would cause again if she wasn't stopped.

The glow surrounding Jacoa intensified as Isra's power slipped through and expanded. Isra soothed Jacoa's breath and was able to take a full inhale along with him. She ran a hand gently through the hair around his injury, helping his body heal itself until the bump disappeared.

Jacoa groaned and arched his spine in a slow stretch. He pushed himself up onto an elbow, hanging his head as he adjusted to his new state of being. Isra supported him as he stood, then he stumbled a few steps to lean against the stainless steel of his over-sized refrigerator door.

"Isra, can I wish that something horrible happens to a djinn?"

"We would have to choose the words very carefully." Isra glared at Maram, who ignored it by focusing on her nails.

"Or we could talk," Ward suggested.

Jacoa massaged his forehead, looking at his friend from under the tent of his fingers. Maram watched from the far edge of the island where she sat in lotus pose, knees resting high on the chunky soles of her boots. Isra squared her body between Jacoa and the sorcerer, a thread of awareness always focused on the djinn.

"Are you actually my friend?" Jacoa pushed from the fridge and faced Ward head on.

"Jacoa." Ward's eyes softened and his lips eased from a scowl to a frown.

"Or have you simply been hanging around waiting for Isra to appear? Just like Aali. And Maram?" he guessed, glancing toward the djinn, who gave a noncommittal shrug.

"At least Isra has been honest about what she wants," Jacoa accused.

"Mostly," she murmured in the spirit of all or nothing. Jacoa lifted his lips in a half smile. He breathed out a combination of hope and amusement, and Isra took it in, letting it curl up around *Anahata*.

"What the hell was that?" Maram demanded, her eyes narrowed at the space between Jacoa and Isra. "What are you two now?"

"What do you mean?" Isra's question flowed in a steady stream, though her heart pounded. Had Maram caught the exchange between her and Jacoa? Did her surprise indicate it wasn't something she understood? Or did she know exactly what was happening when Isra didn't?

"Do it again," Ward said.

Isra gasped at the command and grit her teeth as her chakras reversed direction, sending her energy toward Jacoa, who gripped his lower abdomen. He appeared to dislike being forced to use their connection as much as she did.

The sorcerer's aura pulsed for half a heartbeat before he tamped it down, but not before Jacoa's own aura flared in response. Maram slid off the island. As she moved, the chunky heel of her boots shrunk on themselves to become a pair of narrow red stilettos.

"What's going on?" Jacoa asked. Isra shook her head and maintained her guard while Maram's shoulders rose to her ears.

A slip of Maram's power wrapped around Ward and stiffened in place, becoming a spiral of stone as thick as the sorcerer's thigh. Ward thrust his palm against the middle of the curve, but the rock did not break. The length of his arm trembled, and veins appeared in his neck as he struggled against the shrinking structure.

"Let me go." Ward's words didn't have the same effect on the ancient djinn that they had on Isra.

"Save yourself," Maram charged.

"Stop!" Jacoa tried to push past Isra, but she fanned her hair out and solidified the strands to keep him back.

"What are you trying to prove, Maram?" Isra demanded. "You already have your answer."

"Don't think djinn are the only ones to play games, little draconian." Maram's eyes locked on the ever-shrinking space around Ward.

"You seem to be the only ones playing with other people's lives," Jacoa said.

Maram curled her upper lip, and the stone jerked into a smaller spiral, trapping Ward's arm against his body.

"Isra," he gasped.

"Haven't we already established that the baby genie cannot fight me without the boost of her curse?" Maram asked. "Come on, sorcerer. Show us your greater power."

"Shit." Jacoa stopped pressing against Isra's barrier. She dropped the tension in her hair now that he understood. Maram was baiting Ward, trying to get him to use his magic to spark Jacoa's own. The djinn wanted to verify that Jacoa's involuntary surge of power wasn't a fluke.

"Ward Emrick, you have permission to use magic in my home!"

The stone shattered into pieces on the tail of Jacoa's shout.

The house shook with the force of Maram's rage. Isra pressed her body into Jacoa's, sending reassurance and determination through their chakras. At this distance, their energy flowed freely, rings of infinity twining them together.

Maram's eyes danced as if she followed the signature of those figure eights and her lips thinned.

"Well. That settles that." Maram disappeared before her last word was spoken. The three left behind didn't move.

"I don't feel her anymore, but she can hide herself from me," Isra said.

"Oh, she's gone." Ward rubbed his arm where the stone had pressed into the muscle.

"Are there so few sorcerers?" Jacoa asked.

"That wasn't all that spooked her. I understand why you don't know, Jacoa. Do you realize what happened, Isra?"

"That she doesn't want to tangle with a sorcerer, even if you can't control her like you can me?"

"I can control you because you're draconian, not because you're djinn," Ward countered. "But this isn't about sorcerers. This is about you two."

"How many riddles do we have to fail to answer before you tell us?" Jacoa asked.

"The way energy flows between you is practically unheard of. In fact, in all my centuries, I've only seen it once."

Jacoa coughed. "Centuries?!"

"What does that mean?" Isra asked.

"It means your connection is incredibly unique. It means our future choices become more complicated."

"Our choices?"

"Yes. Like it or not, you two have fallen into a plan that has taken five hundred years to put together."

The timeline was not lost on Isra. "Explain."

"The other couple I saw with a chakra-bond are directly related to this plan. With that in mind, I'm going to ask you both to trust me."

"Trust?" Jacoa scowled. "Damn it, Ward, how am I supposed to trust you? In fact. Isra, should I take away his permission?"

"Isra, tell him who protected Ruby."

"Ward did."

Isra bit her tongue and curled her fingers into fists. The words had fallen out of her mouth without thought. The power Ward had over her sent sparks flying across her nerves, evidence of how her chakras stuttered, then spun at an accelerated rate.

"How can you make her do that?" Any placation Jacoa might have received from Isra's answer was erased by Ward's ability to affect her. Her master's energy flowed into her, providing the stabilization needed to breathe and realign.

"I can control her because she is young and draconian-born. The latter is actually in our favor. Jann didn't think through their game when they made her a genie."

"That was by chance, though," Isra said.

"A happy one, perhaps, but Jann wouldn't have chosen you if you didn't fit their scheme."

"Which game are you referring to?" Isra asked.

"It's not a game," Ward said. "Jann was the most powerful being in existence for thousands of years. And then the Second Djinn formed a chakra-bond. The pair shared energy, doubling their individual power as long as they were together. Jann's strength was surpassed, so they looked for a way to correct that."

Ward met Jacoa's eyes. "Jann reached out to different sorcerers until they found a set that would help them."

"What are you talking about?" Jacoa asked.

"The genie curse," Isra said. "Jann instigated it?"

"With purpose," Ward agreed. "Some tried to counsel the bonded pair against playing Jann's game, but they were convinced their combined energies would always best Jann. In the end, the First Djinn was trapped as a genie. The Second Djinn was transformed into a vessel."

"Wait. Mine?"

"No. I don't know what her vessel looks like, or where it is. But I know where to start looking."

"What is so special about this Second Djinn that you would go to all this trouble?" Jacoa asked.

"Her bonded is my brother."

"Wait. Are you talking about Will? Your sick brother?" Jacoa gaped at Ward, his slack jaw showing this was as much a surprise to him as it was to her. The back of her knuckles brushed his clenched fist. He was not taking his friend's revelations well. She would take point for both of them.

"Where is your brother?"

"In a magically-induced coma. I had to force him there before... Let's just say he didn't handle it well when his bond was ripped apart."

Isra flinched at the thought of someone tearing Jacoa from her. They hadn't been bonded long, but the flow between them was already as natural as breathing. She understood Ward's motives, but wasn't sure that was enough to inspire trust.

"So you want to save the Second Djinn and your brother? Where do I come in?" she asked.

"Jann was tired of their trap, but the contract they constructed stated there must be a djinn tied to what is now your vessel. Without that, the Second Djinn can be freed. I imagine they thought making a draconian into a genie would create a scenario in which no wishes were granted. Her draconian family would be hesitant to kill her."

"That is up for debate. They came straight for me in Death Valley."

"A situation you survived," Ward pointed out. Isra swallowed the bitter reminder of Aali's dagger.

"Forget the draconian for now. If wishes can free the Second Djinn, then why are you against Jacoa asking for them?"

"Everything has to happen at the right time, and in the right order."

"And you inherited this plan?" Jacoa asked.

"No. I've been involved in the whole process."

"For five hundred years. Alive for hundreds of more years than that? And this has been to help your brother, who is also a sorcerer? I don't know you at all, do I?" Jacoa wilted, his shoulders curled in, and his head dipped. His energy lagged, and Isra remembered he'd been trying to make food before all this started.

"Jacoa, I am on your side," Ward said.

"Are you really, though?" Isra demanded, conjuring up a burger and fries, which Jacoa dove for as soon as they shimmered into reality.

"More-so than the djinn you impulsively aligned yourself with. I'm certainly the ally you need against the draconian collective that are surrounding the house right now."

Isra stared at Ward, not bothering to look through the windows for creatures who were well-versed in desert camouflage. Her hair twisted into dozens of tiny braids. She crossed her arms to hide the trembling in her fingers when Jacoa looked at her and she offered a tight smile.

"We will be okay," Isra said, even as she worried it was a promise she couldn't keep.

"Of course we will," Jacoa agreed. Only, he sounded like he believed it.

CHAPTER 25

Jacoa

Jacoa hid the effects of his blurred vision by focusing on his food. Eating was helping, but only by relieving the weakness that he'd experienced before his fall. He chewed slowly to keep the reverberant noise of each bite low, so he wasn't flinching each time Ward or Isra spoke in their sharp, short sentences.

"How many?" Isra asked.

"Enough," Ward answered.

"Can you control them like you do me?"

"Only a few of the youngest ones. But only if they hear me, and that is a bit close range."

Jacoa's food was gone, but the clenching pain just above his right eye was not fading. He rounded the island and pulled out a small bottle of pills he kept in the drawer next to the sink. He grabbed a pint glass from an upper cupboard and filled it from the tap before popping four tablets and gulping the whole sixteen ounces of water. When Jacoa turned, Ward was at the back window and Isra sat on one of the bar stools, shifting her eyes between him and the sorcerer.

"None of your magic works against them?" Jacoa asked.

"Draconian were bred specifically to be immune," Ward

answered. "They have been tied deeply to *Vasundhara* and completely blocked from *Sutara*. Magical energies flow around them instead of through."

Jacoa recoiled from Ward's easy explanation about magic. Many of the things he used to wonder about his friend suddenly made sense. But now Jacoa wasn't sure they'd ever been friends. At least the information he shared in this moment seemed honest.

"*Vasun*... what are these things?"

"Chakra points," Isra explained. "You're aware of them, even if you don't recognize their names. Here's *Vasundhara*."

Jacoa gasped when he felt a flow of energy swirl beneath his feet, as if the power was what supported him instead of the tile. Isra's eyes glimmered, and she leaned toward him.

"Next is *Muladhara. Svadisthana. Manipura. Anahata. Vishunddha Anja. Sahasrara.* And then *Sutara*."

With each of Isra's words, a new point in his body flared and warmed from his tailbone to above his head. The combination of her soft voice and the rush of energy increased his blood flow, and the last of the dizziness faded. He breathed deeply, the air cooling.

"Thank you." As he spoke, he completed the connections between them. Grounded and pain free, he refocused on the problem at hand.

"So, the draconian are blocked at the top? And that means magic can't affect them, so they can fight the djinn."

"A well-placed draconian attack could destroy even the First Djinn's palace in the sky, should they reach it." Ward sounded excited by the possibility, despite their current circumstances. "It's why I had Isra take you into the desert. No djinn dares approach them."

"Do the draconian know Isra was born one of them?"

"No," Isra answered. "At least, they don't realize I was turned into a genie."

"Your dad would have kept that secret?" Jacoa asked. "Why can't we just tell them about you?"

A low, hissing sound pressed between Isra's teeth. "My

father would have told them the only truth that matters. Isra the draconian has died. If they knew otherwise, they'd still execute me, though it would be out of compassion rather than duty."

The image of Isra's father melting down her vessel to create a dagger filled his thoughts. The burger hardened in Jacoa's stomach when he remembered Isra herself admitting she'd once wished for Aali to do just that—kill with kindness.

Jacoa stared at his beautiful genie, her hair shifting in waves of black and white, braids twisting and freeing themselves. She moved so organically, lived so freely.

"I don't understand." How could anyone want to hurt this amazing creature?

"Because djinn are all the same," Isra snapped. "Dangerous. Manipulative."

"Not all of them." Ward left the window and claimed the stool on the other side of Isra. It was the same place he'd sat during Jacoa's wished-away party. Did his so-called friend remember both versions of that night? Had he pretended not to when he'd shown up the second time?

"The draconian can't see the djinn objectively." Ward nodded to indicate Isra as an example. "They don't recognize that djinn are diverse individuals, just as with any species."

"You know this, how?" Jacoa asked.

"He helped make us."

"No." Ward spoke sharply. "I had nothing to do with the perverse creation of your people. I was - am - part of a different faction."

"Yet you can control her?"

"Call it a perk."

Jacoa's fists clenched on the counter behind him, and he struggled against the urge to throw a right hook into Ward's jaw. This person was not his friend. Jacoa separated the two Wards in his mind. He couldn't handle dealing with the sorcerer in front of him without the break.

"What do you mean when you say you're from a different faction?" Isra asked.

Ward leaned into his stool and twisted side to side in thought. Jacoa kept his focus on Isra. Her shoulders eased away from her ears as she watched the soothing motions of Ward's swaying, though her lips pursed and her eyes locked. She was no longer ready to pounce, Jacoa noted, but she was far from relaxing her guard.

"Jacoa?" Ward asked. "Where is the rest of your inheritance?"

"I'm not sure what you mean. The fairytales from my mother?"

"They're in your room," Isra offered. She must have sent them there at the time she'd placed the glass tree on the cloche during their excursion in Death Valley.

"No, the last box," Ward said.

"There aren't any more boxes. I opened them all."

"Jacoa Wicker, where is the oldest box you inherited from your sorcerer ancestors?"

"It's in the hidden cupboard in my office."

Words spoken as if he'd always known the answer. As if he hadn't been just as confident a few seconds ago that there was no such hiding place.

He would never get used to this layering of realities caused by magic.

"Let's go, then. The draconian won't wait for us to be prepared." Ward rose from his chair.

"What are you talking about?" The strength of Isra's voice stopped Jacoa's forward movement.

"The last box has the first Wicker journal."

"How do you know this?" Isra demanded.

"I have known the Wicker line long before that was their surname," Ward claimed. "I invented half the tricks they use."

"Only half?" Jacoa's jaw tensed when he realized he fell into old habits. Ward didn't seem to notice his ire, responding with a wink.

"The other half don't work, so they're clearly not mine."

Jacoa needed out of these fuzzy feelings and turned to Isra.

"It's okay," he said. "Let's go see if he's right. If something goes wrong, I can always wish."

"I wish you would stop saying that," Ward grumbled. The sorcerer's discontent seemed to please Isra, and a tiny smile curled her lips.

"Relax. He still has eight left."

"What? How have you asked for ten wishes in a week? Your ancestors are cursing you from beyond!"

"I thought you were from a different faction." The sing-song nature of Isra's voice untied a few of the knots in Jacoa's stomach. Ward pressed away from the island and stomped toward the floating stairs that led to the lowest level of Jacoa's home.

Jacoa chuckled at the situation's expense. Isra narrowed her eyes on him, but she didn't ask for clarification as they made their way down to the office.

The journals were scattered around the room where Isra had left them. Papers spread out wherever they'd been dropped after her quick appraisal. Ward stood in the doorway, scowling at the mess and raising a brow.

"Yes?" Jacoa asked as he collected and stacked the delicate books and their accompanying documents. Isra perched in the ergonomic chair behind Jacoa's desk.

"I haven't been in here since you moved, I guess. The rest of your house is just so neat," Ward said.

Jacoa didn't appreciate the reminder of the years Ward spent spying on him under the guise of friendship.

"And?"

Ward stepped into the room now that there was space. He gave a frustrated grunt, as if Jacoa should let him off the hook rather than make him state the obvious. Jacoa had no intention of helping Ward feel better.

"I suppose all of this has been the messiest part of your life," Ward muttered. Jacoa shrugged and finished tidying so they could get this show over with. He studied the office, trying to remember what Ward had asked him that unlocked the memory.

Where is the oldest box from my inheritance?

Jacoa stopped turning when he faced the lines of bookshelves behind his desk. Most of the spaces were deep enough for the hardcovers and knickknacks. The shelf in the outer back corner was shallower than the others. The room jutted in from what appeared to be a supporting pillar. Yet that's the spot that drew him when he thought of this box he couldn't quite picture.

He ran his hands along the hand carved strip of this last piece of built-in shelving. One of the ornate, hand-carved swirls twisted beneath his fingers, and the panel popped forward. The opposite side sunk in. The shelf swiveled on an off-center pivot.

On the floor inside, a small wooden box about the size of a desk drawer gathered dust. Jacoa squatted and easily pulled it out through the cavity, turning it around in his hands. The contents within shifted until he located the latch, though he didn't move to open it.

"That mechanism is very human." Isra studied the bookcase and its hidden compartment with intense interest. Jacoa smiled. Once again, his genie found something to marvel at, even in the midst of this tense moment.

"It's good to know we can impress you," Jacoa said with a wink. Isra let out a short chuckle and shook her head.

"You're only a pretend human."

"And what's in this box will prove it." Ward ruined their attempt to find levity. The sorcerer stood in the middle of the room, his eyes locked on the box Jacoa held. With the desk covered in journals, he placed their find on the small round table in the corner next to the sliding glass door. Ward swept away the for-show chess set to make more room.

"I need you to trust me and give me permission to open this."

"No." Isra appeared at Jacoa's side with the word, keeping him from having to say it.

"I have been his friend for years," Ward said. "You have known him for days."

"You have lied to him for years."

"You agreed to let a djinn put him in danger."

Isra flinched but did not back down. Jacoa shook his head at both of them.

"Why can't I open this myself?"

"There is a letter on top that tells you to secure the box in a secret place, then to forget that it's in your possession. You know it works because you've already seen it. You found it because you are the one who put it there."

Isra hissed a curse in a language Jacoa didn't understand. The answer didn't surprise him, and he doubted it surprised her. Isra reached for the box, and Ward shrugged as if to imply it was her mistake to make.

Her fingers came within four inches before she cried out. The flash of light that stung her was gone before she'd vocalized. Apparently, Jacoa's wish for her to touch the journals did not extend to this box.

"And only a sorcerer can open it," she concluded.

"Okay, Ward. I give you permission." Anything to get this over with.

Ward's breath quickened. His fingers spread wide around the box. He moved gingerly, as if not convinced Jacoa's words were enough to allow him access.

A quiet knock rang through the room, followed by a heavier, metallic thump. Ward's hands froze as they all turned to see Aali, his long lizard's nose drawn down so his eyes pressed close to the window. The simple dagger he'd made in the forge was pinned between the glass and his scaled hand.

CHAPTER 26

Isra

Isra stared at her father's familiar face through the glass as he shifted between his lizard snout and his human-like features. She wasn't surprised to see him. In fact, she wondered what had taken him so long. He'd had five hundred years to hunt her, and he'd known where to find her vessel that whole time.

Even with that dagger in his hand, it wasn't fear that left Isra trembling.

She had failed him. She had put herself into the position of being trapped as a djinn. And now that he'd finally come to end her curse, she did not want him to.

Jacoa eased closer, but didn't send her comfort through their link; probably cautious after the event with Maram. The ebb and flow between Jacoa and herself was not forced or enhanced, but simply existed in the moment, offering the support of presence.

"We should let him in," Ward suggested.

"You are insane." Isra gave a sharp shake of her head, curls tightening.

"He's here alone. We can handle one. If the others follow..." Ward shrugged. "Jacoa?"

"Won't more come either way?" Jacoa asked.

"Eventually," Ward said. "But if only one comes, it may be for negotiation. They likely only want the genie."

"They won't get her." Jacoa took a half step away from the window, his body guarding hers as she had done for him in the kitchen.

"Let's buy some time," Jacoa decided. "Ward, let him in."

Isra swallowed her frustration. Jacoa leaned in to kiss her crown, whispering a word against her hair in a soft reminder that he had wishes to spare. She tried to take strength in the faith he had in her magic as Ward approached the glass. The sorcerer flipped the latch and walked backward from the opening as he pulled the door with him. Jacoa scooped up the box. He eased Isra away from the tall draconian as he entered. Ward shoved the slider hard enough that it fastened closed, then moved deeper into the room as well.

The four stood without speaking, tension pulling goose-bumps along Isra's flesh. She pursed her lips to keep them from trembling and glared so they would perceive any dampness in her eyes as anger.

Jacoa broke the silence. "You didn't tell me you were going to make a dagger."

"Why would I share my plans with a boy whose first thought was to claim my daughter? So much that you have her leashed," Aali hissed, pointing to where Isra's hair wrapped around Jacoa's hand. Jacoa raised one of his dark brows along with the appendage in question, opening his fingers for show. Isra added more strands to those already in place, knowing what he wanted, but not entirely certain what they were proving.

Yet it appeared to be the exact right thing. Aali dropped his accusing finger, then glanced over his shoulder at the desert. "We don't have much time."

"Let me have the case," Ward requested, reaching from where he stood by the desk. The energy in the room shifted. Isra looked between their two surprise guests. They were unexpectedly comfortable standing so close together.

Isra and Jacoa took a step away from them in synchronicity. Ward leaned against the bookcase. Aali held the knife at his side, blade at rest, though his cloak blocked much of the view through the window.

"What's going on?" Jacoa asked, hugging the box to his ribs.

"Bad timing, which tends to be the case when you have little of it," Ward answered. "The short story is, Aali and I have been working together for some time."

"Take back his permission," Isra told Jacoa, urging him to restrict Ward's use of power in his home.

"Then you won't get what you want," Aali argued. Isra bared her teeth at him.

"What I want is for you to take that filthy blade away from me."

"Is it pointed at you? You have forgotten your training, Isra. You aren't the only one who's been bound by this metal."

The volume in her hair collapsed and her mouth dropped open.

"A plan that took five hundred years." Isra put the pieces together, few as they were. "You don't mean to use that knife on me."

A kaleidoscope of thoughts and emotions danced within Isra as she met her father's eyes. There was too much to process, so she utilized her training. She set reactions aside for later and focused on the facts. Aali hadn't come for her because he had a different goal.

"You're going after the First Djinn," she guessed. "Are the other draconian helping you?"

"Unfortunately not," Aali replied. "They are here for the djinn tied to the Wicker line. Even if they learned of your birthright, they would—"

"I know." Isra turned her face away. She felt Jacoa's warmth, recognized he was waiting for her lead before deciding what to do with the box.

"Will the knife work on a djinn no longer bound by the contract?" she asked.

"It may not be a death blow, but it could weaken them greatly. I am happy to try." Aali's smile showed off the points of his teeth.

Isra took his words for what they were: a reprieve. She was being given the time she'd asked for. But what was the price?

The dagger wasn't meant for her. That didn't erase all the distrust that had built between them. She needed leverage. That this was Jacoa's home base was their greatest benefit when faced with the sorcerer who could control her and the draconian she didn't fully trust.

"Take away his permission," Isra said again.

"Ward, you may no longer work magic of any kind within my walls."

The energy in the house hummed loud before dying out, as if a power surge had affected the home's electricity. Jacoa flinched as the clunky vibration jerked through the room. "Was that an earthquake?"

"You are recognizing magic." Ward shrugged to show he didn't know why. "You've experienced a lot of it lately. Maybe you're becoming accustomed to it?"

"The answer may be in the first journal," Aali offered.

"What do you know of the Wicker records?" Isra's eyes narrowed on her father.

"He knows what I've told him," Ward deflected. "The memoirs Jacoa has are decoys. Retellings of disgruntled young men who didn't get their way. The first one, however, speaks of Jann's curse. It should tell us about the Second Djinn's vessel."

"Abraham would know that?" Isra asked.

"This journal is not Abraham's. He is where your djinn journey started, Isra, but is far removed from the information we're looking for," Aali answered. "Ward refers to when Jann created the contract."

"Truths impossible to see, now that you've followed the genie's suggestion," Ward accused Jacoa.

"Well, Isra." Jacoa's tongue rolled over her name, his voice soft and teasing as it drifted through his smirk. "What monstrous scheme do you have for me?"

Isra buzzed with that heightened sense of hope and excitement she'd come to associate with what Jacoa felt about her. Only this time, he wasn't sending her the energy; the emotion was her own.

He trusted her despite their rocky beginning. Now she hoped her inkling of a plan worked.

She maneuvered them toward the hallway door, as far from her father and the sorcerer as possible. Isra released her hair from his hand and directed Jacoa to hold the case between their bodies. She placed her hands on his, locked her yellow eyes with his green, and connected them through the third eye chakra, the one that was easiest to access across the distance.

"Close your eyes and open the box."

Jacoa's inky lashes brushed the tops of his cheeks. He flipped the metal latch on the lid and opened it, keeping the wooden case balanced in his grip.

The power of the letter unfurled as soon as it hit the air. Isra exhaled her energy toward Jacoa, even as she activated each of the magic centers in her body. The spell reached for her master, but could not touch him through the protective layer of her own essence.

As his genie, it was Isra's job to protect him. The magic in this letter threatened him. If he lost his memory, he could not be whole. Isra shifted reality, redefining her purpose to include protection of who he was as Jacoa.

The spell fell apart. The ancient parchment crumbled into ash. Isra reversed her energy until the ebb and flow returned to its normal, gentle levels.

"I don't feel an urge to open my eyes anymore," Jacoa said.

"It's safe," she promised. Jacoa's eyelids rose his attention on the revealed contents. He brushed the disintegrated paper away from the bottom. With an upright jerk, he turned toward Ward, upending the box, sending ashes across the tile floor and area rug.

Ward's hands clenched at his side, his eyes blazing.

"Your mother." Ward said the words like a curse. Isra startled at the force of Jacoa's in drawn breath. "I hadn't believed her. Damn it!"

"I don't understand." Jacoa perfectly enunciated each syllable as he stared at Ward. His features shuttered, and his chakras all but stopped turning, leaving Isra off kilter in the wake of his emotional shut down. Her hair fluttered toward him, but stopped short of touching. She wasn't certain he needed or wanted contact right now.

"Riti was always clever," Aali said. "She had sworn she would keep the journal on her person. I guess that means it had been with her when she died."

"Why would she do that?" Jacoa asked.

"She never trusted us," Ward answered. "That diary is likely to hold the location of the Second Djinn, but she would never confirm it. She wanted the curse broken first. Her intention was always to protect you."

"I guess even she knew you better than I do." Jacoa flinched and Isra brushed his skin with her hair. He didn't latch on to her, but he didn't move away, either. She took it as a sign to simply stay by his side.

"How did you know Jacoa's mother?" she asked for him.

"Among its many secrets, the journal spoke of the draconian. Riti wanted to meet one," Aali answered.

"You were caught?" Isra demanded of her father. Aali spread the fingers of his empty hand without removing his protective stance at the window.

"It was intentional," Ward said. "I suggested Riti fight the ruling on her inheritance. I recommended the right lawyer and got her in front of a sympathetic judge. Our intentions had been to introduce her to a djinn friend."

"Friend." Isra's head spun when she found no sign of disgust on her father's face. "I really don't understand."

"From the beginning, then," Aali said. "When you disappeared, it did not take me long to discover what happened. The Wicker who freed Jann came to me, in fact, desperate to have the First Djinn targeted since he had failed in his duty to keep them contained."

Ward continued the story. "I heard a rumor about the First Djinn's release and went to investigate. That's when I found Aali threatening Jacoa's greatest-grandfather. I convinced Aali to allow the poor sot to live, at least so the consequences of his wish could be fulfilled and Isra could return to this realm."

"Why?" Isra demanded. "Sorcerers have no love for djinn."

"You forget so quickly," Ward said. "The Second Djinn was bonded to my brother, a sorcerer."

"Wait, is that why Isra and I are connected? Because she's djinn and I'm kind of a sorcerer?"

"No, Jacoa. Your connection is rare," Ward reassured his friend. "In fact, you are only the second pair I know with it, at least of power."

"Ah, Isra," Aali's quiet exclamation hissed through the room. "I see now why you have fought so hard for this master. I am sorry."

"Sorry. Why?" Jacoa snapped out of his gloom and inched closer to Isra.

"Souls are not meant to blend within the physical realm. When they do, it is both a blessing and a curse."

Aali's last word whispered into the air as magic stuttered. Isra winced, her connection to *Vasundhara* faltering.

"We're out of time." Ward faced the darkness outside the window.

"What do we do?" Jacoa asked. "Do I make a wish before they cut off your magic again?"

"Not necessary." Maram's voice drew everyone's attention to the space behind Isra and Jacoa. Her smile was thin and unforgiving, though the lashes around her over-wide eyes trembled and locked on Isra's with an odd mix of desperation and apology.

"It's your lucky day for an escape. You're all invited to the First Djinn's palace."

CHAPTER 27

Jacoa

Jacoa was walking on clouds. Unfortunately, it had nothing to do with him and Isra or the relationship forming between them. In fact, it was far more unnerving.

He stood between Isra and Maram. Aali and Ward appeared on Maram's right. They were surrounded by an empty expanse of blue sky and a blanket of white vapor which acted as their floor. Jacoa turned to Isra whose hair had fallen flat, though not like it had when guided by her emotion. Instead, it fell like normal hair, as if there wasn't anything special about her.

Jacoa found it hard to breathe, and his aching throat constricted around a forced swallow. He tensed his arm and made a fist, stopping himself from reaching out to touch her. It would feel strange if the strands didn't respond.

"Isra."

Maram shushed him, eyes narrowed with ire. "You are in Jann's palace now."

The edge on her voice was sharp enough to cut. The firm pressure of her hand on his shoulder presented the words as a warning rather than a threat. That this fiery djinn had gone from attacking him to cautioning him made Jacoa pause.

"Are you the messenger?" he asked. "Or our escort?"

"Maybe," she agreed with a swift nod, her voice unwavering, confident in her ability to not clear anything up.

He looked over Maram's head at the draconian and sorcerer she'd also brought along. Jacoa wondered if they'd be in this position if he'd trusted them, an echo of what they thought Riti should have had done. He couldn't find fault with not believing them. Jacoa was confident his mother had felt the same. He wished he'd had the chance to know for certain.

Jacoa leaned toward Isra, pleased the height of her female form placed her ear well within each reach of his mouth as he whispered.

"Can I hold your hand?" He wasn't sure how Isra wanted to approach Jann.

"No," Maram snapped from his other side, even as Isra's fingers wove through his. He ignored the smaller djinn's seething and allowed this moment of connection with Isra to fill him with triumph. No matter what happened, Isra was his genie.

She kept her energy to herself, though, and he worked to do the same. Being so close to her without that gentle sharing felt strange, but after hearing about Jann's history with chakra-bonds, he understood the need.

What came next was a wind tunnel with no wind. Whether the cloud moved around them or they traveled along the path, Jacoa didn't know. White and blue blurred, yet his stomach didn't experience the pull. In fact, when he closed his eyes against the nausea caused by the sea of motion, he couldn't tell he was moving at all. He chose to continue on without looking, giving random peeks to check if they'd arrived.

After a few minutes, their passage slowed enough that he could pay attention to the space. They continued forward on the cloud, though now beings lined up on either side of their pathway. Some stood alone, some in groups. All turned to watch them pass. Their eyes slid over the newcomers until they caught sight of the imposing Aali.

Jacoa tried not to stare and failed. Few of the djinn appeared human, as Isra and Maram chose to do. He swore they passed a gorgon, though he couldn't tell exactly what the thick threads of her hair had been. Many had exaggerated their bone structure with cheekbones that jutted out farther than their brow. Spikes were a common accessory. Some preferred their heads and hands to be covered in tiny pyramids and others liked long, curved projections from their joints. The one he tried to keep in his sight the longest, he'd thought had been a draconian at first. As he stared, he realized the multiple horns around the djinn's skull and the spines on his back and tail were pure dragon.

A bull-headed djinn paced alongside them, glowering with red eyes that glowed with an inner light.

"I see Jann brought us some sport." The bull jabbed toward Aali. The draconian casually gripped the offending djinn's wrist. The bull shouted out as the thick layer of buff fur disappeared. Horns shrunk until the base, thin, and very human form was left behind.

"A fun game," the draconian agreed, then tossed the djinn away. Instantly, the bull façade reappeared, though the djinn was already sinking into the cloud, eager to escape Aali's reach.

"Isra!" someone called out. Jacoa searched for the voice's source. After Aali's show of power, the other djinn maintained a healthy distance, and it was impossible to figure out which one was speaking. "How many wishes?"

Isra narrowed her eyes and pursed her lips, making it clear she had no intention of answering.

"Hmm, isn't that an interesting question." A voice of velvet night and starlight filled the air, as if invisible speakers hid in the wisps of cloud around them. The scattered djinn were pressed away from the path that pulled Jacoa and the others forward, all at the will of the First Djinn. From before them, an ornate white throne approached. The waves and swirls that made up the chair's frame were carved into an odd, polished material Jacoa couldn't place despite a lifetime of studying artists' work.

The creature cradled in the center of the throne sat at ease, leaning against one of the arms as they watched their small group approach with eyes that burned like tiny suns. Their skin echoed the pale blue of the sky above and their simple white toga was tied at the waist with a belt of golden strands.

Jann's starlight eyes reflected off their cheeks and brow. Their gaze roamed over Maram as if she were a prisoner, too. Perhaps her flippant 'maybe' from his earlier question wasn't far off the mark. The First Djinn's eyes flared until the upper half of their face appeared aglow before solidifying into tiny bright spheres, so contained that Jacoa noticed the djinn's eyelashes for the first time.

"For crimes against the djinn as sorcerer and draconian." Jann's unfinished sentence ended in a yawn. They lifted one finger up, thrust it down, then Ward and Aali sank through the cloud. Jacoa startled at the sudden movement, though Maram and Isra didn't move.

The small reaction brought Jann's attention to Jacoa, and the fact that he stood hand in hand with Isra. The First Djinn tapped their fingers in a wavelike motion against the throne's armrest as they studied the physical connection. Even as seconds drew on to minutes, Isra showed no desire to remove her hand under the force of Jann's stare. Jacoa was happy to follow her lead, especially after seeing how quickly and easily Ward and Aali had been separated from the group.

Jann sucked in an audible breath and focused blazing eyes on Isra's face. She did not adjust to meet their gaze, but looked straight ahead past the throne.

Jacoa couldn't stand as still as the djinn. Though he tried, an itch formed between his shoulder blades, and he switched focus between the triangle of magical beings around him.

"I believe congratulations are in order for our newest genie. Ten wishes in only eight days, a record for you. Is this, by chance, because our feisty Maram has taken you under her wing? Or does it have to do with the... relationship that has formed between you and this particular master?" Jann's lips popped hard on the final *p* of 'relationship.'

Jann received silence as an answer. "Perhaps I should ask the Wicker myself."

Isra's fingers stiffened within Jacoa's, but she did not pull away.

Jann rose from the throne as if riding the wind. They approached Jacoa and ignored the female djinn who stood on either side. Their starlight eyes met Jacoa's, a bright light that somehow did not blind him.

"In all honesty, I had hoped to never see a Wicker again. You are, for all intents and purposes, the last of the main line, though. The rest weeded out and watered down." Their attention flickered over to Isra. "Easy enough to snuff out."

It was bait Isra did not ignore.

"Even you cannot break the contract." She'd schooled her voice to sound apologetic. Her eyes remained stoic.

"No. But a year is such a short time. I have slept through quite a few of them myself. But that isn't my concern. His ancestors would not have wished for protection against djinn magic, as he had done for his precious cousin. And to have a genie who offered such an anti-djinn suggestion..." Jann tsked at Isra.

"She's just a human girl." Jacoa swallowed a rush of bile. He could handle almost anything else, but realizing they knew about Ruby and might see her as a threat sent frozen terror through his blood.

"Lucky for her," Jann agreed.

Maram dropped her gaze to her toes. Because it was unexpected, Jacoa automatically turned toward it. Her chin-length hair swayed as if she'd given her head a small shake. Was she apologizing somehow? Trying to tell him Jann's attention was brought by something more than the wish for Ruby?

Without mind reading abilities, Jacoa didn't know. He refocused on Jann, startled to see the djinn's face had moved within an inch of Jacoa's own.

"You have been well studied, Wicker, but I suppose that's becoming clear to you now that you're surrounded by so many paranormals. That being said…"

Jann turned toward Isra without changing the distance between themself and Jacoa. "You've met her father, but have you seen *her*? Oh, of course you haven't, thanks to your fourth wish. Really, Jacoa. Chaining her to human form was not very polite. Let's fix that."

The First Djinn returned to their throne with a soft swagger. They collapsed sideways and the elaborate chair instantly shifted into the wave of a chaise that allowed them to remain mostly upright.

"You are so right, little Isra. I cannot break the contract between you and this master. I would have hoped, however, that you remembered I am very skilled at manipulating them."

Isra looked at Jann voluntarily. She crept closer to Jacoa, her hand tightening around his.

"Wish," she whispered, but Jann laughed at her attempt. Jacoa tried to do as she said, but when he lowered his jaw, the skin tightened under his nose. Reaching up with his free hand, his eyes widened. His mouth couldn't open because the First Djinn had removed his lips and fused the skin of his face over the space.

Jacoa's stomach clenched. He brushed his thumb along the back of Isra's hand, consciously keeping his energy tight within his body even though every part of him wanted to reach out.

He hadn't understood her worry, or that of the others. He'd thought his wishes would trump anything the djinn threw at them. He should have wished them out right away, given them the protection of the magic that spun between them. Now they were trapped; Isra's least favorite place to be.

Jacoa turned, trying to apologize with his eyes, but she kept her full attention on the threat before them.

"A little late for wishes." Jann smiled. "Good effort, though. Beyond that, this connection between you two is really sweet. Unique, even, since no other djinn would consent to enjoying time with their master, much less whatever this thing you're doing is. Of course, it just brings us right back around to how exotic you are, doesn't it, Isra?"

Jann held the silence for a long moment. Isra ripped her eyes away and stared past the throne once again. Jann tilted his head in laughter as they slapped their hand on a raised knee.

"Right, right," the First Djinn said. "You want to know my solution. Fair enough. Well, it's simple. The contract is for Isra Almasi and the Wicker family. There is no specific line within the agreement that states you have to be in djinn form."

Maram's head snapped up with Jann's announcement.

"He wished for her to stay in his presence as a human."

"Oh, Maram. That's the easy part," Jann purred.

Jann lounged back. Isra refused to meet their eyes. It didn't matter, since the First Djinn's attention was on the slow movement of Isra easing her grip from Jacoa's. He wanted to hold her, to tell her not to give up. Instead, he applied enough pressure for a loose embrace. And then he let her go.

As soon as the contact ended, Isra's smooth skin rippled into overlapping scales the color of sand. Her bi-colored hair melded to her body, becoming alternating lines of black and beige along her back. Pale white scales lined the bottom of her chin and down her chest. She kept a humanoid face and posture, and her clothing remained the same, but Isra was once again a draconian, with her thick tail curled elegantly around her feet.

The lines of her jaw and curve of her head were more delicate than Aali's, more streamlined. Jacoa stood in awe of this creature, so strong as she faced a bully without backing down. To be transformed against her will with a tilt of pride at her chin. Jacoa reached for her, to let her know he didn't care what form she took. Isra evaded his hand as she avoided his eyes.

"Perfect," Jann announced, regarding the transformation and, Jacoa guessed, Isra's avoidance of him. "Now, why not have a lovely family reunion with your father?"

Isra dropped through the cloud without warning. She didn't

make a sound, but Jacoa shouted for both of them, his mouth freed with Isra's disappearance. He sank to his knees and pressed into an unforgiving surface.

"Oh, don't worry about her. She'll be fine," Jann said. "Maram, would you show our guest to a comfy room?"

"What?" Jacoa demanded.

"You are as hapless a victim in this whole escapade as the poor genies trapped in vessels. I am a big enough djinn to admit part of that is my fault. For the time being, please allow me to offer you some magical hospitality."

Maram yanked Jacoa to his feet as if she were three times her actual size. She swiveled and pushed Jacoa forward. At first, he tried to keep Jann in sight, but the cloud either moved them out or Jann away. He refocused his glare on Maram.

"What's going on?"

"Learn to follow along," she growled, gaining height as the stilettos on her feet grew a deadly sharp heel. Her jumpsuit shifted into a shiny corset and skin-tight pants as she strode through the field of clouds.

"Jann has no interest in you and Isra making wishes together." Maram flapped her hand toward him. "Or love, for that matter. So they manipulated the contract."

"How long does this last? How do we get out of it?"

"Pay attention! This is Jann's palace. They made Isra a draconian and sent her to the dungeons with the others. All they have to do is keep you apart for a measly year, and they've won."

"What? No. No! Take me to Isra."

He grabbed for Maram's arm, but she twisted out of his way.

"Like I'm going to give you the chance to mess this up any more than you already have. We are going to your room."

Maram lengthened her stride, passing Jacoa and leaving him with the option to follow or be lost in the nothingness of Jann-land.

CHAPTER 28
Isra

Isra fell through the layers of Jann's palace, clouds always blocking her vision so she couldn't gather information about their creation on the way. Even if the space was malleable to the First Djinn's whims, a draconian might notice weaknesses in the design to take advantage of.

Teeth bared in a draconian smile, Isra sent a silent promise into the blinding cloud. She would find the loopholes, anyway. Whether it was within this year or after she returned from the void, she would beat Jann at their own game.

Her calm descent ended in a rush the moment she reached her cell. Isra grunted as her body hit the hard black floor. She lay still as she took in her surroundings. The floor, walls, and ceiling were made of the same black material. The dark bars separating the cells had a shine that the matte stone did not.

She was four cells from an outer wall, empty cages in all other directions as far as she could see. The entrance and exit to these enclosures were at the top and bottom, so there were no doors. It wouldn't surprise her if Jann manipulated sizes at times, making themself incredibly large as they peeled off the lid of their jail to look down at their caged collection.

Isra strode to one wall of bars, studying how they sunk into the floor and ceiling, checking their diameter and the space between, finding nothing helpful.

How had Jann bent the rules around Jacoa's wish? Her master's words had been specific. The Wicker journals taught him how to make his wishes as concise as possible.

"I wish for you to remain in my presence, in human form, until our time ends."

Jann may have messed with the definition of 'in my presence'. Isra had done that herself over the past week. She'd kept Jacoa in the same room to irritate him, and within easy contact while she'd been waiting for him to finish with the police after Ruby's misadventure. Isra lowered her lash-less eyelids and focused on bringing him within touching distance.

Nothing budged. With a frown, Isra checked her chakras. *Vasundhara. Muladhara. Svadisthana. Manipura. Anahata. Vishuddha. Anja. Sahasrara.*

Her lower energy discs rotated unhindered, and she used each of them to support the healthy spin of the other. But that last, distant chakra of the heavens was out of reach.

Of course, as a draconian, her access to *Sutara* would be cut off. Which led to the second part of Jacoa's wish.

How in the hell had Jann manipulated her human form? They'd told Maram it was simple. They might have lied, but it was just as likely they'd found an easy loophole to exploit. That was their specialty.

Had they altered the time piece of the puzzle? Jacoa had meant until their year together was up. Isra could have manipulated that one as well when she'd been his genie, deciding to end her time with him whenever she wanted. With Jann's intent to keep her away from Jacoa, it was the most likely exploitation.

Whatever avenue Jann used, she wasn't gaining any insight on how to get out of this trap. She'd made a complete round of the cage at this point. Nothing.

There was one more thing to try, but did she want to?

She could reach out to Jacoa through their chakra-bond. The

way their energy linked was not magic, but a simple energy flow. Unique, beyond rare, but basic in essence. Like the wind moving between the trees, or waves crashing on the sand.

If she tried and it worked, she risked Jann noticing. Isra didn't believe they knew about the connection. After what she'd learned about Jann's reaction to the only other chakra-bond Ward knew about, she doubted the dramatic First Djinn would have been able to remain so calm.

Isra's breathing labored as her chest tightened. What she shared with Jacoa was more than a quirk of the universe. It was unique because it linked them together. Beautiful because of what they received through it. Intimate because it was theirs.

This might be her loophole. How long could she put off trying? If it didn't work and became another way Jann tortured her, what level of regret would that bring? If it worked, how much would she hate herself for not attempting to connect sooner?

Isra laid on the floor. One hand at her heart, one hand over her stomach, she filled her lungs and expanded her rib cage. She expressed it slowly, noticing each minute shift of her body as it moved with only the force of her breathing.

In Jacoa's bed, the energy intertwined them with effortless grace. Streams of hers went into him, wrapping around his chakras. Her ends remained with Jacoa, even as she took in the edges of his. They'd tangled up in each other during the night, completely unaware of what it would mean.

The first time she'd touched Jacoa, her lips brushed his ear as she asked for him to wish. The energy had flared in excitement, binding them more tightly.

Then in the desert. Forehead to forehead. Chest to chest. Hips to hips. Their energies burned within their passion, fusing them together. It became possible to ease in and out of each other through the draconian den, and while face to face with Maram and Ward.

Isra's chakras spun to the beat of her heart, counterclockwise to pull energy in, to hold her thoughts and memories inside herself. When she claimed them all, she exhaled and switched their direction. Clockwise, the disks eased her energy into the world. She sought the other half of herself, grappling for traction, longing to curl around and within Jacoa again.

She could not find him.

Whether he was too far away, or if Jann prevented them, she didn't know. Perhaps it was her draconian form that kept her from connecting.

She stopped trying and opened her eyes to the darkness. The floor wasn't warm or cold, but at the point where the temperature itself seemed invisible against her body. She realized why Jann made this dungeon as they had. Black on black on black.

It echoed the netherworld. The great void had been her home longer than any place on Earth. That this was only Jann's representation didn't matter. The effect was the same.

No one to talk to. No one to touch. Just her thoughts in a space darker than night. Her prison until Jacoa turned nineteen. Her trip around the sun would be complete, and Jann would win.

CHAPTER 29

Jacoa

Jacoa paced across the thick fur of the rug at his feet. He had taken off his shoes to enjoy the silky texture. He hoped the material wasn't a complete djinn creation, because he wanted this in his bedroom. If it was, maybe Isra would make it for him, if they ever reunited.

Which brought him back to pacing. Even his appreciation of the bright white fur did not stop his need to move. Somehow, Jann manipulated the nature of Jacoa's wishes. Isra should not be this far away after his fourth wish.

Jann had found a workaround, obviously. In fact, they may have even created it in the moment they needed it. The thought of their easy power sent a shiver along Jacoa's spine. The First Djinn even intimidated Maram, who'd done their bidding without a second thought. She led Jacoa on a brisk hike across the clouds, then dropped him without ceremony into an empty suite one level down.

The place was magnificent, of course. Exactly the opposite of the draconian den, as Isra had said. This rug, for one. Everything was done in shades of white, sky blue, and gold. The long, deep couch appeared as luxurious as the postered and draped circular platform bed across the room. A gauzy curtain separated this main area from a bathroom with a pearlescent tiled tub the size of a small pond.

Another time, Jacoa would have examined the room as if it were an exclusive art gallery. However, he'd only gotten as far as taking off his shoes, so the rug caressed his feet while he attempted to pace a hole through it. Because the main problem was there were no doors.

If Jacoa was a djinn, he would be a very comfortable guest. For a human, this was simply a cozy trap. It was probably better than wherever Isra landed. Jacoa clenched his fists against his ribs. He turned about face and set off for another pass.

A bell chimed and Jacoa looked around, then up at the fluffy cloud ceiling. The polished steel underside of a pair of stilettos lowered, the exaggerated toe almost as sharp as the pin-point heel. He eased out of the way of the weaponized footwear.

"Maram," he greeted as soon as he was certain it was her.

"You are the most irritating human."

Jacoa raised a brow. "The most? Out of all of them?"

"See what I mean?" Maram stalked to the couch, where she spun to sit down, arms and legs crossing in the same movement.

Jacoa curled his toes in the creamy fabric under his feet. He bit his tongue against the hundreds of questions and thousands of accusations he wanted to throw at her. First and foremost, he wanted to ask about Isra. He kept his silence, however. Maram's presence must mean something was starting.

"Why couldn't you have rapid fire asked for your wishes?" Maram tilted her head back on the couch, staring at the cloud rather than him. "So fast even they couldn't stop it?"

"Maybe I was too busy trying to stay alive."

"Nothing a few wishes couldn't take care of."

"At the time, I was debating trusting Isra again, and considered banishing her."

"Impulsive!"

"Self-preservation. And if I had, it would be your fault for starting that nonsense."

Maram's lips thinned into glossy lines.

"The. Most. Irritating."

Jacoa crossed his arms. "You're lucky I'm even still talking to you after you dragged us here."

"Me?" Maram demanded, her body snapping into ninety-degree posture on the couch. "You have no idea what is happening. Don't you dare blame this on me, when all I was doing was damage control."

"You're claiming to be selfless right now?"

"Hardly. If Jann knew about…" Her lips thinned and she looked toward the ceiling. Her arms hugged her ribs, and she curled around them, finishing her sentence with a glare.

"Is this room bugged?" he asked quietly.

"Please. As if a djinn would use a bug. Think of it as a notification system tied to particular words. Speak about certain things, get more attention than you bargained for."

"So why are we here?" If he knew what she'd told Jann, he could figure out what he shouldn't say by default.

"Because your long-time friend is a sorcerer who was trying to rope you and Isra into some kind of deal."

Jacoa rubbed his eyes. That's exactly what had been going on. What else was there? Maram blew out an unnaturally powerful breath that hit him in the chest, drawing his attention to her. She made small figure eights with one of her fingers.

The chakra-bond.

"Oh."

Maram relaxed back onto the couch, her glare not as sharp now that he understood they needed to speak around the important things.

"So this isn't only about my wishes?" The idea was more appealing to Jacoa than he realized. If Jann had mentioned Ruby only for intimidation purposes, he'd feel a lot better right now.

"Maybe not for Jann. That is all I care about."

"Why are you so interested in how I wish?"

"I don't care how you wish, as long as you do. I want the genie contracts canceled."

"Ward said some of them should stay trapped."

"If there was a choice, I would only free one." Each word fell out of Maram's lips with hesitant deliberation.

"Then getting me to wish is the wrong tactic."

"As if I haven't tried others over the past hundreds of years," she lashed out. "I cannot find his vessel."

"Why didn't you ask Isra for help finding it, rather than involve her in this wish scheme?"

"What could a baby genie do that I couldn't?"

"Not much. But she's also draconian."

Maram's eyes widened until they were oversized. Her lips softened and parted on a gasp. With a vicious curse, she pressed herself from the couch. Maram grabbed a silvery, twisted sculpture and threw it against the wall. It shattered into a million sparkles, only for the entire process to reverse. The repaired piece settled on the table. Maram's fingers clawed toward the abstract statue, but she stopped inches from its surface and turned her back on it.

"She wouldn't have helped. She only listened to me this time because she'd finally lost faith that her father would find her."

"After trying every other thing, I'm surprised you didn't even ask once."

Maram snarled in warning. Jacoa caved just a little. Not because she threatened him, but because he recognized her driving force. Helplessness.

"What do you need from me?"

"Oh, you're accommodating all of a sudden. Good. Here's the plan. You go entertain Jann. Keep them occupied. I will..." She mouthed "*help your girlfriend escape.*"

"I'm going to - you're going to what? How?"

"Don't worry about me. Just do your part."

"And distract the most powerful being in the universe?"

"One of the most, but yes. Monopolize their attention. It should be easy for a boy from Las Vegas."

"And I'm supposed to get to them how?" He swept his arms out to indicate the room with no doors.

"I'll drop you somewhere. I'm sure one of their minions will find you soon enough. Then, you'll explain that something weird happened, and you got lost."

"Maram—"

"You'll be fine. Remember the stakes."

"Why are you helping us?"

"Because then you and Isra will owe me." Maram made a show of rolling her eyes, her scowl reminding him he was irritating. "The rest doesn't matter."

CHAPTER 30

Isra

"Isra."

The voice sounded familiar and came from the depths of her childhood. It was odd that she heard anything in this place of nothing. But then, this wasn't the netherworld. It was Jann's invention. It wasn't surprising they would encourage a few hallucinations to make the cell more tortuous.

"Isra."

Her father's voice filled her thoughts without echoing. Surely that meant it wasn't real. She lay still, unwilling to respond to a trick of her mind.

She was not used to this body anymore. Even immobile, she adjusted to the added fluidity in her spine and the stiff armor of her scales. The heaviness left her feeling claustrophobic in her own physique. She needed time for her brain to catch up, to recognize she could not transform into something more comfortable or suited to her mood.

Then again, perhaps this body was perfectly suited to being locked in a cage. And what did Jacoa think of it? This reptilian form had no business existing and wasn't compatible with his. She couldn't bear to look at him as Jann forced the shift. She didn't want to see his shock or horror. Or if he had a collector's gleam in his eyes.

"Isra."

She closed thick lids over her eyes and ignored the voice, stuck in thoughts of what she'd lost. What Jann had taken away with a simple djinn thought. Her freedom of movement. The man she loved.

Hot tears slipped over the layers of scales at the sides of her head.

"Fight it!"

What was left to fight? Jann won. They were impossibly powerful and had shown it without bothering with fanfare. In fact, they'd seemed wholly bored. How was she supposed to challenge that?

"You are draconian." The depth of Aali's voice cut through the lethargic force that wove between the cells like a cool breeze. She opened her eyes and turned her face toward it.

The cell next to hers wasn't empty. She recognized the outline of Aali through the gloom, standing with his taloned fingers wrapped around the bars.

The anger she'd held onto during her descent through the clouds burst into life. Her heart thumped in her chest, pumping hot blood through her veins. She pushed herself to her feet and shook her head, clearing out the tangle of shadows and sleep that had pinned her with more ease than any shackles and chains would have done.

"I cannot believe I fell for that." Her words formed natural slurs as she forced her human-like mouth to work around a set of sharp draconian teeth.

"You have lived in a different head for a long time," Aali reminded her. He studied her form, though his features were carefully neutral. "It is good to see you, Isra. I am sorry it is like this."

"What? You mean locked in some djinn's dungeon?"

"Trapped."

"Story of my life."

"No. The story of your life is that you fight for yourself and your freedom."

Isra's dark eyes met her father's.

He hadn't abandoned her. He'd had a plan the whole time, just a different one from hers. Her father still worked toward the goal they'd had when she'd been draconian - changing the fate of her birth.

"I'm sorry I lost faith," Isra murmured, bowing her head as she wrapped her hand around the cuff inscribed with draconian script.

"That is easy to do when you are alone in the dark," Aali soothed.

Isra's throat thickened, and she managed a nod, blinking her eyes to swallow the tears. This was her father and mentor who raised her to have confidence in herself. She hadn't allowed herself to realize how much she missed him, not when he was the one who would track her down to end the curse. Yet, he'd clearly thought of her every day.

"How did you fight it?" she asked.

"This place cannot affect me. I am immune from djinn spells," he responded with the ridge of his brow raised, as if he wasn't sure why she didn't recall this basic knowledge. "They can manipulate the world around me, but they cannot alter what's inside."

"I don't mean this place. I mean my curse. It is draconian nature to hate what I am. You claimed my vessel, but not to use the weapon against me. You want to help me."

"You are my daughter. That is reason enough to change my blanket hatred of djinn. Now come. Ward is that way." Aali redirected their attention to the task. Isra looked in the direction, tapping into her training from centuries ago. She made out a hazy spot within the empty room. A low red flame only draconian eyes could see marked the presence of a sorcerer's magic.

Aali pulled a thin wire from his cloak and wrapped it around one of the bars between him and Isra.

"Jann will have based their palace on the nine chakras," Aali informed her. "What level is this?"

"*Muladhara.* The Root," she offered after recalling her drop through the clouds. The level just above the lowest, where it would be easiest to prey on a being's energy, anxiety, and fear, leaving them indolent.

Aali began a chant using their ancient draconian language, long connected with the ability to undo magical energies. The wire between his hands glowed a deep purple. The bar it encircled vibrated, then dissolved until there was nothing left. Aali repeated the ritual until enough bars disappeared between them and he stepped through.

Memories flooded Isra as Aali stopped before her. He used to stand over her like this just before they'd start a mission. He would have a similar posture with a bowed head when he offered her a gift. She'd sat across from him at so many campfires, dinner tables, and in their own underground home, staring into those dark eyes.

His presence grounded her in time and secured her within this body. It was stiff, yes. Not preferred, absolutely. But she knew how to use it, thanks to her father.

"It will take too long to get through the maze if I'm the only one canceling out magic."

"I'm ready," she promised.

"Good." Aali's tone held surprise and pride. He handed her one side of the thin chain of silver. They wove it between four of the bars, each holding an end. When Aali began the chant again, Isra joined her voice with his. The draconian words flowed from her lips as if she'd never stopped speaking her birth tongue. In less time than Aali dispersed one bar, the four they worked on together flickered from existence.

Jann's few prisoners were easy to sneak past as they laid on the floor, staring at the ceiling. The draconian avoided opening the occupied cells as they made their way toward where Ward's sorcerer flame burned.

When they reached Ward, he wasn't lost to despair. He sat in lotus form, hands resting on his knees as he muttered a counter curse against the depressive magic pushing in. Aali and Isra made quick work of the bars and slipped into Ward's space, careful not to startle him mid-spell.

"Ward," Aali called. The sorcerer opened his eyes. When he saw Isra and Aali, he stopped his chant and stood. The force of movement had him swaying on his feet and Aali hesitated only a moment before placing his large hands on Ward's smaller shoulders. With the draconian's touch, the spell around Ward shattered back into its raw energy form, flapping away like tiny bats until they dissolved into the stagnant air.

"Thank you," Ward said.

"There is further to go," Aali warned. "Keep contact with me or Isra."

"Right."

Isra was startled at the ease between the males. "You two don't sound surprised we're here."

"I told you we had a plan." Ward tested his balance, then brushed off his jeans as well as he could with Aali attached at his elbow. "As much of one as you can have against the First Djinn."

"You intended to use Jacoa and me."

"Yes," Aali said. "The original Wickers were the architects of both the genie curse and the draconian race. This is as much Jacoa's destiny as yours."

"The Emrick line, my line, never wanted this," Ward added. "We believe coexistence is not only possible, but as nature intended."

"Even though the djinn are dangerous?" Isra asked.

"They weren't always," Ward said. "Neither side is free of blame, but it was the work of sorcerers that made this world perilous for djinn. What enslaved, besieged being wouldn't fight with every tool in their arsenal, especially if one of those skills was magic?"

Isra glanced between the two men, her frown harsh.

"I have met many of them. They can be incredibly destructive!"

"But how often are they?" Aali asked.

"And for what reasons?" Ward asked.

Isra prepared a collection of answers that would include Maram's attacks on Jacoa, and the djinn who had battled over the lives of a nanny and Jacoa's cousin, Ruby.

But she stopped because Ward's words sunk in. The reason behind those dangerous actions was to free their djinn brethren from captivity. The djinn in the bar she'd met Maram in had kept to their own kind. Earth was not overrun by djinn magic or realities, despite the possibility. In fact, humans no longer believed in paranormals.

"You must let go of your draconian instincts on this one," Aali counseled. "As I had to, in order to see you for Isra and not a monster."

Jacoa's words echoed in Isra's mind. Was she a monster or a fairytale? She'd worried that he was looking for a princess. He'd only wanted her.

And Jann was intent on taking that away far sooner than Isra was ready. She wasn't even being allowed the one year of time promised by Jann's own contract.

"There must be a loophole." She stared at her clawed hands, then at her father. "What can a draconian do against the First Djinn in their own palace?"

Aali pulled a dagger from the sheath at his waist. The bronze sheen was a bright spot in this dark place. A freshly minted weapon recreated from the vessel that bound her. But there had been a different djinn attached to it before. Her father had made a blade Jann wouldn't know to fear.

CHAPTER 31

Jacoa

As soon as Jacoa had agreed to cooperate, Maram wrapped her fingers around his bicep and hauled him toward the cloud ceiling. She didn't continue up, though, using the cover of the milky interior as she moved them in a confusing zigzag through indecipherable space.

Jacoa closed his eyes to combat the threat of nausea. Even that didn't help when Maram's smooth motion came to an abrupt halt. Jacoa opened his eyes when Maram released a strangled scream. Her hair rose straight up as if someone had grabbed it and was pulling her through the cloud bank. Maram's fingers wiggled and though it seemed she tried to let Jacoa go, something wasn't allowing her to.

That something was Jann.

The First Djinn waited for them at the top level of the palace. They stood before their throne as Jacoa and Maram rose from the floor.

"It pains me to see my guest has been bothered." Jann's blue lips dipped into a deep, over-exaggerated frown. "I really am so sorry, Jacoa. It seems you'll be safer in my presence after all."

An ornate chair a quarter the size of Jann's formed from the clouds. Without moving on his own, Jacoa found himself siting in the replica with his next blink. Vines of the marble-like material wrapped Jacoa's wrists and around his chest, pinning him.

An audience of djinn fanned out before the throne. The eclectic collection of creatures stood spaced out in an odd scatter of symmetry, as if even they were placed in the exact spot that pleased Jann the most.

Jacoa settled deeper into the chair and pinched his lips together. He had nothing to say, yet guarded against speaking. Whatever was happening with Jann and Maram, he didn't want to risk making it worse.

"Now, what to do with you, Maram," Jann said. "You generously come to tell me our youngest addition is playing with sorcerers. But then I catch you sneaking around, my guest of honor in tow. Very troublesome."

"Banish me from your palace. It wouldn't be the first time."

"Exactly," Jann agreed. "And yet you haven't learned your lesson. Let's try this. We'll pretend you are the Court Genie, and you have to grant each of us a wish."

"I wish for Maram to service me in the—"

The djinn who spoke lost his coveted spot three spaces deep from Jann. He flowed through the others to be settled much further toward the back.

"You have forfeited your chance because you didn't wait for the rules. First, Maram must remain here where all can witness her wish granting. And please remember we have a young guest with us. Keep it human-appropriate. The rest of you will line up."

"You would make me act like a servant." Maram spoke through bared teeth.

"I would make you do anything I cared to," Jann responded.

Jacoa shifted in his chair, his blood pumping in reaction to Jann's treatment of Maram, his body uncomfortably warm in his trapped position. There was no give in his elegant shackles, and he doubted he could stop Jann's play.

The djinn floated across the cloud, following Jann's directions. Jacoa kept his attention on the First Djinn themself. His tongue swelled, his throat dried, but the drive to do something grew inside him until his chest felt compressed.

Jann's starlight eyes softened at the show of djinn obedience as they followed instructions. The First Djinn moved to their throne and lounged so their upper body leaned toward Jacoa.

Maram stood stock straight, lips screwed together when the first wish was asked of her. Jann grinned.

"Tell them 'wish granted' as you complete their wishes." The vibration of magic rippled out in forceful waves. Maram snarled the required words in the same way Isra reacted to Ward's commands. Jacoa's stomach dropped as thoughts scrambled, some too quick to grab, some sharp enough to make him wince. To stop the rush, he grasped on the first full sentence his brain formed.

"Maram told you about Ward."

"Oh, yes," Jann nodded. "She raced up here and shared every detail of how your latent power responded to his active sorcery. It was very kind of her, actually. We haven't located any free sorcerers in quite a long time. Acquiring Ward is almost as exciting as having a draconian bound within my palace."

"Ward said he was from a different faction than the Wicker line."

"Of course he is, if he still has his power."

"If he hasn't attacked, why have you imprisoned him?"

"Crimes!" Jann exclaimed, a false innocence raising the tone of his voice. "Against the djinn."

"So you said. What crimes?"

"I'm sorry, Jacoa, but you are from the Wicker line. I'm unlikely to give you clues to the inner workings of the djinn."

Jacoa had started his questions out of desperation to still his thoughts, but now he wondered if he could learn something. Maram's plan hadn't gone as expected, but perhaps he could adjust it. He'd work to keep Jann talking and see where that led.

"Insights I'm not getting by watching Maram grant wishes for pet dragons and... was that really Botticelli's sketchbook?"

Jacoa leaned against his restraints and squinted toward the book.

"If it was wished for, then it was."

"Can't the djinn get these things for themselves?"

"Of course. But you have a genie and have been prolific with your own wishes despite being able to claim virtually anything you like via your fortune. You must understand the draw of making someone else do the work for you."

"Is that something you enjoy as First Djinn?"

"Obviously."

"Have you always had this position?" Jacoa asked. "Was another djinn ever more powerful?"

Jann stiffened. "I was born from the first perfect alignment of universal energies that occurred here on Earth. All other living beings have come since. That is why I am First Djinn. It cannot be earned or taken away. The position, as you call it, is simply who I am."

The light in Jann's eyes sent rays of concentrated beams over his skin as they turned to Jacoa. Their voice rose in volume with each word spoken.

Jacoa had struck a chord. Upsetting the First Djinn hadn't been his plan, but perhaps heightened emotion would make Jann more free with their words.

"I see. It's just, I had thought..."

"Thought what?" Jann asked.

"There had been mention of a djinn more powerful than you, is all."

The string of wishes stopped. Silence fell in a stagnant blanket as all djinn eyes turned to Jacoa. Those who had finished their wishes sank into the cloud, clutching whatever trinket they'd forced from Maram. The line drifted away, the djinn settling back into their symmetrical places.

"And where did you read this? One of the thousands of lies written in the Wicker journals, I assume."

Living in Vegas, Jacoa had long practiced his poker face. He didn't reply to Jann, wanting the assumption to stand. Jann had given up another useful piece of information with his question. Even the self-proclaimed most powerful First Djinn feared what was inside the Wicker journals.

"The hierarchy of the djinn is clear." Jann's velvet voice floated over the cloud, a resonating hum that sunk into Jacoa's chest, and likely did the same to the djinn who remained. "It is impossible to usurp my place. Energy is energy, and the universe frowns on those who try to change their nature. Truth remains. The older the djinn, the stronger they are. There are none older than me."

Another few djinn disappeared into the cloud. Jann didn't seem to notice as their eyes burned into Jacoa's. Beyond the throne, Maram struggled against the bonds that held her in place. If Jacoa continued to question Jann's position, would they lose their grip on Maram and allow her to slip away?

"Yet you were trapped as a genie."

"By choice! I wanted to taste the power of creating true reality. Once I had my fill and was ready to return, it was child's play to trick your weak ancestor into wishing that cocky draconian into my place and—"

Jann straightened on their throne. The surrounding cloud boiled and rolled. Jann's eyes condensed into a light so bright, Jacoa had to look away. He flinched at the First Djinn's next words.

"Speaking of Isra."

CHAPTER 32

Isra

"Aali, a little closer," Ward whispered, then cursed. "Too close!"

Aali grumbled as he leaned away. His job was to negate just enough djinn power without affecting Ward. Too close and Ward's work shattered. Too far and the djinn magic was too strong.

Aali's low hum filled the cloud, his eyes narrowed in concentration.

"Stop," Isra hissed, and both Aali and Ward froze as they listened to the silence through the milky fog. Isra waited as the djinn power signature she'd sensed moved away. Once it was safe again, she nodded to signal they could continue.

Getting through Jann's vertical palace for non-djinn proved a tremendous effort, but something else Ward and Aali had prepared for. With Aali canceling out djinn magic, the sorcerer set to rework the vapor into a zigzag of stairs leading them upward.

The three kept inside the cloud that separated the levels and the rooms, though remaining in it left them blind. By creating a delicate balance of magic nullification and sorcery, they moved through the palace undetected.

"How did you learn to do this?" Isra asked them, studying the well-practiced motions between the two.

"It isn't only sorcerers who have separate factions of belief," Aali told her as Ward struggled to form another layer of stairs. "Ward has introduced me to djinn of a different set. It seems you and I were born into one side of a war. Not all djinn and sorcerers want to battle. After a millennium and a half of fighting, I'm inclined to see the benefits of peace."

"After half a millennium of Isra being djinn," Ward corrected with a low chuckle.

"It was a necessary catalyst," Aali agreed, winking at Isra without adjusting his distance from Ward's work.

They rose another floor, then took a moment to rest. So far, they'd created seven staircases, placing them one level from the top where there would be no place to hide.

"What will you do?" Isra whispered as the three knelt together.

"The goal is to get as close to Jann as possible," Ward murmured. "We could only plan for so much."

"I can do it," she offered.

"What are you thinking?" Aali asked.

"I can beg to be returned to genie form. It would likely amuse them enough to let me come close."

"Not close enough," Ward argued. "Not in your current form."

"It wouldn't matter." Aali bared his teeth in a draconian smile. "It is a distraction. I have excellent aim, and they cannot stop a draconian-made weapon. We will try your plan, daughter, but remain alert for additional opportunities."

They set to the delicate work of creating their final staircase. As they rose onto cloud nine, they eased their heads through and then pulled up, Isra and Aali on guard. With Ward the last to ascend, the three stayed low on the mist, using the wisps floating from the floor to their advantage.

A slow, repetitive clap filled the air. Isra's sense of triumph shattered against the heat of her anger. Dozens of djinn power signatures sped toward their location from every direction—blue flames where Ward's was red.

Isra surged to standing, claws curled into her scaled palms and her tail lashing through the puff of vapor at her feet. Aali and Ward rose more slowly, their attention focused on the brightest blue flame.

Maram stood just before the throne to Jann's right, facing the room. Her posture was too stiff. Her lips trembled, but she did not speak.

On Jann's left, there was now a smaller chair that held Jacoa. Though he appeared comfortably seated, bands of thick white crossed his chest and wrapped his wrists to hold him in place.

A knotted ache bloomed at the base of her skull. Isra suppressed the need to reach her power centers toward Jacoa. She could not blend her chakras with his, anyway. In her draconian form and unable to access *Sutara*, their connection was impossible. It was likely a blessing, as they were so close to the First Djinn. Knowing was not enough. She forced herself to swallow her heartache.

"What an enlightening display. I am truly impressed with your ingenuity." Jann spoke as if offering high praise, though their lips curled away from the words. "I'm curious about how this happened. There are so many conflicting motivations, yet look at this level of cooperation. So, new game. Maram, since your wish granting was cut short, you can start this one."

Maram's spine bent back in a small crescent, her head tilted so her chin pointed up. The stiff, quick movements were reminiscent of a marionette, one Jann controlled.

"This will be a game of absolute truth. What is your purpose here?"

"I would see Ansel freed."

A deep, quiet chuckle bounced through Jann's chest until it exploded in a bark of energy.

"Your once upon a time lover? You have wasted your efforts. That fool's curse isn't tied to a vessel."

With a wave of their hand, Jann released the invisible hold they had on Maram's body. She fell onto her hip with an angry growl, then twisted to face Jann while scrambling away on hands and heels.

"You told me—" Maram said.

"Think carefully," Jann interrupted, "and you'll find I hadn't."

Maram's body vibrated. The back of her hair shortened while the front elongated into points on either side of her chin. Shimmering spikes burst across her shiny black corset and atop the already lethal pair of stilettos.

Isra's breath pulled shallow and slow. This wasn't their planned distraction, but it was a good one. Her tail flickered toward her father. The movement proved unnecessary. Aali's knife was on its way.

The thrones shimmered. The blade flew true and straight, landing deep in Jacoa's chest, just to the right of his heart.

Isra could not move. Her chakras stopped turning. Her feet rooted, and it had nothing to do with magic.

Ward ran toward the young man, but never moved an inch. Aali pulled his cloak around him, solidifying his neutralizing power. A cage of clouds surrounded him and Isra. Aali reached for one of the bars. It shifted just out of his reach without providing a gap large enough to escape. Aali used his shoulder to force the contact. The cage solidified, bringing Aali to a halt. The vapor reformed before the draconian had time to neutralize any part of it.

Isra's eyes locked on Jacoa as he tried to pull his arms free and reach for the knife. He gave up with a grimace, the color draining from his cheeks. Blood dampened his black button-down in an expanding oval.

Her body trembled. She stood, a useless draconian, trapped within djinn power and losing Jann's well-played game. Always trapped. Always with few or no choices. And now she watched as the one person she wanted bled red over the white bars holding him.

"Oh, I've learned from your draconian-sorcerer alliance," Jann purred. "As I said earlier, it has been an enlightening display."

Jacoa's soft chuckle floated above the cloud. Isra could not look away as he narrowed his eyes in defiance, mocking Jann with a sideways grin.

"What is so amusing about your death?" Jann demanded, their voice shaking at the edges. "Your curse will not end with you, you know. It will simply transfer to the next Wicker in line, weak as their blood may be. This is not the end for Isra. Even if it is for you."

"I find your arrogance funny." Jacoa gasped between his words, then grit his teeth.

Jann eased back on their throne, staring at Isra who never took her eyes from Jacoa. Her heart burst with his courage. She would give her chance at freedom for the ability to connect her chakras to his and take on his pain, to have her own heartbeat strengthen his until its last beat.

"Your master is delusional," Jann said to Isra.

"Right." Jacoa coughed. "As her master, Isra is mine. And you have convinced *my* genie of a reality where she is a creature immune to magic."

Jann's brow furrowed. Isra's eyes widened. She raised her wrists and unwound the leather strips that remained. The branded words of *My family shall be known* disappeared into the heavy mist at her feet. Copper and iron wrapped her forearms. She'd become so used to the cuffs that she'd forgotten them. Yet there they were, marking her as one bound by the genie curse.

No matter what loopholes they found, not even the First Djinn could break this contract.

Isra seized her chakras, propelling them to life. She spun them counter-clockwise, pulling in djinn power. *Sutara* burst into her senses and it was as if she could breathe for the first time since they set foot in Jann's sky palace.

Then there was Jacoa. Weak, in pain, but there. He had been reaching for her all along. When their energies blended once more, the strain on his face relaxed.

"No." Jann's voice came rough and low as he gripped the arms of his throne. "You cannot be chakra-bound. I refuse it!"

Isra reached out a taloned hand and the cage of cloud fell away at her touch. Jann thrust their version of reality into the realm they'd created. They sought to trap her once again, and struck at the very cords that wound between her and Jacoa.

But Isra had also learned from Ward and his work with Aali. She charged her scales with the gifts of her draconian blood, accepted her birthright as part of the power that flowed into Jacoa. With every step forward, she defied Jann's will and strengthened her own.

The surrounding djinn stood as statues, only their eyes moving from between the First Djinn and the draconian who stalked them. She felt Jacoa's lifeblood fading and her call as his genie filled her with purpose. He would not die. The blade reversed from his chest and flew into her hand. His body stitched together even as hers rippled with change.

Her master had wished for her to remain in his presence, in human form. Shimmering scales smoothed into rich brown skin. Her hair burst free, black framing her face, white cloaking her shoulders and back. It flowed around her, reached toward the First Djinn, ready to lash out at the being who had taken its freedom.

Jann ripped Jacoa from the ties of the small throne, holding the human against their body as a shield. Jann's twin sun eyes blazed at Isra who bared her teeth in a draconian smile.

"Any last wishes?" Isra asked.

Jann's starlight eyes flared until he and Jacoa were flooded with light. Isra launched forward, dagger held high. That Jacoa was between the blade and its target was of no concern. She could never hurt her master. In her hand, the weapon would only find Jann's flesh.

The First Djinn twisted space, trying to ensnare Jacoa in the same flow of power. A tornado spun wisps of cloud into the air, creating a funnel around the throne. Isra slammed her body into the storm, one hand reaching for Jacoa, the other armed with Aali's blade.

The white rise of Jann's magic blinded Isra, but did not hinder her aim. The knife met resistance, then passed through flesh. Jann's high-pitched scream pulsated through each of the palace's nine levels. Isra fell forward, her hand clasping Jacoa's through the maelstrom even as Jann pulled him away.

In this, her will was stronger than the First Djinn's. Jann could not take what was hers and hers alone. Her chakras twisted, gripping onto the energy connected to her master. Talons erupted from her human hands, digging into Jacoa without breaking skin, pulling him back from the whirlwind and into her arms.

CHAPTER 33

Jacoa

Jacoa wrapped his arms around Isra, pulling their hearts as close together as their bodies allowed. He had missed every inch of her, even how she made him work for each piece of her story. And how she taught him to look for moments of joy in any situation. Bleeding out, certain he would die, it was her presence that gave him the strength to stand up to Jann.

His lips nuzzled through her hair. He sought out the curve of her ear to whisper words he should have spoken as soon as he'd understood what his fourth wish had done to her.

He didn't get the chance to make his new wish. Jacoa lost his breath as he was hauled to his feet. He blinked through the dizziness to startle at Aali's visage close to his, though the draconian was quickly replaced by Ward, who wrapped him in a rib-cracking hug.

"Damn, Jacoa. For someone who doesn't enjoy parties, you sure know how to be the center of one." Ward let go with a relieved laugh.

"Not my intention." Jacoa placed a hand on his chest and winced. "If I'd known there would be flying knives, I might have stayed home."

"My apologies." Aali bent in a small bow. Jacoa's cheeks

heated, and he lowered his head, unsure how to interact with Isra's father now that they were on better terms.

"It wasn't your fault," Jacoa mumbled.

A phoenix burst into yellow and orange flames as it dove toward Isra. Aali grabbed for the creature, but only caught a feather, which dissolved in his grip. Jacoa tried to block the assault, but wasn't fast enough.

Isra didn't need him.

His genie pressed her djinn powers into her aura. The attacking djinn was older, and her automatic defense wasn't enough. Jacoa winced when the bird's crown struck Isra's sternum with a deep, broken sound, knocking her back so she crashed into Jann's throne.

Isra's arms wrapped around the djinn's head and the flames wavered. The bird molted, red and orange feathers blanketing the cloud floor. Thin legs thickened. The creature shifted from an armored phoenix into a face that appeared very human as it stared into his genie's angry yellow eyes.

Jacoa had seen the same happen when Aali had grabbed the bull. A djinn stripped of their powers appeared remarkably human. Even frail. Isra was neither of those things. She stood, her grip never relaxing as she forced the attacking djinn to her feet.

"Are you going to kill me, too?" the molted phoenix asked. "Show your roots and your blood. Prove yourself unworthy of the djinn power in your soul."

Jacoa glanced around the silent cloud to find every other being stared at Isra. Eyes wide and faces slack in the face of her power. Jacoa grinned, focusing his relief and pride on Isra with reverent wonder.

"Death is a freedom you do not deserve. You should fly far, far away before I teach you what is worse." Isra released the djinn who burst into flames once more, this time her feathers carrying her into the pale blue sky.

"Gorgeous," Jacoa said.

A surge of amusement and joy filled Jacoa as he reached Isra's side, but her attention wasn't fully on him as she took in the potential threats in the room.

"If you want to talk," Isra shouted into the large space. "You are welcome to stay."

"What is there to discuss?" the bull demanded, peeking around a dragon-shaped djinn. "Why don't you just leave?"

Jacoa felt Isra's slight jerk before she looked to Ward and Aali, as if asking them for their help. Before any of them answered, the dragon djinn eased forward and stopped at Maram's side.

"What does all of this mean? What has happened to Jann?"

"They're dead." Maram's sharp words pulled gasps from around the room. Over half the djinn disappeared with the announcement and a few others move timidly toward the group standing at the foot of the thrones.

"Are they really?" A soft-spoken wisp of a ghost floated forward, startling Jacoa into stepping back.

"It's possible." Aali exchanged a glance with Ward, both their brows wrinkled in apprehension. "They have been separated from the vessel for five hundred years. It is difficult to know what potency it has over them."

The dragon hissed at Aali, though the ghost seemed more willing to accept the draconian's assessment.

"But what does it mean if they are dead?" the wisp demanded. "What will happen with the First being gone? Will the universe fall apart?"

"Hardly," Ward answered with dark confidence. "Djinn are spontaneous creations, just like any living creature. The universe will survive with or without any of us."

"How would you know?" the dragon asked. "You are nothing but a magic-thieving sorcerer who is but a speck compared to a djinn."

"And yet I'm powerful enough to break into the First Djinn's palace and help knock them off their throne."

Jacoa frowned, not sure Ward's defensiveness was the right move. Yet, he wasn't sure he was qualified to add to this conversation between magical beings. A small yearning for his sorcerer's blood surprised him. He wanted to stand with Isra as her equal. His ability to wish using her magic made them partners, but for how much longer?

A sorcerer's abilities were a complication he didn't want added to his life. Jacoa was a collector, not a creator. He would bring value in another way. Magic needed a balance, after all. Perhaps that's what he could offer.

"I doubt the First Djinn is the linchpin of the universe." Jacoa looked at his feet the moment all eyes turned on to him, suddenly certain he should have stuck to his first instincts and remained quiet.

Aali broke the silence, allowing for Jacoa's participation.

"Of course they are not. And the djinn are not dependent on them. There is the hierarchy to consider. The Second Djinn is only moments younger than Jann."

"Who?" the wisp asked. Jacoa scanned the djinn who had moved in to listen, all of them with questioning expressions.

"Obviously, there'd be a second," the dragon agreed. "Who is it?"

A low murmur filled the room.

"It doesn't matter," Maram said. "We'll figure it out. For now, we need to talk about the Wicker wishes."

Jacoa winced as attention fell on him. The weight of expectations convinced him he was better off without a more permanent magical legacy.

"Yes!" The bull djinn pushed forward, a heavy red-eyed glare warning Aali to keep his distance. "Make the rest of your wishes, Wicker. Free our kind!"

"That may be hasty," the dragon said. Jacoa stared at them in surprise. "Remember, Gothric is one of the cursed."

"And Sylthen," someone spoke from the crowd. The uneasy silence that followed suggested all the djinn preferred that these two, at least, were not freed to roam among their ranks.

"What if we use the draconian?" Maram asked.

"We will not become djinn servants," Aali hissed.

"Why not, when you've served the sorcerers for all of your existence?" Maram asked.

Aali had the grace to lower his head. "It is that truth that will make an alliance nearly impossible. We have been created to loathe your kind."

"You don't seem to despise your daughter," Maram said.

"And I am ashamed to admit the strength of effort that took. Without my connection to her, I would not have been able to fight my predisposition."

Jacoa slid closer to Isra, placing his hand on her back. Isra smiled at him, and the peace he saw in the soft curve answered his silent question. She'd reconciled with Aali. A deep tension within Jacoa melted away, along with the fearful guilt he'd carried since handing over her vessel. Thank goodness his instincts had led to the outcome he hoped; father and daughter, reunited.

"An alliance is worth considering." Ward raised a hand to stop Aali's objection to his suggestion. "A compromise, Aali. No one made to serve. You have worked with sorcerers and djinn, and we have discussed the possibility before."

"What djinn have dared work with you?" the wisp asked.

"It doesn't serve anyone to point them out, if cooperation is what the future brings," Ward said. "And with Isra now able to use djinn powers and harness draconian resistance, she could act as ambassador."

"Wait a long minute—" Isra pulled away from Jacoa, shaking her head. Jacoa had objections of his own and stayed close, ready to offer his support.

The low rumble of thunder trembled through the white cloud. From the edges of their vision, waves of mist rose toward them as the field of vapor writhed around them. The few remaining djinn disappeared between one blink and the next. Even Jacoa's temporary ally, Maram, was gone.

"The palace is failing." Aali's warning came as his leg fell through a hole in the cloud. Ward reached for him and held him steady. The rescue lasted a mere second as the ninth level flickered out and they dropped, hitting the door of the apartment cubical below.

"We have to go," Jacoa said.

"It's not that simple," Ward argued. "Aali will resist any magic, even that meant to save him."

Why did they keep forgetting Jacoa had a trump card?

"Isra, I wish for you to bring the four of us back to my house."

"Jacoa!" Ward bellowed as the floor of the apartment cracked. "Stop wishing!" His shout filled Jacoa's small office, standing where they had before Maram dragged them to a palace that no longer existed.

"Because you'd rather be falling to your death?" Jacoa asked.

"You don't understand." Ward's voice sounded oddly quiet now that he wasn't yelling.

"Then it's time to tell them," Aali said.

CHAPTER 34

Isra

"We need to check if the draconian are still here," Isra said. Everyone turned toward the window as if expecting a line of lizard faces. All they saw were the dim lights reflecting off the surface of the pool. Jann's palace had been lit up like the middle of the day, but stars speckled the dark desert sky outside Jacoa's home.

"I forgot that part when I wished," Jacoa said.

"How dare you, considering the circumstances?" Isra offered Jacoa a soft smile along with the teasing words. Aali slipped out, then returned a few moments later, his shoulders relaxed and his cloak free-flowing.

"They have abandoned the house. We should be fine in the short term. I would worry more about Jann."

Jacoa stiffened. "Wait, Isra stabbed the bastard."

"I can't find them." Maram appeared on Jacoa's desk with her legs dangling, the spikes still present on her clothes. "It could mean they're dead. Or they're in hiding, feeling like a wounded animal and becoming more dangerous because of that."

"What are you doing here?" Isra demanded.

"Setting up protections against the djinn, of course," Maram said. "You'll have to do your own for the draconian. After the palace fiasco, I figured you might want a barrier between you and any flying phoenixes or the like."

"We can do that for ourselves." Isra's hair looped into a rope braid, though she would prefer to wrap the length around Maram's neck.

"Yes, but as the strongest djinn present, I'm best for the job. Even Jann will have trouble getting through the layers of misdirects I left."

"Why?" Isra was done assuming. She wanted all Maram's cards laid out.

"Jacoa gave me the idea to ask for help." Maram spoke through her teeth. "Nothing else I've tried worked, so why the hell not?"

Isra's frown cut deep as she looked at Jacoa. His eyes held the width of surprise and approval. What had happened between them while she was fighting her way through Jann's palace?

"Don't let her fool you too much," Jacoa cautioned. "From what I understand, this is more of a trade."

"For what?" Isra asked.

"Ansel." Ward answered. "I have heard of him."

"Do you know where he is?" Maram's arms uncurled and the spikes on her clothes dissolved.

"I do not." Ward held up a finger, asking the volatile djinn to keep listening. "Ansel's name came up in my search, but he had not been who I was looking for."

"I know of Ansel's curse." Aali offered, his eyes flickering to Isra, then to the door behind her before settling on Maram. "He is restricted in the use of his powers. He may only practice them within human dreams."

"How do you know?" Maram's stiletto heels deflated.

"His ability to dive into a human's mind has enabled him to evade us on multiple occasions."

"So he's free; Jann didn't lie, and getting Jacoa to ask for his wishes won't help me?" Maram asked.

"Not with Ansel, no. But if you are willing to assist us, we would return the favor."

"Ward," Isra growled. A velvet caress on the inside of her wrist caused an automatic flutter of her lashes.

"It would be a fair trade."

Perhaps, but Jacoa was the one not playing fair. He clearly knew how she felt about his fingertips if he was using them purposefully to alter her mood.

Maram snorted. "I think that's for me to decide. What would I be helping with?"

Ward hesitated. "That is complicated. We don't know everything that will be required. But the more allies we have, the better our chance of success."

"What does that mean?" Jacoa asked.

"There are other risks beyond freeing dangerous djinn from the genie curse. Jann has locked away far more threatening beings that will be a problem," Ward explained.

"You're talking about those sealed away." Maram narrowed her eyes on Ward. "Jann is many things, but they are good at their job. You don't have to worry about any of those criminals breaking free."

Ward shook his head. "Unfortunately, in their effort to escape the deal they'd made with the Second Djinn, they inadvertently created a skeleton key for all their locks."

Aali and Ward looked at Isra.

"You mean my vessel."

"We mean you," Ward said.

Isra's braid fell apart, her hair halving in length with corkscrew curls. She backed into Jacoa. Her chakras reached out on their own, seeking his calmer rhythms to steady their own stuttering pace.

"Please understand. We didn't know for certain until your victory at the palace." Pride lengthened Aali's posture even as his words carried a thread of uncertainty. "But we expected it would be possible."

"Hoped." Ward pressed his hands together at his chest as if expressing a prayer, or pleading with them to consider joining his cause.

"So Isra is a super being now. Ansel isn't a genie. Just keep Jacoa from wishing and all will be well." Maram shrugged as if it were that simple. Ward crossed his arms, a sign that it was not.

"Jacoa absolutely needs to wish, just at the right time."

"And what, exactly, is your end goal?" Jacoa asked, his quiet voice laced with suspicious accusation. "I'm tired of your riddles, Ward. Tell me what this is really about."

Ward closed his eyes on a calming breath, then opened them to focus on Jacoa.

"I want to find the Second Djinn for my brother. Her name is Teacia."

"This is not our agreement."

The sand-grit voice poured in from the hallway. Isra and Jacoa spun, realizing their backs had been in a vulnerable position. A tall, thick draconian appeared from his hiding place, his muddy green cloak held tight as he stepped through, onyx eyes boring into Aali.

A strangled sound expelled from Maram, and she pulled magic in. The draconian threw a fistful of dust her way and the flow stopped. Only a combined mix of ground djinn and draconian bone could have such an effect, a rare commodity for any draconian to have. Maram collapsed onto the desk with the normal weight of her body. She trembled and slid to the floor, keeping only her eyes and fingertips within view.

Isra lowered her gaze in respect for the elder who entered Jacoa's office. Her hands shook in the male's presence. If she had returned to the collective at eighteen, Terron would have been the one to sentence her to the brood den. Why was he here? Did that mean her father had lied about all the draconian leaving?

Isra wrapped her fingers around Jacoa's, intent not to leave his side. No matter Aali and Ward's arguments, she would not sacrifice her master's wellbeing for any of their best laid plans.

"Terron." Aali curved his back to lower his head, no sign of surprise in his movements.

"We had not agreed on anything, except to continue negotiations once we were certain Isra could play her part." Ward said, proof he was also aware of the draconian presence. Isra's body vibrated with the need to move, yet she held herself still, knowing it was prudent to see how this confrontation played out.

"And can she?" Terron asked.

His arm swept around toward her, another puff of bone dust filling the air. It entered Isra's lungs and settled into a fine layer on her skin. She winced at the contact, her chakras spinning in self-defense. With her draconian energy utilized as a shield, her djinn magic pushed out her aura to remove the offending particles.

The powder reversed its course. Terron waved a clawed hand to clear the air, eyes wide with wonder and perhaps a little distress.

Isra tilted her chin at the show of weakness and her proof of strength. If Terron's bone dust couldn't affect her, then surely she had no reason to fear this elder, no matter the role he would have played had her life been different.

"It is still not enough to convince me to help you free the Second Djinn," Terron declared. "She is the worst of these creatures and deserves her fate after trying to encompass too much of the universe within her realm."

"I would not have expected a draconian to fall for one of Jann's lies," Ward charged.

"And I should believe a sorcerer instead?" Terron showed his teeth.

"How about proof? Maram?" Ward strode to the desk and gripped the djinn, lifting her as if she were truly a small human woman.

"I will not be involved in this!" Maram pulled with her captured arm and pushed with her free hand, digging her nails into Ward. He did not let go.

"I assume you'd like to know how to get your powers back,"

Ward remarked. "Here is your chance to earn that information, Eighth Djinn."

The draconian in the room rose to their full height, and Isra's mouth fell agape. Maram stopped fighting Ward and slipped behind him, putting his wider frame between herself and her predators.

"Would you accept her explanation?" Ward asked Terron.

"If she can speak the truth, then yes," the draconian agreed with caution. Maram remained out of sight.

"Would you give her the antidote to the bone dust to inspire her assistance?" Ward asked.

Terron turned his dark eyes toward Aali, slipping into the language Isra had grown up speaking.

"*I have always trusted you, Aali, but this is asking too much. I did not fully realize your goal.*"

"*It was not meant as a deception. We wanted to allow you time to understand our situation before presenting the whole proposal.*"

"*And have we reached the whole of it, yet?*"

Aali glanced at Isra. "*No.*"

Isra stiffened. Her father's answer was meant for her as well. There would be more to come that she wouldn't like.

"What is your truth?" Terron asked. Ward side-stepped and pulled Maram forward, demanding her compliance through the force of his gaze. Maram's lips pressed against their trembling.

"I am one of the nine oldest," she confirmed. "When Teacia formed a chakra-bond, there was a threat of a civil war between those who would follow the First, versus those who would follow the strongest. Jann presented a plan that appeared as if it would remove them both from power to preserve peace. It was part truth, part lie."

Maram twitched, wincing when Ward's grip held her in place. With a nervous glance toward the ceiling, she continued her explanation, nearly whispering as if she wasn't certain the protections she set would block any determined eavesdroppers.

"Jann became a genie, and Teacia transformed into a vessel.

They were not bound to each other. Teacia's vessel is lost to time, and Jann has erased much of her memory among the younger djinn. Her erratic removal caused the temporary fluctuation that rippled through all magic, rather than by an attempt to grow her realm."

"Jann's game did not cause the cataclysmic wave of magic." Ward's hand cut through the air to refute Maram's claims. "Teacia was ripped from her chakra-bond, and the sorcerer went mad. He nearly shredded a large chunk of reality before I could subdue him. He's been in a coma ever since."

Jacoa shifted, and Isra looked up to see he'd turned his head from Ward, his jaw tense. Ah. Ward spoke of his brother, and Jacoa was hurting from his friend's deceptions. She sent a soft wave of her hair around his arm, and he managed a tight smile to acknowledge her comfort.

"I had thought to hear the truth," Terron said. "But it seems you are not capable. Chakra-bonds are a myth."

"My daughter is part of such a bond," Aali spoke quietly. Isra glared at him. That was not his information to share. Now she and Jacoa were under Terron's scrutiny.

The draconian noted her protective stance beside her master, the way they laced their fingers together. Isra eased her chakras into a steady turn, pulling Jacoa's energy into hers on his exhale. As the spool reversed on her out-breath, Jacoa breathed in, and her energy seeped into his.

Terron's beige scales paled to a light gold.

"Did you plan this as well?"

"You know that is not possible," Aali countered.

"I see." Terron shook his head, but not in denial. "The Eighth Djinn's truth is powerful. Isra's ability to retain her djinn magic in the face of draconian charms is impressive, but it would not be enough to change the tide of destiny. A chakra-bond, however..."

The elder bowed to Isra and Jacoa, arms stiff at his sides.

"I cannot ignore such a sacred sign. None of the draconian will be able to disagree. We will pledge our service to your cause."

"Um, what?" Jacoa asked.

"They've volunteered me for something," Isra answered.

"What is Isra's part?" Jacoa's voice was laced with fatigue and frustration. "What is the cost? What does she get out of it? Aali, you said you had a way to free her. That's why I gave you her vessel. Is that your plan?"

"I assure you, her freedom has always been my goal." Aali's lips fought a sneer, a reaction Isra recognized as her father trying to keep his temper. "Remember, we must neutralize rogue djinn before we free Teacia. We have limited time, and your wishes have to be well used. The draconian can relieve much of the weight if they agree to ally themselves with us."

"And it would help to have a powerful draconian genie to enforce the rules. We eliminate only dangerous djinn, leaving the passive djinn be," Ward said.

Terron stiffened at the sorcerer's addition, but did not protest.

"Wait," Maram said. "You're talking about freeing all the genies, but without the mass release that would come from all eighteen wishes?"

"Yes."

"You are insane," Maram declared.

"One by one, we have a chance," Aali argued. "If they attack together, we will lose."

"But how does that free Isra?" Jacoa's fingers tightened on her shoulder. "You said we have a limited amount of time to accomplish this. You mean until I turn nineteen and Isra disappears. That is not what you promised me, Aali."

"I promised nothing except a chance," Aali countered. "Teacia—"

"I'll make them all." Jacoa's chakras pulled her energy into his, as if he could absorb her into his body to save her from the nether.

"Jacoa," Isra soothed. "What you're feeling is because of our bond. Being apart would be painful for us. We need to remember we are not the only ones. Would you agree to this, to try my father's way first, to free Teacia and return her to her chakra-bond?"

Jacoa frowned. "I think we should make a condition."

"Oh?" Terron asked, brow ridge raised.

"Yeah." Jacoa's voice gained confidence, evidence he'd made a decision. "You said we need all the help we can get?"

"Yes," Aali agreed.

"Okay. Then we should have every hunter involved. Even the females."

Isra's heart soared before her brain caught up to what Jacoa meant. He intended to force Terron to awaken the females in the brood den. They would be free. Awake and alive.

She turned her back to the room and wrapped him in a hug, their chakras aligning as their bodies made contact, spinning together in perfect time.

"It is impossible," Terron said.

Isra twisted to argue the old draconian's words, but his wide eyes were on her and Jacoa, his hands held out as if tempted to touch them.

He was reacting to their alignment, not to their demand.

"Will you agree?" she asked.

"The reason I allowed your father and Ward to pull me into their plan was for the promise of ending our people's long failure," Terron said. "We aren't meant to be part of this world, proven by the very need for the brood den."

The elder bowed again.

"We will offer every hunter available to this endeavor. Our objective will only include the djinn who pose a threat to the natural order. And then we shall return to the sands for the last time."

"Great. It sounds like you don't need me anymore." Maram crossed her arms over her chest, her shoes half their usual height and the toes without their spikes or chrome point. "Get this gross dust off me so I can go."

"We could use a high-ranking djinn ally as well," Ward said. "I offered you help to find Ansel, and that stands."

"If I want to find him, the deceitful bastard," Maram muttered the words as she wiped her hands down her face, shaking them over the desk. "Fine. Whatever. I still want this crap off me."

"A shower will wash it off." Terron smirked.

"Bathe? Like a human?" she gasped.

"There's a bathroom across the hall." Jacoa gestured in its direction. "In fact, can we be finished? I know we're not done with everything, but I'm exhausted."

"Do we need more safeguards?" Isra asked.

"I will go speak with our people." Terron included Isra in the statement and she blinked in surprise. "Once they are convinced, we'll set up a guard."

Ward grinned like he'd just won a double-or-nothing bet. "There's a lot to figure out, but with the dream team together, I'm sure it will get done. Later."

"There are two guest rooms," Jacoa said. "If you sleep, you're welcome to them. If you don't... Do what you do."

Jacoa pulled Isra from the office and up the stairs. She tried to judge his mood through their connection. It was impossible to sort out her mass of emotions from his. Once safely in Jacoa's room, he closed the door with his foot and twisted the lock with a jerk.

"Are you okay?" she asked.

Jacoa lifted Isra's hair to his lips, and she felt the gentle contact in each of her nerve endings. Goosebumps danced across her skin.

"All of that was really heavy. I know we should talk about it, but I don't want to."

"Alright," Isra agreed.

"The thing is, there's something I've wanted to say for a while. But someone took away my ability to speak." His self-deprecating smirk pulled a bubbly chuckle from Isra.

The sound cut off when he dropped her hair to grasp her arms, turning her until her back pressed against the door. He peeled his fingers from her skin and placed his palms flat against the wood on either side of her shoulders. Leaning in, he closed the distance between them but refused to touch her with anything more than breath.

"Jacoa?"

"You asked me once what I meant when I said I want you to be mine." His eyes blurred before hers, they were so close, but she didn't dare look away.

"In my head, you've been a fairytale. A shadow. Sometimes, a monster. Except none of those ideas of you were true. None were right. And frankly, I don't want any of those Isras. When I say I want you to be mine, I mean you. Not as someone else makes you out to be, all of you as you are. So, what do you think, Isra? Would you be mine?"

Isra's chest was so full of love and hope, she didn't know if she was capable of speech, but pushed out the words as best she could.

"If you'll be mine."

Jacoa's lips parted in a wide smile and his nose brushed back and forth over hers.

"You are the only one I want to give my whole self to."

Isra's chakras ignited, burning away the day's wariness and destroying the darkness that had tried to settle in. She shoved Jacoa. He stumbled, his hands lifting as if he were about to offer an apology, clearly misinterpreting her actions.

Isra's hair flared around her, reaching for the buttons on his shirt and snapping the threads that held them on. She opened the cloth with her hands even as she pushed him harder toward the bed. With a laugh of relief, Jacoa relaxed his posture and allowed her to tumble them onto the mattress before he stilled her searching fingers against his chest.

"I wasn't finished. Please let me, Isra."

A puff of impatience blew through her lips. She had few defenses against the way he rolled his tongue over the center of her name. She offered a small nod even as she closed her eyes to focus on how the long strands of her hair fell over his body, their touch creating a tactile picture within her mind as she waited for him to finish with words.

"Isra Almasi, I wish for you to be whomever you desire to be. To be wherever you want to be. Your form and your place are yours to choose in your time of choosing."

Isra gasped. She straightened her arms to peer into his face. Magic flooded her system and her lashes fluttered with the rush. Invisible bands fell away from the structure of her body, and Isra was weightless in her freedom.

Her molecules burst apart as she became the wind, ruffling through Jacoa's hair. She tightened her form just a little, condensing into a fine mist that kissed his face. Tiny drops danced at the tips of his lashes. Jacoa's laugh vibrated through her own chest as she solidified into her female physique, unable to contain the joy that lifted her mouth in a grin, no matter that they'd broken the rules.

"That was your twelfth wish," she whispered.

"Don't tell anyone," he whispered back, as if they were conspiring children. "We'll have to be extra careful from here on out. But if there are any wishes I regret, this will never be one of them."

"Thank you." She leaned forward to match her mouth to his, pausing just before contact. "But there's another of your promises I'm more interested in right now."

"Hmm?"

"Don't stop touching."

Acknowledgments

This story almost never happened.

Quill and Cup came at the exact right time. Because of this group of dedicated, mindful women, I knew I could find the right balance between work and play to get this story done, even if I wasn't as enthralled with it as I hoped.

Then came Lauren, my BFF (Best Feedback Friend), and her quiet joy and deep insights that showed me there was more to the words I put on the page than I had thought. Isra and Jacoa's story is amazing because her enthusiasm made it so.

A special shout out to Sage, who was my shining light of a cheerleader at the very end when I needed it the most.

And as always, to my family who puts up with a writer's schedule simply because they see the joy that it brings me.

All of you have my thanks and my love.
C.K. Sorens

About the Author

CK Sorens lives with her husband, Kristoffer, their three sons, and their dog, Pippin. She enjoys days at the beach, day hikes, and sitting on the patio with a small fire and a glass of wine. To keep tabs on future books, you can find her on social media and at her website, www.cksorens.com.

Sign up for C.K. Sorens Newsletter (found on her website) for updates sent straight to your inbox.